THE BLOOD INSIDE ME

A Legacy of Blood and Loyalty

ANNE BROOKS

Anne Brooks

THE BLOOD INSIDE ME

Copyright © 2024 by Anne Brooks

All rights reserved. No part of this book may be reproduced in any manner whatsoever without written permission except in the case of brief quotations embodied in critical articles and reviews.

First Printing, 2024

Contents

Author's Note		1
Acknowledgments		2
Prologue		4
1	Chapter One	6
2	Chapter Two	16
3	Chapter Three	33
4	Chapter Four	41
5	Chapter Five	45
6	Chapter Six	60
7	Chapter Seven	66
8	Chapter Eight	71
9	Chapter Nine	95
10	Chapter Ten	102
11	Chapter Eleven	111
12	Chapter Twelve	140

13	Chapter Thirteen	145
14	Chapter Fourteen	152
15	Chapter Fifteen	164
16	Chapter Sixteen	177
17	Chapter Seventeen	182
18	Chapter Eighteen	189
19	Chapter Nineteen	202
20	Chapter Twenty	208
21	Chapter Twenty-One	213
22	Chapter Twenty-Two	220
23	Chapter Twenty-Three	225
24	Chapter Twenty-Four	241
25	Chapter Twenty-Five	251
26	Chapter Twenty-Six	254
27	Chapter Twenty-Seven	263
28	Chapter Twenty-Eight	270
29	Chapter Twenty-Nine	276
30	Chapter Thirty	281

Author's Note

The development of this story started in my 3rd grade class with a group of students who wanted to write a book. Our journey began with a simple, popular idea - *werewolves*. Each week, the students would huddle together to discuss their characters in the story, while as an entire class, we discussed story development, plots, and themes. At the time, for me as the teacher, this was purely educational, but as the students became more invested in their story, it developed a life of its own.

While we didn't complete the novel that year, it stayed with all of us in our minds. As we geared up for the next school year, I was determined to complete this story for the students, who continually begged for the final copy. As they prepared to leave elementary and embark on the first phase of their next life, I wanted to make sure they had a piece of our time together to take with them. There in lays the production of *The Blood Inside*.

It was always our collective dream to hold this story in our hands. I am honored and proud to be able to give this published book as my gift to them at their 5th grade graduation.

This book is for all you...

Acknowledgments

I am forever grateful to Heather McLeod for letting me highjack her writing unit to help these students develop this story. She was an inspiring and dedicated teacher who nurtured her students' creativity. I am thankful to Mr. Larry Knight, our Principal, for allowing me to develop and print this story for our students.

To the students, class of 2021, who helped develop this story, I was and always will be impressed by your passion, creativity, and dedication to not only this project but your education as well. You have accomplished a great thing with this story - be proud! Celebrate your accomplishments in your life and learn from your failures. When things are hard, and they will be, remember that hardship breeds passion and grit. Both of which you will need to succeed in life, which I know you all will.

Take your time, as we did in developing this story, to develop your own passion. Take your failures, as I did so many times with my first novel, which is now published, to learn how to succeed. Take your fears, as we all do, and conquer them head-on. Take a risk, do something scary and amazing, to develop that grit you will need in life. Never. Give. Up.

This one is for my students ...

Prologue

The full moon illuminated the night sky, full and bright, as faded yellow rays cascaded through the barren woods. Roaming free through the woods, the melting snow crunching beneath his paws, his thick black fur making him appear like a shadow in the night, he felt alive. In these moments he felt like his true self, unencumbered by his secrets and fears. He howled at the moon, releasing all his anxiety, the sound echoing for miles unheard. Then he was gone, racing through the familiar woods.

In the distance, a dark figure crouched, hidden in the blanketing shadows of night. Stalking his prey, he waited for the perfect moment to strike. He could feel the vibrations as the creature's heavy, clawed paws beat against the hard ground and smell a deep, musky scent of spice in the gentle wind. Leaving a taste of iron settled in the back of his throat. Blood saturating the surrounding air. A howling pierced through the thick forest, as the creature came into view.

The man pulled at the black scarf around his neck, positioning it over his rough, scarred face. His bright, green eyes shadowed by his large, black-rimmed hat in the darkness as he slowly pulled the gun from his belt. He aimed ... *any moment now*, he thought.

As his finger tightened on the trigger, the creature suddenly turned, its eyes returning his glowing stare. It was not the first time, nor the last he would face this kind of animal. He knew his aim would miss, graze its shoulder. Wound him, but not kill. He needed to kill him, otherwise, he was dead. Frozen, he waited to see if the animal recognized him as an equal or a threat.

Slowly, the creature moved towards him, massive shoulder blades pushing its large frame into a lumbered trot. He watched as the creature circled the perimeter, appearing to be just as intrigued. Even from this distance, he could feel the heat radiating from the creature's body and smell the foulness on his tongue. We watched the creature, curious of its habits, waiting to see what it would do.

It was a mistake.

As the misty gray glow of the moon broke through the shadows, a swift wind rushed through the cool night air, betraying him to the animal. He hesitated, seeing the animal catching his scent in the wind. Immediately, the creature quickened his pace directly towards him. Then, leaning on its back legs, it leaped through the space between them, its speed unmatched by the man. Just as the creature was about to be over the top of him, he took aim at the end of the long-barreled shotgun and managed a single shot.

The shot rippled through the silence of the forest.

The creature fell to his feet ... *dead*. He had killed the wolf.

I

Chapter One

The wide-opened, green fields rolled by as the Jeep rode smoothly down the barren road that curved through the plains. Elly gazed out the rear window, her mind consumed with the music humming in her ears, as she avoided thinking. If she allowed her thoughts to form she would start to cry again and she had done enough of that in the last week to last her a lifetime. When she had slowly closed her bedroom door just four short hours ago, she felt as if she was being violently ripped away from the only world she knew.

"We are home," Jane announced.

Elly winced at the word *home*. This place would never be her home, as these strangers would never be her family. She had lost both her home and her family the moment she found her mother dead.

Elly barely glanced at her grandmother, who had shifted

around in her seat and was staring at her intently from the front of the jeep. The car turned down a gravel, one-lane road. Tall trees flanked either side of the truck as they slowly bounced through the canopy of leaves.

Knowing that Elly needed time, Jane rotated her shoulders back towards the front, giving her husband a tight smile. In the last twenty years of their marriage, they had perfected the art of having a full conversation without ever saying a word. They both knew it was going to be difficult bringing Elly home, especially after all she just witnessed. However, it was necessary. Now that her mother, their daughter, was dead, it was only a matter of time before Elly started to change. She would need Jane the most, even if she didn't see it now, soon she would.

The trees faded away as they followed the curved path around the waterless, cracked fountain, pulling to a stop in front of the enormous, wooden doors. Elly had no memory of this place, as she peered up at the colonial house with its peeling white panels and tall, thin windows that reminded Elly of an advent calendar she had as a child. Each little window would open to reveal a small snapshot into the family's life at Christmas time.

According to Jane, she had been here once before as a baby. A visit that presumably did not go well considering her mother never spoke of them, except to say they existed, but she could not see them. Elly noticed there was always an undertone of pain when her mother spoke about her parents.

"Austin, will you get Elly's things up to her new room?" Jane asked as she pulled the door open, the hinges screaming in pain. Austin nodded as he got out and walked around to the back of the forest green Jeep. Through the rearview mirror, Elly could barely see Austin through the dust-covered window as he lifted the trunk and pulled out a single duffle bag.

Elly didn't want to get out of the car. There was a finality in getting out of the car. She wasn't ready to accept her new life in this small farm town two hours north of Atlanta, GA. If she could just stay in the car maybe she could wake from this nightmare. As she pulled the AirPods from her ears, the music fading away, she reminded herself that it wasn't a nightmare, but her reality. She knew the moment she walked through the doors, there was no going back. But, then again, there wasn't anything to go back to anymore. She had lost everything.

Her grandmother's thick, black boots beat against the wooden planks as she stepped up to the grand house, pausing at the top to wave Elly out of the car, her plaid shirt and frayed vest a fine complement to her dirt-stained jeans. In the last week, Elly had only known her grandmother to wear the same style of plaid shirts and vest, only changing it out for a solid black dress the day of the funeral. Just as the house, she initially appeared grand in stature but when you took a closer look, she was tattered and worn. Flecks of gray sparkled in her hair as the setting sun highlighted all her aging features, such as the deep permanent lines around her mouth and a cloudy film as a summer heat haze over her speckled green eyes.

"Well, come on," Jane called, waiting for Elly. She stood dwarfed by the towering columns holding up the sprawling front porch. Just then her grandfather slammed the trunk, jolting Elly's mind awake. As much as she didn't want to go, she knew she had to eventually get out of the Jeep.

Elly's grandfather disappeared up the large staircase with her singular bag. Elly followed Jane down the expansive main hallway, as she realized that this place was more of a museum than a home. The walls were lined with large portraits of men she didn't recognize.

"These are all very important people in our family," Jane explained as she caught Elly staring up at the large pictures. Each one equal in size and importance, but different based on the person's contribution to the family.

As they continued to walk down the hallway, Elly noticed a progression of time. The first portrait of a man clearly from the 18th century, his high white-collar ruffled around his neck and a black coat pulled tightly around his slim waist. But, it was the large, pointed sliver of a sword that gave away the time period. The next couple of paintings from the early 19th century, each man holding a different version of a handgun. Elly noticed a familiarity in their features, mostly in the deep, green brilliance of their eyes.

Glancing into each room as she continued to follow Jane down the hallway, Elly noticed they all appeared untouched, the furniture faded by the light and dust visible even from this distance. Jane pushed through the swinging door at the end of the hallway, revealing a glimpse of the kitchen.

As Elly entered, she realized it was the only room that appeared to have been lived in, with dishes dirty in the large, deep ceramic sink on the far wall, a newspaper sprawled open on the small round table tucked away in a breakfast nook area, and jackets hung by the back door.

The white cabinets reached high to the ceiling, as her grandmother stepped on a small stool to reach the cups. Pulling down a single glass, she proceeded to fill it with water. Elly stopped at the large kitchen island, a barrier between herself and this person she should know, but didn't.

"Here." Her grandmother slid the glass towards her tightly wrung fingers.

Reluctantly, Elly released the painful grip she held on her fingers and took the glass. It was cold against her hot, flushed, nervous skin. She noticed the window above the sink was open, the chill of the winter air seeping into the room around her making the sweat that had started to bead on her forehead turn cool.

Elly awkwardly took a long sip, wanting to avoid any conversation with her grandmother, who was watching her keenly. Elly could see in her eyes the want to ask the question she had been asking Elly from the moment she arrived in New York a week ago. Elly dreaded the question, in fact, she'd asked her after the first hundred times to stop asking her how she was doing. There is no way anyone could be anything but shocked, overwhelmed, or numb after finding her mother's dead body on the kitchen floor.

"All set," Austin announced as he entered the room, instantly feeling the tension in the air. He stood between them, his cloudy, grey eyes shifting back and forth waiting for Elly to speak.

"Thanks," she said quickly, taking the last sip of water. She slid the glass back across the counter then turned on her heels, disappearing back into the hallway to find her room.

Upstairs, Elly floundered through the hallway lightly pushing each door as she tried to find her new place in this world. Most of the doors were open, giving her a view of a bathroom flanked on either side by a neatly put together bedroom. It all seemed normal, but it didn't feel that way to Elly. At the end of the hallway, there was a solitary door closed.

Elly gently turned the nod, the door screaming as she pushed it open. Mostly dark, it took a moment for her eyes to adjust, only a small sliver of light finding its way through a split in the drawn curtains. Tentatively, moving into the room, a deep, dark curiosity pulling her in, she drifted over to a dusty, oak desk by the window. Dust danced in the light as it cascaded over the desk, a single item on it. She ran her fingers over the brown leather, picking it up and slowly pulling at the frayed ribbon holding the pages together.

"What are you doing?" Jane's voice caused her entire body to jump, the book dropping back to the desk with a vibrating thud. Her heart raced, as she steadied herself by leaning on the chair in front of the desk. The wood creaked under her weight.

"You shouldn't be in here." Pushing the door open wide, Jane ushered her out of the room. Reluctantly, Elly left the mysterious book behind as she followed her grandmother's orders.

"Your room is this way," Jane instructed, as she closed the door tightly behind her, a pained look washing over her eyes.

Elly silently followed her grandmother to the room located at the opposite end of the hallway. Looking back, unable to explain it, Elly felt drawn to the room and she was desperate to open that book.

There was a brighter glow in her room, the curtains fully pulled back revealing large windows that gazed out over the expansive backyard. Elly could see the entire property from her room, all the way to the treeline. In front of the windows was a large window seat flanked by two hideaway shelves stacked with books. A few scattered pillows were thrown onto the window seat. Elly had a window seat in her apartment where she frequently cozied up to read, but she couldn't see herself doing that here.

"Best to not venture too far. The woods can be - *unsafe*," Jane told her as she stood in the doorway, watching Elly explore her bedroom. "There is a dresser for your things, and a small desk to do your schoolwork."

Elly instinctively shook her head, unable to accept that she would be here long enough to unpack or do schoolwork. It was still hard for her to accept it all. The death of her mother. Moving here. Her life losing all shape.

"Can I be alone, please," she blurted out, filling the tears starting to well in her burning eyes. Her grandmother, filled with pity, gave her a tight smile and nodded as she closed the door.

Alone, Elly could no longer hold her pain back. She could feel the warmth of her tears as they faded down her face. Memories of that day flashed across her mind, as she could vividly see her mother's body, covered in blood, lying lifeless on the kitchen floor. The police surrounded her body, pushing her away. Then, the memories were replaced by a memory of a black dress her grandmother gave her draped across her flamingo bed cover. Lastly, the memory of just the night before. Her last night in the only place she even knew to be her home.

Curled tightly in her sheets, the winter chill turning into a suffocating heat, she thrashed to be free from it all. Her screams echoed through the night, the pain rippling through her entire body. She thought it would never go away when she felt firm arms tighten around her shoulders. Jane had rushed to her side, holding her as her pain released scream after scream into the silent night air.

Jane held Elly, rocking her slightly as she started to settle down after hours of screaming. Gently, she traced her fingers through her dark hair. It was the same color as her daughter's hair. Jane could remember sitting and holding her daughter when she was Elly's age, both of them crying over their loss of innocence. Jane had wished then, as she did now, that she could take it all away, change the world, but she knew it was impossible. Something her daughter never accepted.

A familiar smell of bacon waffled through Elly's room, a clouded morning light creeping slowly across the wooden floor to her bed. Elly had not realized how exhausted she was from the lack of sleep in the last week. It had felt like a dream, rocking in her grandmother's arms last night. As much as she had wanted to push her away her body melted into her comfort, needing someone to hold her together.

Pulling her sore body from the soft, warm, pink sheets, she couldn't decide if she needed to eat or change first. Elly could feel the dampness of her sweat-drenched clothes as they stuck to her warm body. Her stomach cramped, growled for food, but she found it hard to move in her clothes thick with sweat. The night seemed to bring on anxious hot flashes since her mother had died. Now, she'd be forced to unpack her bag. A single, green duffle bag that had belonged to her father held everything she owned.

Come to find out, their cozy two-bedroom apartment in the heart of New York City did not have much in the way of valuables. Besides her personal items, the only other items she took were a single photo book her mother had made just a year ago. The photos, only including her and her mother, started when Elly was two years old after her father disappeared. It was the only thing she could think to take with her in that moment. Everything else just seemed to have changed the moment she found her mother dead.

By the time she had showered and changed, her stomach groaned for substance. As much as she wanted to stay locked away, avoiding reality, she had to eat. From the hallway, the swinging door propped open, she could see her grandmother's back as she stood washing dishes at the sink. Her grandfather was perched on a barstool, coffee cup steaming beside him, as he was enthralled with the daily newspaper. Pushing up the walls in her mind in preparation for the questions her grandmother would undoubtedly ask, Elly made her way into the kitchen.

"Good morning," Elly whispered, as she slid onto the furthest barstool from her grandfather. Cuffing the ends of her sweater into her hands, she hesitated not sure if she should gather the breakfast herself or if that would be rude to presume she could move about a stranger's kitchen.

"Breakfast?" Jane asked, not turning around as she continued to wash the dishes.

"Um, yes ... please," Elly added, still unsure of her place.

Without asking, Jane made her a plate filled with scrambled eggs, bacon, and topped off with a southern-style biscuit. Elly didn't hesitate, eating quickly, as she could feel them both watching her anxiously.

"Jane, you have plans to go into town today?" Austin inquired over the spectacles perched on the tip of his long, thin nose. Elly could feel he was just making conversation to ease the tension.

"Yes, to get a few things for the project. I can go by the grocery store as well, Elly." At the sound of her name, she looked up, catching Jane's eye. "Would you like to go to get some things you like?"

With her mouth full, she only shook her head no.

"Well then." Jane tossed the rag she was using to dry her hands on the marble countertop, appearing defeated. "Guess you can just stay around here."

Elly got the feeling her grandmother was not asking, but telling her she must stay at the house. Not as if Elly had anywhere to go, so she agreed to the restriction.

"Austin will stay here."

"Yes, of course," Austin agreed, sliding Elly a pitiful look. He clearly understood that Elly knew exactly what Jane was doing. She did not want Elly to be left alone. She did not want Elly going anywhere. She felt like a prisoner.

2

Chapter Two

Just as Elly finished her breakfast, Jane having pulled the dusty, green Jeep out of the drive over thirty minutes ago, Austin folded his paper and looked directly at Elly.

"Well, I have some things to get done around the house," he announced. Elly just stared at him. He stared back, unsure if he could trust his only granddaughter. He did not like the feeling.

"I need to go fetch some firewood." He narrowed his eyes at Elly, contemplating what to do. "I think you should come with me," he finally decided.

Not feeling as if she had a choice, Elly nodded in agreement.

Austin led Elly out the back door of the kitchen, handing her a pair of black, rubber boots. Elly struggled to pull the thick, rubber boots over her wool socks. The boots were covered in a thick layer of mud and slightly too big, causing her walk to be clumsy as she reluctantly followed her grandfather to the detached garage. It was clear that the garage was not used for parking their cars as they passed by a rusted, faded-red pick-up truck parked in the covered area between the house and garage.

Elly stood in the doorway as he lumbered to an old, two-seater golf cart with an empty cage attached to the backside. Splintered wood chips sprinkled the black canvas laid in the bottom of the basket, a large ax draped over the side. Hanging from the side walls were an endless amount of tools and a large workbench spanned the length of the back wall. Elly saw a large, metal saw at the end of the table, the tips of the blade rusted. Elly's mind flashed as the rust turned to blood on the end of the blades. Quickly, she shook her head, literally trying to toss the image from her mind.

"Here!" Austin tossed her an oversize, brown jacket with a deep, brown-hue-plaid flannel along the inside. It was the size he should wear, but instead, he intended for her to wear it. "Can get cold out there under the canopy of the trees. Not much light reaches the forest floor out there in the thick parts."

Elly's eyes widen at the thought of getting deep into the woods. Being raised in the city, nature was not something she knew well.

"It's okay," he assured her, slapping his hand on the ax, "nothing will bother us. As long as you are with me, you'll be safe."

Even though her grandmother had told her it was unsafe in the woods, Elly had not felt unsafe, just out of her element, especially since Austin was taking her there now. Yet, there was something about the way he used the word *us* as a collective being out in the woods, that sent a fearful shiver down her spine. Now, as they rode on the golf cart down the grassy hill towards the treeline she could feel the fear creeping into her mind. Holding tightly to the cold metal bar, the golf cart bounced her around as he barreled into the woods, narrowly missing the large tree trunks. Instantly, the light was covered by a blanket of shadows. Thankfully, Austin seemed to be following a well-carved-out path that somewhat alleviated her fears.

They weren't far into the woods when he pulled the golf cart to a stop. The path was blocked by a thick row of trees, each trunk's enormous diameter only dwarfed by the actual size of the tree. He pulled the ax from the back and waved at Elly to follow him. She didn't feel comfortable leaving the speed of the golf cart behind her but she did as instructed, sure he wouldn't just leave her alone.

But his legs were lean, strong, and much longer than Elly's. His stride moved at a quick pace to the point that within a few minutes she had fallen behind. The darkness of the forest had engulfed him, as Elly suddenly realized she was lost. Frantically, she turned in all directions, looking for any signs of her grandfather. But, it was as if he was a ghost. Gone without a trace.

Turning back around, unsure if she was going the right way, she tried to make her way back to the golf cart. Clumsily, Elly slipped over large, moss-covered branches, her oversized boots and jacket making it difficult to stay on her feet. Elly felt as if she was literally crawling through the trunks of the forest.

Suddenly, a faint noise echoed through the silence, causing Elly to freeze. The soft hum of a song long forgotten floated on the wind. It was out of place in the isolated forest. Elly could feel her heart rate quicken, her mind becoming hyper-focused on every single sound around her: the low hum of a fly's wings, the crack of a fallen branch under the weight of something large, and a rhythmic huff in the air. Squinting through the settling fog, Elly scanned the edge of the darkness, straining her eyes to see what was out there.

Something was there.

Something was watching her - *she could feel it.*

"Elly," Austin called, emerging from the other direction, his ax tight in his hands. "Everything okay?"

"Yeah..." Suddenly, the sounds were gone as the forest fell silent again. "I just thought ... I thought something was out there." Austin's face dropped into concern, almost fear as he scanned the encroaching fog.

"We should go," he announced.

Reaching out, he pulled Elly by her elbow, keeping her close, as they walked shoulder to shoulder back to the golf cart. He didn't toss the ax into the back but kept it by his side as they rode back up to the house.

The moment they passed through the treeline, she could feel the instant warmth of the late morning sun pushing away the cold darkness of the forest. Elly took her first real breath since they had entered the forest. She did not understand the feeling she had but the fact that something was out there pulled on her curiosity, making her fearful.

"Uh, Mr. ... um, Aus ..." Elly wasn't quite sure what to call him, as she realized this was the first time she was addressing her grandfather.

It had only been her grandmother that came to retrieve her after her mother died. After two days in the care of her best friend's family, her grandmother arrived, claiming to be her immediate next of kin, which meant she was now Elly's sole guardian. Since her father had disappeared over thirteen years ago, and her only other father figure, her uncle, hadn't been seen in over two years, it was all she had in the way of blood relatives.

Elly was filled with disappointment when Jane arrived, wishing to stay with her friend, Makiyah. She didn't care if she stayed on the couch the next two years, as long as she didn't have to leave her home. However, Jane refused to let her stay, even convincing Makiyah's mother that Elly had to leave with her, staying in her home no longer an option. Losing her mother would've been enough to break her, but being ripped away from her life had broken her spirit.

"Austin is fine, for now," he conceded, a ghostly, painful look draping over his eyes. He had wanted to have her call him granddad, or grandfather, anything other than just his name, but he could tell it was too soon. He, more than she realized, understood it would take time for her to come to know them as family. Austin had suffered through his own painful loss for some time, learning too late that this life is complicated by outside forces all too often.

"Is there something out there?" Elly asked as Austin unloaded the few pieces of wood he had collected. He leaned the ax against the tire of the golf cart.

"Out where?" Suddenly, Jane was standing in the doorway of the garage, her anger palpable. Her fingers tightly twisted around her waist as she glared at Austin. Reading the fear on his face, and knowing without asking, that Austin had taken Elly into the woods.

"The forest," Elly offered, unaware of the shared fear between her grandparents. "I thought I could feel... no hear," she quickly corrected, "something out there." Jane shot an angered look at Austin, who shrugged his shoulders. Another unspoken conversation.

"I'm sure there was nothing out there," Jane assured as she attempted to hide the concern from her face. She did not need Elly to ask more questions. "Why don't you go take a rest. I'm making some lunch." Elly stepped as if she was going to ask another question. "I'll call you when it's ready."

Elly backed down, the cold tension causing a deep, uncomfortable shiver to radiate through her body. She could see that her grandmother was upset, so instead of pressing her, she decided it was best to just do as she asked. She was worried that if she pushed a conversation with her grandmother, it might be turned against her and she'd be forced to talk about her mother. So, she let it go, retreating to her room.

Jane stormed into the kitchen, anger flaring in her eyes that brought a heat to her cheeks. She listened for the close of Elly's bedroom door before spinning around on Austin, who was still sheepishly standing by the door removing his cap and hanging it next to his jacket.

"Why would you take her out there?" Jane accused. "What happened out there?" she demanded, but before Austin could explain.

"Nothing, Jane, it was fine."

"No, Austin, don't do that. What happened?"

"She just got lost for a second. Heard something moving. It was nothing, I checked," Austin assured her.

"What? How reckless can you be?" Jane's eyes flared with anger.

"It was not reckless, Jane, and you know that."

"How far into the woods did you take her?" Jane slammed her hand down onto the counter, her palm instantly stinging in pain, but she didn't even flinch.

"No farther than normal, Jane, I promise," Austin spoke slowly, holding up his hands in surrender. Fighting with Jane was futile, he had learned that one a long time ago as well. "I doubt she saw anything, not that time of the month."

"Oh, please, that means nothing," Jane scoffed, her mind racing with a million thoughts of what Elly could have felt or heard out there in their own backyard. "Austin, if she did feel something watching her," Jane's voice cracked with fear, as she held a hand over her gasp.

"It'll be okay, we will protect her. Even if she is right about something being in the woods, they would never dream of coming this far," Austin affirmed.

Their muffled sounds floated on the wind, swirling through the house, as Elly listened to her grandparents speak in the kitchen. Their words were low, in an attempt for her to not hear. But, Elly slipped into the hallway, balancing at the top of the staircase she could listen.

"Jane, please, it's the middle of the day. Nothing was going to happen." Austin assured.

"You don't know that. Look what happened to..." the words caught in her throat, "to Julianna," she managed to say with a great deal of pain.

"My dear, we don't know that *that* is what happened to her."

Realizing they were talking about her mother, Elly moved, silently down the stairs, as she pressed up against the flowered wallpaper, just outside the closed kitchen door. Elly was desperate to hear what they were saying about her mother's death.

"What else could it be?" Jane's voice was filled with annoyance.

"It could have just been an accident, as the police said."

"No, there is no way. That is not what happened."

"You don't know that," Austin urged, frustration building in his voice.

"I do, Austin. They killed her. And now they are after Elly."

Elly gasped, immediately clutching her hands over her mouth.

Suddenly the door swung open as Jane found Elly eavesdropping on the other side. Jane glared at Elly, who wished she could melt into the flowers on the wall.

"Elly," Jane breathed, realizing what Elly just overheard as her eyes started to turn red with pain. Jane could see the anger and confusion on Elly's face.

"What happened to my mother?" Elly demanded.

"Elly, it's just not the right time."

"The right time? What does that mean? I don't even understand. Who was after my mother? Who is after me?" Elly could feel the panic rising, as her eyes pricked with tears.

"No one my dear, it's not for you to worry about. I promise you are safe here," Jane assured. She reached out to Elly, but she backed away.

"That's not an answer."

"Elly, Juliana had a tragic accident, " Austin injected, flashing a fierce look at Jane. They had explicitly discussed not having this conversation with Elly until she was ready, and she was nowhere near ready to learn the truth, if that was even the case. They had no clear evidence that Julianna's death was murder, only Jane's suspicions.

Elly remembered that after she found her mother she couldn't go into the kitchen, there was too much blood everywhere. Even after they had removed her mother's body, the investigators spent hours looking over every detail, she still couldn't bring herself to leave her mother's bedroom. She had spent hours sitting on the bed in a daze, as the world moved at high speed. Her mind was painfully, slowly going over every detail trying to make sense of her mother's death.

She heard whispers, as the detective discussed the position of the body, the placement of the knife on the counter, the possibility that it was a horrible accident...

"That's not what you said." Elly looked towards Jane, imploring her to tell her the truth.

Jane wanted nothing more than to be honest with Elly. But, she knew deep down that Austin was right. Elly was too fragile right now, she needed time.

"Elly, you misunderstood," Jane started, reaching out to Elly again, who backed away further this time.

"No, I didn't."

Anger blanketed Elly's face. The thought that her mother could've been murdered and these strangers refused to tell her infected her mind. She had failed to realize it until now, all the pieces of her mother's death scattered about in her mind, but the moment she heard the word *murder*, she knew.

"Tell me," Elly demanded, holding back the burning tears. "Tell me!"

"Elly, you don't understand," Jane started.

"No, I think I do."

Pushing through the back door before they could stop her, Elly raced from the house. A wave of burning anger boiled inside her as she took off running across the yard, blocking their calls for her to come back, only stopping when she reached the treeline. Her lungs were tight as she gasped for air. The large trees stood like a wall around the property to cage her in this place. Looking back over her shoulder, she briefly thought about disappearing into the forest, but her fear held her back.

What if her grandmother's words were true? What if someone had killed her mother on purpose. What if someone was after her?

Elly leaned against a lone, smaller tree trunk as fearful tears started to cascade down her hot cheeks. Silently, she cried as the emotions of losing her mother hit against her like waves in the ocean, giving her little time to recover or breathe between each engulfing pressure of the wave.

Her mother was gone. She was alone.

Then, suddenly, she didn't feel alone.

Someone, *or something*, was watching her. Turning, she stared into the darkness of the forest, searching for any sign of movement. Then, she heard the faint whisper of the low, soft song she had before. Without thinking, Elly stepped towards the edge, her foot crossing over into the darkness. Bracing her hand on the tree, she peered into the thickness of trees, the alluring, unknowing sound pulling her into the forest. Just as she felt she was about to fall into the darkness, a voice called her back.

"Are you ok?" Elly turned at the sound of his voice. "Are you hurt?"

"No, who are you... why would you ask me if I was hurt?"

"You are crying."

Quickly, Elly brushed the leftover tears from her blushing cheeks. Fully embarrassed, she shifted awkwardly as she pulled her sweater tightly over her chest, willing it to blanket her from mortification.

"Can I get you some help?" He offered when she didn't answer him. Elly was caught up in his presence, a pressure building on her chest as he stared down at her. His tall, muscular size matched that of the tree trunks. His olive skin and dark features blending into his surroundings.

"No, I'm fine." Elly managed to say. "Who are you?"

"Oh, I am Khalil." He politely offered his hand. Slightly confused, she slipped her hand into his, an instant warmth jolted through her body. Quickly, she pulled her hand away, as if he had shocked her with an electrical current. "I live just across the river," he offered, pointing to the west of the forest. Elly could hear the slow trickle of the water as it flowed over the rocks. "I was just out for a ... run."

"A run? Where?"

"Oh, in the woods. I found it very peaceful there."

"In there?" She questioned, pointing to the darkened curtain behind the trees. "You aren't scared?"

"What would I be scared of?" Suddenly, Elly realized she wasn't quite sure what he should be scared of in the forest. It was just a feeling she had. Something about the fear Jane had in her eyes when she learned that Austin had taken her into the woods.

"I think there is something out there."

"Well," he stepped closer, the heat of his body radiating off her own. "I can assure you there is nothing dangerous in those woods," he whispered, close to her ear. A slightly playful smile crossed his full lips.

"Well, I guess I could take the word of a stranger," she jeered.

"Well, once you give me your name, we won't be strangers anymore."

"Oh, uh," Elly nervously pushed a stray strand of her straight dark hair behind her ear, hoping to hide her blushing cheeks. An overwhelming feeling, one that Elly had never felt before, washed over her entire body. "Elly, my name is Elly."

"It's nice to meet you, officially." Khalil gave Elly a wide, toothy smile. "So, what are *you* doing out here?"

"Escaping," Elly thoughtlessly said, immediately wishing she could take back the word.

"Seems we have that in common," Khalil admitted, a tight smile casting a painful shadow over his face. "What are you running away from?"

Elly hesitated, the question feeling too personal to answer considering she had just met him, but there was this feeling of an imaginary string pulling her towards him. Biting her lower lip, she wasn't sure what to tell this stranger.

"See, I'm running away from my brother, Rex. He's back for a visit and playing dad again."

"You lost your father?" Instantly, Elly felt connected with this stranger.

"Yes, my brother and I were young when he died. Ever since then it's just been us and my mother until…" he hesitated, the pain still raw. "She was diagnosed with cancer about a year ago." Elly braced herself for what she thought he'd say next. "It's any day now," he added, casting his eyes away, unable to say the words.

"My mother died a week ago," Elly choked out, feeling the pressure building in her chest, as her eyes burned to release the pain.

"I am so sorry, I can't believe..." Khalil pulled his thick fingers through his wavy, jet-black hair.

"I'm sorry, I really shouldn't have brought it up. You don't even know me." Elly started to walk away, sure he thought she was crazy for just blurting out such things.

"No, no," he said, reaching her hand just as she swung it back, his fingers instantly wringing within her own effortlessly. A shock exploded through her hand, as he quickly dropped it. "That might just be what we both need right now. All I want is to get away from everyone who thinks they know how I should be handling all this or what I should be doing. Maybe sometimes a stranger, who is unbiased and unjudging of our thoughts, is just what we need."

"That would be nice," Elly admitted, realizing she had no one else she could talk to about her mother's death. Which had just become her possible murder.

"So, what happened?" Khalil asked, as Elly casually nestled amongst the grass, both of them sitting across from each other. Elly picked at the blades, wrapping them around her thin, pale fingers as she thought about his question.

"I came home from school," Elly started, staring down at the blades of grass. "There was blood everywhere." Taking a deep breath she held back the flashes that threatened to consume her mind and the tears that burned in her eyes.

"I can't imagine what that must've felt like," Khalil mused.

"Fear, the deepest I've ever felt," Elly confessed, her cheeks instantly flushing as she realized how vulnerable she was with this stranger.

"Each day, I watch little pieces of my mother fade away, like a flower at the turn of the season. They know they are dying but they hold on, only releasing a single petal at a time until..." the words caught in his throat.

Elly reached out, their fingers lightly touching, as their pain connected them. Even though they were both surrounded by a painful fog, somehow in a brief moment they had found each other, like a light guiding them both to each other in the distance. Elly wondered if Khalil would be a lighthouse for her, or if she was forever doomed to roam lost in the thickening fog that was her grief.

"I worry about what my life will be without my mother," Elly confided, gazing into Khalil's deep, brown irises that glistened in the sunlight.

"I know what my life will be like," Khalil admitted, "and it scares me to my core."

Elly and Khalil stared at each other for several minutes, their own fear reflected back at them. They both feared a life without their mothers and the unknown of what they could become without her in their lives. Elly realized she had been closing her mind off from thinking of what her life would become, while Khalil saw it clearly. The fact that he feared it scared Elly even more.

Khalil found himself strangely vulnerable with Elly, as he wanted to tell her his fear. He wasn't sure what he thought would happen when he emerged from the shadows of the forest, having watched her cry for what felt like hours. Each moment he watched her, he felt drawn to her to make her feel better in some way. Normally, he would've remained hidden, as he preferred it, but his need to comfort her was stronger. Now, he was confessing his darkest fears to her, unsure of where this need to be honest with her came from.

"My brother wants me to go away with him, and without my mother I know I will no longer be able to stop him."

Elly nodded in understanding. But, Khalil knew she could never truly understand his fear, not without knowing the truth.

"I wanted to stay." Elly glanced back up at the large, white house in the distance. She could see the top windows, but the first floor was hidden behind the hill, meaning that her grandparents wouldn't be able to see her talking to this stranger from the kitchen window. "I never wanted to come here, that's for sure."

"Well, I'm glad you did," Khalil confessed, his eyes shadowed by his long, dark lashes. Elly blushed, quickly looking away.

Suddenly, Elly turned, hearing a faint whisper of her name on the wind. Looking back up to the house, she strained to see if someone was calling for her, but she couldn't see anyone. Elly had considered revealing to Khalil that her mother might have been murdered, but the information was still raw and she wasn't sure what she believed at this point.

"I should get back before they start looking for me," Elly conceded. As much as she wanted to keep talking to Khalil, she didn't want her grandparents to find out about her new secret friend, because that is what he would become to her now.

"Yeah, okay." Khalil regrettably said goodbye to Elly, watching her walk slowly back up the hill, turning at the top to give a slight hidden wave in his direction. He raised his hand, feeling hopeful for the first time in years.

"Elly?" Jane called as she walked through the back kitchen door, the screen slapping back against the wooden frame betraying her return. She winced at the noise, knowing she'd have to talk to her grandmother now. "Is that you?" She called again from the living room.

"Yes," Elly answered, as she pulled off the old boots, tossing them by the back door. Jane appeared in the doorway.

"Where have you been? Is everything okay?"

"I'm fine, just please stop asking me that." Elly pushed by Jane, making it halfway to the staircase before Jane's voice stopped her in her tracks.

"We are just worried, Elly." Jane's matter-of-fact tone sparked anger in Elly. As if somehow they could instantly take responsibility for Elly, caring about her whereabouts when they hadn't spoken or even called her the last ten years.

"Why? Why are you so worried?" Elly demanded, standing her ground in the hallway, as Jane lingered in the living room doorway.

Jane stepped towards Elly, attempting to close the gap between them, but Elly moved back at her step unwilling to allow her closer. Elly could feel the burn rising in her eyes, as her mind pleaded for clarity. Yet, no matter how much she wanted Jane to answer her, deep down she feared the truth as much as she did the lie.

"You have suffered a grave loss, we all have. Can't I be worried about my granddaughter?"

"You don't even know me."

"I know you better than you know yourself, just trust me on that."

"Trust you? How could I ever trust you after what you did?" Pain cascaded across Jane's face, as it quickly contorted into anger. Elly got the feeling that there was another piece to the puzzle of her mother and grandmother's relationship. She wondered briefly what had happened between them, her mother never willing to discuss it.

"You don't know," Jane reassured herself more than Elly. Jane was sure Julianna never told her daughter the truth behind their strained relationship because then she would have to tell Elly who she was inside.

"I know that you abandoned us. I know that my mother never spoke of you. Why is that?"

Inside relief washed over Jane as her assumptions were confirmed. Julianna had not told her the truth. While she knew the day would be fast approaching with her mother's death, she wanted to protect her granddaughter, just as she had her own daughter.

"Your mother and I had a disagreement."

"That's vaguely cryptic."

"It would be hard for you to understand."

"Stop lying, just tell me the truth."

"I promise, I have never once lied to you."

"But you haven't told me the truth either."

3

Chapter Three

Elly spent the rest of the day hiding away in her bedroom with her knees curled tightly to her chest in the bay window as she overlooked the yard. She watched as the trees gently blew in the cascading wind, the calm blades of grass, and the moving sun across the clear sky. She could see the shadows of her grandfather in the garage and assumed he was building something. But, as she looked into the shadows of the forest, she didn't see Khalil.

Just as the sun was kissing the treetops, she saw her grandmother walking across the yard towards the garage, then disappearing into the shadows. Feeling restless, she took the opportunity to silently leave the confinement of her room. Moving softly down the hallway she made her way to the closed door at the end of the hallway. Curiosity guided her as she yearned to learn more about the leather-bound book she found.

Gently, she pulled the door open, wincing as it groaned in

pain at the forced movement. Silently, she melted away into the room. Elly scanned the dark room, waiting for her eyes to adjust, the sun so low that only tiny shards of light peeked through the thick curtains. Slowly the shapes of the room took form, as Elly started to walk around. Her fingertips tingled as she glided them across the stakes of books on top of the dresser, dust fluttering up into the flecks of light.

Elly moved towards the desk, the leather-bound book was still there where she dropped it earlier that day. Gently, she lifted the book into her hands, brushing the dust from the top. Her fingers traced the letter J embossed into the leather. She swallowed hard as she realized this book belonged to her mother. Taking a deep breath, she opened the ruffled, yellowed pages of the book seeing her mother's inked letters on the pages. It was *her* journal.

Turning to the ribbon-marked page, Elly read the words written in her mother's hand: The nightmares will not go away. I am afraid to go to sleep at night, knowing they will haunt my dreams. Each morning I wake covered in sweat, fear filling my heart. It calls to me at all hours of the day now. It is getting closer and I have nowhere to hide. I don't want any of this, but she tells me I don't have a choice … it's in my blood. I am marked.

Suddenly, Elly heard heavy footsteps in the hallway. The light that crept under the door, swirled in the shadow of a person as they walked towards the door. Holding her breath, Elly slowly closed the journal and gently placed it back on the desk. The shadow stopped outside the door.

"Elly?" Austin asked as he opened the door, shining a harsh light in the room. Elly squinted at the blinding light, her eyes long since adjusted to the darkness. "What are you doing in here?"

"Nothing."

Austin had a tight smile on his face that was filled with pain as he scanned the room. He refused to step into the room, waiting for Elly to exit. Wanting to take the journal, but knowing he would stop her, Elly regrettably walked towards him without the journal, leaving it in its place on the desk.

"This was her room," Austin whispered, as Elly walked by him out into the hallway. Gently, he closed the door behind her, leaving a pausing hand on the door, as if somehow touching the door connected him to his dead daughter.

"My mom?" Elly asked, a need to be sure of his words. Austin just nodded, a deep pain blinding his eyes as he looked away from Elly. She wanted to ask more about her mother, specifically what happened to make her never return or talk to her mother, but she saw a deep pain in Austin's eyes that stopped her from asking.

"I came to let you know dinner will be ready soon," Austin announced, as Elly started back towards her room.

"I'm not hungry," Elly lied, dreading another conversation filled with lies. Austin nodded as he retreated from the hallway. He paused at the top of the staircase making sure Elly went back into her room before taking the steps down to the kitchen to help Jane with dinner.

Within minutes an expected knock came at Elly's door.

"Elly, dear, may I come in?" Jane asked, only poking her head through a crack, waiting for permission as if she hadn't already violated it. Elly nodded, feeling as if she had no other choice.

"Elly, look, I know you have questions." Elly shifted on the window seat as Jane perched on the opposite end.

"Was my mother murdered?" Elly asked.

Jane sighed, gazing out the window as she considered what she was willing to tell Elly. Jane traced a wrinkled hand over the delicately stitched pillow. She had chosen this room for Elly because of the light, pastel hues. She thought it would make her feel better to be in such a bright place. Yet, she could still see the deep sorrow in her eyes, which Jane should expect. After all, she was still grieving too.

"We are not sure," Jane admitted. "It's still an open investigation."

Elly scoffed at Jane's excuse to get out of being honest. She knew what she heard her say in the kitchen. Jane thought her mother was murdered. Elly couldn't understand why she would keep that a secret.

"I want to tell you the truth. But, it's complicated."

"The truth always is," Elly mumbled, keeping her eyes down, avoiding Jane's gaze. It was what her mother always said when she asked about her grandparents.

"I think we both need time," Jane confessed. "It's only been a week. In time, we will get more answers and maybe we can talk about it then?" Jane offered, knowing there would come a time when she would no longer be able to keep their secret from Elly.

Elly nodded, conceding that Jane was just like her mother: stubborn.

"Dinner is ready, I can bring it to your room if you prefer?"

Jane desperately wanted to build a relationship with her estranged granddaughter, especially before she had to reveal the truth. Yet, she knew it would take time to build her trust. Time she hoped they both had.

"I'm really tired, do you mind?" Elly asked, unsure if her offer was true. Her mother never let her miss a meal together, not always at the kitchen table and sometimes in front of a movie or in silence after a long day, but never alone.

"Sure," Jane forced from her mouth.

Jane returned within minutes with a tray that held a plate with good southern-style cooking of fried pork chops and mashed potatoes, a meal Elly did not find appetizing. After Jane left without saying anything, Elly picked at the food. She looked out the window, the sun starting to spread like melting butter over the treetops.

Night fell like a curtain of darkness over the landscape. In the distance, a faint light glowed like a fading headlight in the night. But, there were no roads. Looking out, Elly tried to see the light more clearly. Slowly, the lights started to move through the dark, the glow intensifying by the second. Elly pushed the plate of food away, pushing her nose up against the window, desperate to see the source of the lights.

Just when she thought the lights would reveal their host, they disappeared, the landscape falling back into darkness. Elly's held breath released as she realized she missed her opportunity. Leaning back on her knees, she pondered the floating lights. She knew they had to come from somewhere or something. She just didn't know what, or who.

Elly tossed endlessly in her sleep, as her dreams were filled with glowing lights and dark shadows in the forest. A low moaning filled her room as the words she read in her mother's journal haunted her dreams. Suddenly, the lights that were dancing about in her dreams burst open, the brightness startling her awake.

Elly's eyes struggled to adjust from the bright burst of light in her dream to the silent darkness of the night. Feeling the quick rise and fall of her chest, she attempted to regain her composure by clasping her hand over her chest. She willed herself to slow her breathing by whispering into the darkness, *It was only a dream.*

Her ears rang with the thunder of her heartbeat for several minutes, as her mind slowly adjusted to reality. That is when she heard it. At first, she told herself it was just the wind, willing herself to return to sleep, feeling the weight of exhaustion on the tips of her eyelids. But, the wind would not stop as it howled past her window. Sitting up, Elly walked over to the window and strained to see through the darkness.

As if on command, the clouds parted revealing a full moon as light flooded her room. Elly found it mesmerizing. The earlier warm, yellow glow of the setting sun was a stark difference from the pure, white, milky glow of the moon. Looking down over the yard, as a Princess from her tower, Elly surveyed the night. It was still; frozen in time.

The wind howled again, pushing against the window, causing the panes of glass to creak as they flexed beneath its power. The whispering rode on the wind as a surfer on the waves, washing up against the windows for Elly to hear clearly. Elly could not only hear the lullaby, but she could feel it pressing against her chest. It pulled at her to move, calling her to its sound. Elly pushed her hand to the glass, the heat of her hand causing an instant fog to form on the cold pane. Her fingers tingled and pricked with nervousness. She felt as if she could feel each nerve dancing with excitement.

Another gust of wind pushed the clouds back over the moon, pulling down a dark curtain over the glow of the moon. In the darkness, Elly could see something moving in the shadows of the trees. Leaning into the glass, her breath hot against the surface, she yearned to see what was moving. Suddenly, the shadows turned revealing two yellow lights flickering in the distance.

The lights!

Elly was hypnotized as she stared at the unmoving lights, more defined and vivid than better. She could feel her heart start to beat wildly, as her mind seemed singularly focused on the lights. She had an unknowing urge building inside her thoughts. She had to get to the lights.

In only her oversized t-shirt, Elly turned, racing to the door, determined to touch the lights. Just as she pulled open her bedroom door, her mind focused on only one thing, she was stopped by a towering presence in the doorway.

Elly's eyes flashed with anger and excitement, each pulling at each other in a tango-like dance. Jane recognized the familiar look as she stood, blocking Elly's exit.

"Are you okay?" Jane pulled her dingy robe tightly around her waist.

"Uh, yes, I just couldn't sleep." Elly's shock was evident, as her mind had been abruptly stopped in its tracks. She shifted awkwardly as the urgent feeling to rush from the house to the lights was starting to dim. She was sure Jane wouldn't understand, or worse she'd try to talk to her about it.

"I was going to get some water."

Jane knew she was lying.

"I'll join you." Jane stepped back allowing Elly to walk from the room. Suddenly, Elly could not remember what it was she was in such a rush for, the feeling of chasing the lights completely gone.

"Actually, I think I'm okay now."

"Are you sure?"

"Yes, I um... I'm just going to go back to bed."

Jane gave Elly a skeptical look as she returned to her bed. She didn't want to leave Elly alone, but she forced herself to close the door convincing herself there was no other way out of this house except through this door and she would guard it all night if she had to. The call was only the beginning of what would happen. Elly was not ready. Neither was Jane.

4

Chapter Four

Elly was not sure when she fell back asleep, only that when she woke the sun was drifting on specks of dust throughout her room. Thankfully, she had fallen back into a dreamless sleep. Last night her nightmares had felt real and reality had felt like a dream. Her ears rang with the lullaby in the wind and her mind could still vividly see the yellow lights moving in the darkness. There was an ominous presence to this place, her mother had felt it when she lived here and now Elly felt it as well. A shiver crept down her spine.

The smell of maple syrup lured Elly into the kitchen, where she saw Jane, still in the same dingy robe, cooking over the stove. *Guess it wasn't a dream,* Elly thought.

"Good Morning," Jane chimed, as she slid the pancakes onto a plate. "I just finished breakfast." Jane took the open container of syrup and poured it generously over the stack of pancakes, without bothering to ask Elly her preference.

Elly pulled her stiff body up on the barstool, as the smell of pancakes melted with maple making her mouth water. She was not used to a home-cooked breakfast, her regular morning diet consisting of coffee and occasionally cereal. However, the warm pancakes seemed to soothe her sore body and quiet the lullaby still ringing in her ears.

"Coffee?" Jane asked, holding the full pot in her hand, the empty cup perched just underneath it waiting for Elly's answer. The deep midnight blue color of the cup morphed to have two yellow lights as Elly stared at the cup. "Elly?" she prompted, pulling Elly from her thoughts as she quickly nodded yes. Jane glared at her as she slid the cup of coffee across the counter.

"Where is - uh - Austin?" Elly asked, attempting to divert the developing conversation in the awkward silence. Jane winced at Elly's use of her husband's name, feeling a sting of sorrow over the absence of the relationship they should have with their only granddaughter.

"He's out this morning," she motioned out towards the garage, "building a bench, I believe."

Elly glanced out the window but didn't see Austin, or anything else for that matter. She shifted awkwardly on the stool, wishing she could think of a reason to leave so she did not have to be left alone with Jane; who had made it perfectly clear to Elly that she needed time before discussing her mother's possible murder. Elly still wasn't sure if she was angry with her or sympathetic. Suddenly, she found herself wanting to discuss it with Khalil, which was odd considering she barely knew him at all.

"I think I'll just go for a walk," Elly announced, thinking this was the only way she might get the chance to talk to Khalil.

"Just stay on the property and don't go into the forest." Jane glared at Elly attempting to read her mind but failed. "And be back about lunchtime, okay?" Elly nodded in agreement, as she shoveled in the last bite of pancake.

Jane watched Elly as she walked past the garage, then just to the edge of the forest. For a moment, Jane thought she would have to run after her into the woods, unsure if she was deliberately defying her orders or mindlessly entering the woods. But then, Elly turned to trace the treeline with her feet. Jane watched until Elly was out of her eye line from the kitchen window.

"Anymore left?" Austin asked as he stomped his dirt-covered boots by the back door, pulling Jane from her trance.

"On the counter," Jane announced, not taking her attention from the dishes she was still washing. She was still mad at him for taking Elly into the woods yesterday. Only when she heard the screen door make its final wail did she turn around to see Austin taking the last pieces of pancakes in his raw, greasy hands.

"She went out for a walk," Jane announced, her anxiety showing through in the way she wrung the dishrag in her fingers.

"I am sure she will be fine," Austin offered, gently pulling the dishrag from her hands. Softly he slid his own hands around her arms, quelling her anxiety instantly. "She is safe here."

"What if she goes into the woods?"

"I don't think she will. The last time scared her pretty badly. Besides I'm sure we have more time," Austin affirmed, without any facts to back it up which infuriated Jane.

"You don't know that for sure though. And last night," Jane

paused, knowing what she felt last night and that Elly felt the same. "I don't think we have as much time as we thought we would."

"Trace will be here soon, I am sure we can wait until then," Austin urged, attempting to pacify her anxiety.

"I'm not really sure what difference that makes," Jane confessed, noticeably exasperated with her husband's attempt to avoid the truth that she felt was slapping them in the face. "Nor do I think it is best to wait for him either. We should just tell her before all of this just gets out of our hands."

"No, Jane, now we talked about this," Austin's voice firm, as he squeezed her shoulders. "She just lost her mother, it's too much right now."

"We just lost our daughter," Jane interjected angrily.

"We are adults, Jane. She is a child. Give her time to grieve, adjust. It's the best thing for her, don't you want that?" Jane nodded, knowing he was right. "She has an affinity to Trace, it will help to have him here." Jane nodded again, knowing that it was best, especially since it was her plan from the beginning. But having Elly here, knowing that she was starting to feel the pull, she worried that if they waited it would be too late. The change would happen and she'd be unprepared ... unprotected.

5

Chapter Five

Elly walked along the treeline, her eyes trained on the shadows under the thick canopy, looking for Khalil. When she first made it to the trees, she thought maybe she'd hear the lullaby again or feel the pull towards the woods, but nothing. It only made the events of yesterday feel more imagined than real.

She stood by the singular, towering oak tree at the edge of the property. The place she had seen Khalil the day before. Leaning against the firm, rough trunk, she gazed out over the open fields that led back up to the house. From the back, she noticed that most of the windows had the curtains drawn closed, pieces of the siding on the second floor were starting to crack and peel, giving the home a more neglected feel than the front. Elly considered it might be difficult for her grandparents to care for such a large house just the two of them.

"Hello." Elly jumped, his voice immediately jolting her from her thoughts. "Fancy seeing you here again." She looked up at him just in time to catch the sun gleaming off his overly white teeth as his smile revealed a deep dimple on his left cheek.

"Hi." Elly nervously bit her lower lip, eager to jump into a conversation with him, desperate to work through her thoughts, but holding back unsure if they could just pick up in serious conversation.

"Something on your mind today?" Khalil asked, his playful smile fading into concern. He could feel her nervous energy, sense the anxiety in her fidgeting body, and smell the fear on her skin.

"It's just that - " she hesitated, unsure how to even begin to describe what was happening. "Well, it's my grandmother - she's just not..." her words trailed off again.

"It's okay, remember no judgment," he added, holding up his hands in surrender. The gesture comforted Elly, as she realized she now wanted to confess it all to Khalil, assured he would understand. There was something about the way he looked at her, coupled with his playful demeanor that eased her anxiety and made her feel as if they were long-time friends, not strangers that met yesterday.

"My grandmother is lying to me, I know it."

"Do you think it has something to do with your mother's death?"

"I know it does," Elly affirmed. "There's something else too." She winced, dancing on her feet, as she mustered the strength to tell him. "I don't really know my grandparents. In fact, I have no memory of them at all. My mother stopped speaking to them when I was a little girl. I asked my grandmother what happened, but she's refusing to talk to me about it, which just makes everything more confusing and suspicious." Elly exhaled the breath she had held in the entire time, realizing that she had just blurted everything out.

"Wow, that's a lot," Khalil admitted. He moved around her, nestling in between the large roots of the tree. He tapped the protruding root next to him, motioning for her to sit by him. Elly didn't feel much like sitting, in fact, she felt like running very far away, but instead, she nervously perched on the root.

"When my father died, I promised my mother that I wouldn't be anything like him. See, he was careless - well, more reckless than anything else. He did things that initially put him in harm's way, and us as well. As long as my mother is around, my brother is kept at bay in his feeling of forcing me to follow in our father's footsteps." Khalil let out a deep sigh, as sorrow flashed across his face. It was clear to Elly that he loves his mother very much. Their pain over their mothers' lives being a tethered rope pulling them closer together.

"That must be so difficult," Elly offered, looking down at her hands, as she knew there was really nothing she could say to make it feel any better.

"I'm eighteen, in a couple more months," he offered.

"Should I say Happy Birthday then?" Elly giggled and he vehemently nodded.

"I worry that then my brother, Rex, will force me into the family business." There was seething anger to his tone, as he hissed the words *family business*. Elly got the impression but was too afraid to ask point-blank, that it was probably something illegal.

Elly just watched as Khalil tore at a leaf he had been turning over in his long, slender fingers. She knew more than most that this was a moment in which Khalil needed silence. There were no comforting or supportive words he needed to hear, but more he just needed her to sit there and allow the silence to slowly heal his wounds.

"I don't plan on going though," Khalil announced, breaking the silence between them, as he tossed the last piece of leaf.

"Well, I'd jump at the chance to leave this place," Elly confessed, attempting to ease the growing tension.

"Really, why is that?"

"Well aside from having to deal with my grandparents I don't really know, there is something about this place," she glanced towards the woods, "that gives me a creepy feeling." Elly shivered at the thought of the howling winds and unknown glowing lights.

"Well, maybe we should change that," Khalil said, as a sly smile slid across his perfectly framed face. He held out his hand for Elly, who hesitated only slightly before conceding to follow his lead. Elly slid her hand into his own, forgetting all about the millions of things she wanted to say.

Khalil pulled her to the edge of the woods, then stepped under its canopy, waiting patiently for Elly to trust him. As much as Elly did not want to go into the woods, she didn't want to let go of his hand. It was not lost on her that she was about to follow a basic stranger into the one place Jane told her not to go. She hesitated, unsure of how much trouble she would get into if Jane found out, or worse if she heard the lullaby in front of Khalil. She wondered if he'd think she was crazy. Against all her better judgment and fears, she allowed Khalil to pull her deeper into the woods.

She followed him in silence, as he navigated through the tall, thin trees. The earth was moist under her boots causing them to sink with each step. Khalil kept them in an area that still allowed light, but just beyond she could see the tree trunks grew thicker and the shadows darker. Her heart quickened, but Khalil seemed to feel right at home, a smile permanently plastered on his face.

"There is a hidden beauty in these woods," Khalil offered in an attempt to make Elly feel more comfortable.

"You like to be hidden?" Khalil stopped in awe of Elly's intuitive observation.

"I guess so," he shrugged as he tried to hide his own vulnerability. Khalil always had to hide his true self even from his own family. Only his mother knows the truth.

"There is a sense of peace out here," Elly offered to ease the growing tension in Khalil's shoulders. There was a lost look in his eyes as his hand squeezed slightly tighter, his thoughts clearly bothering him. "You said you run through the woods?"

"Oh, uh - yeah, I do." Khalil pushed the thoughts aside.

"So you live on the other side of the river?"

"And through the woods," he joked, poking fun at the old children's tale, a smile returning to his face. Elly realized she preferred him smiling, as she could see his dimple and a softness in his deep brown eyes.

"Very funny," Elly smiled, feeling comfortable in the woods for the first time. "Is it far from here?"

"Are you inviting yourself over to my house?" He teased.

"Oh - uh - no." Elly's eyes were wide, as her cheeks flushed with embarrassment. In her attempt to make small talk to distract Khalil from his painful thoughts, she inadvertently made it seem as if she wanted to go to his house. "I was uh - just asking."

"No, it's okay, I know. Another time."

"Agreed," Elly said too quickly.

"Can I show you something else though?"

"Yes." Elly was grateful for the change in subject, as she followed Khalil deeper into the woods. Keeping them just on the edge of the thicker parts of the forest, Khalil easily navigated his way through the woods, as if he was following some unseen path.

As they approached a rather larger tree compared to the others around it, Khalil stopped and pointed his free hand to the treetops. Looking up, Elly saw a thicker area of leaves, or so that's what it initially appeared to be, but as her eyes adjusted she realized it was something built into the tree.

"It's a treehouse," he smiled, "for lack of a more mature term." Elly giggled, as she pictured Khalil as a small body bouncing through the woods. Of course, she couldn't see how he would get up into the massive tree that was a least ten feet off the ground. Seemed unnecessarily dangerous, especially for a child.

"Did you build that?"

"Oh, no, I found it a few years ago." They both stared up at the dark figure hidden in the shadows of the large tree branches. "Want to go up?" he asked, gently pulling on her hand. He had not let go of it since they entered the woods.

"It's very high," she hesitated.

"It's okay, I'll catch you if you fall."

A laugh escaped Elly's lips as if Khalil catching her was even a possibility. Yet, there was something serious about the way he assured her that he could, that made her feel safe, so she allowed him to pull her closer to the tree. Stepping over massive roots as they carved a maze in the ground, they made their way up to the enormous trunk. Up close, Elly could see the loosely hanging boards that climbed up the tree.

"Are you sure?" She asked, her foot perched on the first board.

"Yes, I've climbed it plenty of times before," he assured her, gently placing his hand on her lower back. Elly knew she needed to return home instead of climbing into this hanging death trap with a complete stranger, but there was something about the way Khalil looked at her that made her forget things. Things like the recent death of her mother, or the secret her grandmother was holding, or the indescribable feelings she was having in this place. Elly liked being able to forget, so she started to climb.

Khalil remained right behind her the entire way to the top. Even though Elly couldn't bring herself to look down, she could feel that he was there. Reaching the last board, Elly lifted her hand through the dark hole in the floor. For a split second she imagined that instead of pulling herself up, something, or someone would grab her, forcing her into the darkness.

"Are you okay?" Khalil asked behind her, as she hesitated to go into the treehouse.

"Uh, yes. Are you sure it's okay to go inside?"

"Yes, I am sure, trust me." Elly thought about that for a moment - *can she trust him?* It seemed ridiculous, but she did actually trust him. She reached up and pulled herself into the darkness.

There was no light in the treehouse, the leaves blocking any stray rays. Elly stood uneasy as she waited for her eyes to adjust, the smell of moist moss and musty mold giving her the feeling she was underground instead of so high above it. She felt disoriented as if she was about to fall over when suddenly Khalil was beside her placing a stabling hand on her back.

Gently, he walked around her, pulling a small flashlight out of his pocket and immediately shining a dim light into the darkness. Elly blinked, her eyes adjusting to her surroundings as she took in the deep, vibrate green color of the leaves. They draped across the ceiling then entangled around each other over the manmade windows on either side of the treehouse. Elly felt as if the tree was reaching out to hug her.

The flashlight cast a ghostly light on Khalil's face, highlighting the slight stumble on his squared chin that she hadn't noticed before which made him appear even older. Suddenly, Elly realized that she was much younger than Khalil. She had only just turned sixteen in a month ago, which would make them at almost two years apart in age. She found herself wondering if he thought she was older than that, or if he knew she was younger.

"What do you think?" He asked, opening his arms encouraging her to take in the full scope of the treehouse. Elly noticed he was proud of this place, even though he admitted to just finding it.

"How do you think someone built this?" Elly wondered out loud, as she walked around the edge, slowly sliding her fingers over the molded, rotten boards. She could feel the moistness within the boards from the unknown amount of rainstorms it had survived.

"Someone skilled at climbing," Khalil offered, as he watched Elly, amused by her astonishment. He couldn't reveal to her that he had, in fact, built it. "Most likely strong, nimble ... " she turned to him, "or so I would assume," he quickly added, attempting to cover his lie.

"I guess that would make the most sense." Elly reached a darkened corner, unreached by the light, but she could still tell there was something there. Bending down, her hands caressed something hard. She smiled as she realized what it was.

"Are these yours?" She asked, pulling one of the books into the light.

"Oh, uh, yes, they are," Khalil admitted. "I often come here to read - alone."

"Don't you basically live alone?"

"Well, yes, but only for the last couple of months. Before that ..." his voice trailed off, as he did not feel like having another conversation about his family, partially when it was in regards to his brother, Rex.

"I like to read as well," Elly offered, opening the book in her hand and tracing the words on the page. "What is this one about?" She asked.

"Oh, uh, that one," he stepped closer, so close Elly could feel the heat of his body against her own as he leaned down over her shoulder. "Ah, that is *Bisclavret*."

"I don't think I've ever heard of it."

"It was originally written in French in the 12th century."

"Oh, so you are one of those," Elly jeered.

"What is that supposed to mean?"

"You like antiques."

"If you mean do I appreciate some of the first literature ever written, then yes, I do," he confessed, pulling the book from

Elly's hands. It slammed closed in his palm, as Elly feared she offended his taste in reading materials.

"So, what is it about?" Elly faked interest in the book in an attempt to recover from her blunder.

"Well, if you must know," he teased, showing her the cover of the book. Elly noticed it was leather-bound with the title inscribed in gold across the front just above the gold outline of a wolf. "It's a redemption story."

"How is that?"

"Well, it's a story of a dishonored man who is cursed, forced to live a life as a werewolf." Khalil studied Elly's reaction, as she scoffed at the idea. "It was his punishment," Khalil added, as Elly saw a flicker of sadness in his eyes. She wanted to poke at the idea of the story but realized that a part of Khalil was attached to this story. "But then he is redeemed through his loyalty towards the king. In return, he is transformed back into a human."

"Can I read it?" Khalil looked shocked by her request. Elly realized that if this story meant something to Khalil then she was desperate to read it and figure it all out.

"Uh, sure." He flicked the book into her open hands.

"So, you like running and reading," Elly dictated as she walked around the treehouse, tucking the book under her arm, "is there anything else you do?"

"Well, I don't want to brag, but I am a pretty good cook. At least my mother told me so and well, I have never cooked for anyone else."

Khalil had a tight, forced smile on his face, as Elly saw the raw pain of his words. He didn't enjoy cooking, it was something he was forced to learn in the absence of his family and his mother's illness. She briefly found herself wondering what was worse: Khalil watching his mother slowly die or the abrupt way she lost her mother.

"I can't cook," Elly admitted. "Yet, neither could my mother. We were a *pick up an order for two* type of duo." Elly could feel the tears threatening the corner of her eyes as she mentioned her mother.

"Where did you live with her?"

"New York City."

"Oh, wow, I didn't realize you were a city girl." Khalil flashed her a warm, playful smile. "This must all seem so - mundane to you."

"Not really, actually," Elly confessed. Even though she harbored anger towards her grandparents for forcing her to move down here, she did feel as if the city would've only made it harder to move on from her mother's death. There was a part of her that was grateful for it, but also resentful as well. "I do miss my friends, the energy of the city, and everything my life was with my mother." Elly paused, feeling the sharpness of the cold air against her raw wound. "But, I couldn't have that anymore there, so ..."

"I feel the same about this place," Khalil divulged, shoving his hands into his pockets which made him appear even taller. "That was until I met you."

Elly's breath caught in her lungs at his words, as a powerful warmth flooded over her entire body. She considered that she misunderstood the meaning of his words, that he was only making an observation, not a statement of feelings. But, it sure felt like a statement of his feelings.

"I feel the same way," she admitted, her eyes casting down towards her shifting feet as she was not able to look into his eyes as she said the words. She knew she would see that he did not feel the same as she did. After all, he was two years older than her. He probably saw her as a child. Coupled with the fact she only just meant him, she was assured she misunderstood.

Gently, he slid his fingers under her chin and lifted so her eyes met his own. She could smell the sweet lily of the leaf on his fingers from earlier. Slowly, she raised her eyes to meet his, seeing the intensity in his deep brown irises. She could feel her heart stop as she felt frozen in time.

Elly knew that he was about to kiss her, his breath hot against her lips. She was surprised how much she was willing to allow this stranger to kiss her, something she had never done before this moment. Just before his lips touched her own, she hesitated, her body flinching in fear of the idea of her first kiss. Khalil immediately pulled back, dropping his hand.

"Uh, it's getting late," Khalil said, shifting away from her, as he realized he had overstepped the imaginary line between them both. Even though he barely knew her, he felt drawn to her, as Elly did to him in a way neither of them could fully explain.

"I told my grandmother I'd be back by lunch. I should get going." Elly moved to the hole, but Khalil pulled her back.

"I'll go first."

Elly watched as Khalil effortlessly lowered his body down through the hole, then she followed with a lot less grace as her arms struggled to hold her weight. Elly could feel his hands catching her weight around her waist as she found her footing on the first board. Instinctively she looked down, which she immediately regretted, as her head started to spin realizing just how high off the ground they truly were. She could feel her legs going weak, the fear rising as she realized she was going to fall. She panicked, having no illusions that Khalil would be able to catch her in this position.

Suddenly, Elly was on the ground, cradled in Khalil's arms. Blinking, she tried to remember how it all happened. The last thing she remembered she was at the top of the tree, falling, but now she was on the ground.

"What happened?" Elly groaned, feeling a deep pain spreading over her forehead.

"You started to fall," Khalil explained, still holding her in his arms.

"Did I hit my head?"

"No, I caught you - as promised," he smiled. Gently, he placed her down amongst the roots, ensuring she had her footing before releasing the stabilizing arm he had around her waist. "You okay?"

"Uh, I think so, but how?" She gazed up into his eyes, confused how he could possibly have gotten her from the top of the tree to the ground. She searched his eyes for answers, a flicker of the truth to what happened, but he just stared down at her, his eyes blank.

"We should get you back." He turned and started making his way through the trees.

Even though Elly wanted an explanation, she also did not want to get lost in the woods. But then, just as she was about to start following him, she heard it; the low hum of the lullaby. Turning, she saw it was coming from the darkest part of the forest. In a daze, her mind still reeling from the possible fall she had no memory of, she mindless walked towards the sound.

"Elly," Khalil called in the distance, but he was too far away. Suddenly, the humming stopped as Khalil's hand slid into her own. "Elly," he urged, pulling on her hand.

"What?" Elly's mind shook from its daze as the forest fell silent again.

"You were going the wrong way." Elly looked around realizing that she was no longer standing behind the treehouse. In fact, she didn't see the treehouse anywhere as she looked up at the treetops. *It only felt like a second, so how could she have gone so far?*

"I'm sorry, I must've gotten lost."

"You shouldn't go this far into the woods," Khalil warned.

"I thought you said the woods were a misunderstood place?" Elly questioned, even though she felt the fear creeping into the corners of her mind. For a moment, she considered telling him about the lullaby she kept hearing in the woods but hesitated.

"There are darker places in these woods," Khalil assured her, looking over her shoulder into the thickening darkness just a few feet away. "If you stay in the places that still have some light, you can find your way out. But, if you go in there," he motioned towards the black curtain, "it'll be next to impossible to find your way out."

"What if I take my own light?"

"Doesn't work that way, you need the sun's guiding light to get out of these woods."

"Is that how you know where you are going?" Khalil nodded. "I can't ever seem to get my bearings in this place."

"Well, then stay close," he said, squeezing her hand to ensure she didn't let go.

Khalil's face was filled with concern, having only turned away from Elly for a second, knowing that it could not have been long before he noticed she wasn't behind him. Quickly, he retraced his steps back to the treehouse, then he followed her footprints deeper into the forest. He wasn't sure what drew her deeper into the woods, but he had his suspicions. As much as these woods were a second, isolating home for him, they were innately dangerous by nature.

Holding tightly to her hand, Khalil followed the path lit by the sun back through the woods to Elly's house in silence. Just before they reached the edge of the woods, Khalil stopped and turned to Elly.

"I have to go back home now, but can you hang out again tomorrow?" Khalil asked.

"Under one condition." Elly glanced back at the woods, an unsettling feeling causing her body to fidget. "You don't take me in the woods again."

"Deal."

6

Chapter Six

At the top of the hill, Elly turned hopeful to see Khalil, but he was already lost in the shadows of the forest. She had learned so much about her secret friend in the last twenty-four hours, making it feel almost unbelievable that they hadn't known each other for years already.

Elly was returning home well after lunch, so when she saw Austin sitting outside the back door, his straw hat pulled over his face, and the slow rhythmic breathing of his chest, she tried her best not to wake him up. Silently, she climbed the concrete steps to the screen door, barely pulling it open so it would not groan in pain.

"Elly," he coughed, the slight squeal of the springs announcing her return. "Is that you?" Austin lifted his hat back onto the top of his head.

"Yes."

"Where have you been?" He glared up at her, the sun forcing his eyes to squint so that she was unable to read his feelings. Elly debated whether or not to be honest about going to the woods... or being with Khalil.

"Just walking around."

"Find anything interesting?" Austin asked.

"No, not really."

"Not much around here really."

He gazed out over the vast fields that Jane's family had owned for generations. It was never where he saw himself living, but it was the only choice for Jane when her parents died. So when they married, it became his only choice as well. Over the years, he had come to enjoy his life in the country, though he would've preferred to travel more frequently and have more friends to spend evenings with for various reasons. He always considered himself a social person, but Jane was the opposite. She was reclusive and content hiding out in the country.

"Nope. Did I miss lunch?"

"I think your grandmother - uh, Jane - left something out for you."

"Where is she?" Elly nervously looked around, assuming she would be upset that she didn't come back. Somehow she felt as if her grandmother would instantly know that she had disobeyed her and went into the woods.

"Gone into town to run an errand, I believe."

"Oh, okay." Elly pulled the screen door again to go inside.

"Just stay around here the rest of the day, okay?" Elly understood that he was not asking, but demanding her presence in the house the rest of the day. Suddenly, she got the feeling he was well aware of the fact she went into the woods.

Elly pulled the book from underneath her sweater once she was in the isolation of her room. Pulling out the top drawer of the desk, she tucked the book Khalil had given her into her t-shirts. She did not want to have to explain to either of her grandparents where she acquired this new book.

Closing the drawer, Elly had decided she needed to take a shower first. She could smell the dampness of the woods against her clothes, which she realized Austin would've most likely smelled it as well.

Maybe that was how he knew.

Elly had to wash the evidence away before her grandmother returned. She was sure she would not give her as much grace as Austin had just now.

As Elly was drying out her hair, she saw Jane pulling the pick-up truck back into the driveway. Slowly, Jane backed the truck that was filled with wood into the covered parking area. She watched as Austin greeted Jane, an exchange that most likely had to deal with Elly as Jane did not appear happy. Not wanting another conversation with her grandmother, Elly curled up under the covers. She only planned to pretend to be sleeping when Jane came to her room, but when her eyes opened back up, it was dark outside.

Her hair had dried frizzy and wild, her body chilled to the bone as the cold winter night air had settled around the house. Pulling a sweater over her shivering shoulders and fuzzy socks on her bare feet, Elly proceeded to make her way downstairs. As she reached the last stair she paused, hearing voices coming from the living room.

"What would you have me do?" Austin said.

"Watch her - is that too much to ask?" Jane retorted.

"I was watching her," Austin affirmed.

"Doesn't sound like it."

"Look, you are making this a bigger deal than it needs to be. She is here. Safe, there is nothing to worry about."

"But for how long, Austin."

Suddenly, their voices cut off. Jane appeared in the hallway.

"Elly, you are up," Jane stated, appearing flustered. "Would you like some dinner?" Elly wasn't sure she could speak, so she just nodded instead. "Well, come along then." Elly followed Jane down the hallway into the kitchen, where she immediately took her place on the barstool.

Dinner had already been prepared. Elly could see the used dishes in the sink and knew they had already eaten. Pulling the sleeves over her cold hands, Elly waited for Jane to scold her, as she was sure they were aware she went into the woods. Anxiously, she waited.

Elly was halfway through her dinner before Jane finally spoke.

"You know I only want to keep you safe."

"From what?"

Jane sighed, glancing out the window. "I know your grandfather would like to think those woods are harmless, but I assure you they are not. There are things in those woods. Things you need to stay away from." Elly suddenly got the feeling that Jane might be talking about Khalil.

"What things?" Elly probed, attempting to find out how much she knew about her time in the woods.

"An array of animals first of all." Jane's eyes were wide with fear. "Most of them are poisonous as well. What if a snake bit you?"

"I didn't go far," Elly whispered, ashamed that she had been so reckless. Of course, at the time she was with Khalil and it didn't feel so dangerous, but she couldn't tell Jane that piece of the story.

"I think it's best if you don't take any more walks," Jane announced. Elly wanted to argue, if it was her mother she would've, but there was a cold glare in her eyes. Elly didn't know how angry Jane could get, but she feared it was much more than her mother.

Elly nodded in agreement and the rest of the dinner was spent in silence. Since Jane had made it abundantly clear that Elly needed time before she would talk about her mother, Elly had nothing else she cared to talk about with Jane. A part of her wanted to learn more about Khalil but feared if she asked about the boy through the woods it would reveal her secret friendship. There was no guarantee they even knew Khalil or his family.

After Elly finished dinner, she excused herself back to her bedroom, under the ruse she was still tired. Back in her room, Elly softly opened the top desk drawer and pulled out the thin, old book. Elly pulled her knees up to her chest as she cozied up on the window seat. Elly took in the smell, a mixture of oak, leather, and Khalil. The book fit nicely into her hands, its small, thin stature making it easy to hold. She thumbed through the lightly browned pages.

It was the original version, written in poem form. Each page felt as if it would disintegrate right through her fingers as she gently turned past the first few pages to the start. As she started to read it was as if the words glowed on the pages, the front a flicker of gold in the ink making the words come alive.

Elly read well through the night, finishing it in the early morning hours when night still blanketed the land. Slowly, she closed the book, her mind lost in the detail of the elaborate, magical story of *Biscalvret*.

Her eyelids felt heavy, as images of a large werewolf creature floated through her mind - *the bisclavret*, which she assumed was the French word for werewolf. Elly found herself wondering which part of this particular story had drawn Khalil to hold it in such high regard. There was a poetic rhythmic beat to the read, as Elly herself became engrossed in the tragic betrayal of the man's beloved wife. The knight, who became trapped as the werewolf, no thanks to his horrible wife, was not beastly as they all assumed. He befriended the King, who saw a human nature to him...Elly's eyelids slid closed as she thought about the story of the knight, his face quickly taking a likening to Khalil.

Chapter Seven

Jane allowed the cool water to rush over her aching hands, as she gently massaged her swollen knuckles. Her fingers grazed over the thin, gold band that had bound her to Austin all those years ago when they were just a couple of kids. It had not been her choice, just as much as it had not been his choice as well, but like everything in her life, since she was born, Jane had little control over the matter.

"You are pushing her away," Austin cautioned as he stood next to Jane slowly drying each plate before slipping them away in the cabinet just above his head.

"Don't you think I know that," Jane snapped, immediately bracing her hands on the edge of the sink and taking in a deep breath to calm her nerves.

Austin reached out to her, but she pulled her hands away. Jane was always strong, stronger than any person Austin had ever met in his entire life. He knew his place was to stand behind her, not next to her.

"There is so much at stake here ..." Jane's voice trailed off.

Suddenly, a ring vibrated through the kitchen, pulling Jane from her thoughts. Austin answered the yellow plastic phone attached to a long, curled cord on the kitchen wall and spoke for only a minute before passing it to Jane. She knew who was on the other end.

"Trace, how are you?" Jane breathed into the phone. Abandoning the dishes, Austin naturally taking over solo, Jane paced to the other side of the kitchen.

"Things are well, mother."

Jane breathed a sigh of relief. Trace's endeavors were always dangerous with deadly consequences she understood all too well.

"When can you get home?"

"It's taking longer than expected," Trace admitted. Jane could hear the strain in his voice. He was tired and defeated.

"Anything from Hunter?"

"I called him first, he is still running some tests on the blood samples you sent, but nothing so far." Jane clenched her jaw in anger. "It appears the genetic markers are there, but there is something else as well," Trace paused.

"Well?" Jane probed. Austin glanced over, but Jane turned away from him.

"He's still running some tests, so he wouldn't say."

"Trace, things are not going well here. We need to address this as soon as possible with Elly. We need that information from Hunter," Jane urged.

"I understand, mother, he's doing his best."

"Clearly it's not good enough," Jane snapped again.

"Look, I should get going, I have to get back to uh -" Trace's voice trailed off as if he turned his face away from the phone.

"Get here as quickly as you can."

"Is that an order?" Trace jeered.

"It always is."

Elly could feel the brisk wind against her hot skin that chilled her body causing her to shiver in the darkness. Fog swirled around her in a kind of Van Gogh Starry Night motion as her mind attempted to make sense of what was happening. In the distance, a glowing light drifted through the fog carving a path through it like a maze. Elly reached out as she realized the source of the light - *the moon*. Looking up she saw it through the thick, green leaves. She was in the forest.

Unsure of how she arrived in the forest, her chest rose quickly in fear. Elly could feel the chill of the wind, the moist dew of the fog, and the hairs on the back of her neck prickled in suspense. Her eyes darted around, as she desperately searched for a way out of the forest. Then she saw the glowing, yellow lights. Without thinking, Elly started to run, chasing the lights through the forest. Suddenly they stopped, going black then yellow again in a pulsating motion. As if hit by a bolt of lightning, Elly realized that she was looking into a pair of eyes. Just then, a piercing sound vibrated through her entire body.

Elly's body jolted awake. Elly's fears calmed as she realized she had fallen asleep. *But it felt so real.* Her body was flush with heat, her clothes damp with her own sweat. She had read about night terrors, how they can affect people after trauma, which is what she assumed just happened until she heard it. A howling shook the window panes, prickling the hairs on the back of her neck for real this time.

"It was just a dream," she whispered into the darkness, attempting to quell her growing fear. Jane had said there were animals in the woods, could there be wolves? Or was she still fixated on the story of Bisclavret?

The dream had not been long, as the sun was still not waking up. Elly's mind refused to return to her nightmare, so she didn't even try to go back to sleep in her bed. Her throat felt raw as she swallowed. Elly feared it was from screaming in her sleep again.

Fetching water from the sink in the bathroom was not enough, it was warm and tasted like metal, so Elly tip-toed down to the kitchen. Thankfully, she didn't find Jane outside the door again. Elly filled a glass with filtered water from the fridge. Turning around, her eyes gravitated towards the forest in the distance just outside the window over the kitchen sink. A part of her was afraid to look, that the lights would be staring back at her. *Could they really be eyes?*

"Another nightmare?" Elly jumped at the sound of Jane's voice.

"What?" Elly turned to see her standing in the kitchen doorway. "No," Elly added quickly.

"You have been through so much." Her voice sounded so nurturing, but yet she still stood there, stiff and cold in the dark, like a statue.

"Just needed something to drink." Elly lifted the glass of water. Jane glared at the glass as if it would somehow corroborate her story. When Jane didn't respond, Elly moved towards the doorway, eager to escape the awkward silence.

"Are you sure you are okay?" Jane probed, noticing the remains of sweat still glowing on her pale skin in the moonlight.

"Yes, I'm sure." Elly waited for her to move from the doorway so she could pass, but she didn't move. "I promise," she added.

Jane reluctantly stepped aside to let Elly pass, even though she had heard Elly screaming in her room. Jane knew she had another nightmare. All she could do was hope they would pass after tonight, but a part of her knew they would not.

8

Chapter Eight

It was two days before Khalil knocked on Elly's front door. She had spent her days reading various books from her grandparent's library by the window, stealing moments to gaze out over the yard and down to the tree to see if he had arrived to see her, but nothing. Jane kept a watchful eye on her, so waiting by the tree would've raised suspicions or worse questions she wasn't sure how to answer.

In the last two days, she realized that she knew very little about Khalil, starting with his full name or any other markers for that matter. But, just as she thought she didn't know him, she realized she knew some of the deepest parts of him. She justified that meant more than knowing his last name.

"Elly," Jane called from the foyer, her eyes trained on the young man standing in her doorway. She could smell the must of his shirt and saw a familiarity in his deep brown eyes that she couldn't place in her memory.

"Elly, come down here," she called again, eager to learn of her granddaughter's connection to this stranger on her porch. She found it hard to believe Elly had already acquired a friend in the area, especially considering she hadn't left the house since they arrived five days ago.

Slowly Elly made her way down the staircase, feeling as if she was on display as Jane and Khalil stared, gauging each step. In the last two days, Elly never imagined that Khalil would show up at the door. She more imagined him beckoning her down by throwing rocks at her window as they did in the movies.

"Elly, you have a friend?" Jane's eyes raised in question, waiting for Elly to explain.

"Uh, yes, this is Khalil." Elly glanced at Khalil for help, but he just smiled, clearly enjoying the awkward tension he was causing. "I met him while I was walking."

Just then, Austin appeared in the hallway, his hands still greased as he wiped them off on his dingy overalls. Jane glared at his dirty boots, before signaling to him to interject.

"Hello, who is this?" He offered his hand, which Khalil didn't hesitate in shaking despite the fact it was covered in grease.

"Khalil, sir." Austin smiled, impressed with his polite response. "I'm a friend of Elly's," he added, motioning back to Elly who still hadn't stepped off the last step.

"Oh, I see," Austin shot Jane a look of satisfaction that was quickly debunked by Jane's deep eye roll.

"I was wondering if I might take Elly out for the day."

Elly attempted to hide her excitement over the idea of leaving the house, especially leaving with Khalil.

"We were talking, when we met on the walk," he paused, winked at Elly to show he was in on an unknown plan that her grandparents assumed was concocted as well. "She talked of wanting to learn to fish. So, I thought I could take her." Elly had a hard time hiding her confusion.

"Oh, well, where do you plan to take her?" Austin asked, still appearing impressed much to Jane's dismay. Little did Khalil know that Austin was an avid fisherman.

"Just down to Carters Lake." Austin nodded, familiar with the place. "We will be back before nightfall, " Khalil assured. Elly waited perched on the edge of the step, silently hoping that Jane would allow her out of the house.

"I think that sounds fine," Austin said, as Jane glared at him over Khalil's shoulder. Before Austin could change his response, Elly pushed by them both.

"Thank you." Elly moved quickly, grabbing Khalil's hand, spinning him around on the porch, and dragging him towards what she assumed to be his bronco parked at the bottom of the steps. She didn't want to give Jane any time to refute Austin's approval.

Khalil stumbled behind her down the stairs. Pulling back on her forceful hand, Elly slowed, as Khalil motioned her to the passenger side of the bronco. Elly initially thought his gesture to help her into the bronco to be overly masculine, until she realized that she was physically too short to get into the bronco without help. She felt his hands lightly support her back, as she lifted her body into the truck. Blushing at his touch, she quickly glanced away hoping her grandparents didn't notice as they stared at them from the porch. Out of the corner of her eye, Elly could swear she saw Jane slapping Austin with the dish towel in her hands.

Elly thought the bronco would be bumpy and uncomfortable judging it solely by its exterior presence. It sat at least four feet off the ground with huge tires and a roughed-up, faded green paint job with many dents. But, the warm, soft leather molded to her form, cushioning her as Khalil drove down the gravel driveway. A miniature Christmas tree dangled from the window, giving the car a pine fresh smell. Though it was old, Khalil certainly took good care of it. The dash was polished and there wasn't any dirt in it at all. Glancing back, her grandparents still on the porch watching her drive away, Elly realized the back of the bronco didn't have any seats, just a metal frame filled with fishing stuff.

"That was risky," she said, breaking the silence between them. Elly was still in stock that her grandparents let her leave with a stranger.

"Well, I waited."

"What? No, you didn't, I was watching."

"I was there, waiting for you to come out of that room, but you seemed enthralled with your book." Elly knew he was referring to Bisclavret.

"Well it was ... enthralling," she jeered.

"Did you finish?" Elly nodded yes in response. "What did you think?"

"It was a quick read, more like a poem." Khalil glanced at her and she realized that was not what he was asking her about the book. He wanted to know how she felt about the story itself. "The story was ... well," Elly bit her lower lip, thinking of how to explain her feelings. Khalil waited patiently. "I think if I could describe it in one word it would be sad."

"Sad?" He questioned, a puzzled look on his face.

"Yes, this woman he trusted with his darkest secret betrayed him and abandoned him." Elly's voice cracked. "I know what that feels like," she whispered.

"Your father?" Elly just nodded, holding back the burning tears. "But he was a beast," Khalil offered in defense of the wife's actions of stealing his clothes, leaving him captured in his wolf form for years.

"No, he wasn't actually. The King saw that and his humanity saved him in the end, despite the fact he was considered an animal. The only time he was animalistic was in vengeance." Elly could hear the passion in her voice, having found herself more empathetic towards the werewolf than anyone else in the story. Her mother had always taught her never to judge someone or feed into stereotypes, but to always form her own opinions of people and things.

She flushed with embarrassment, as a wide smile spread across Khalil's face.

"I like your thinking," he admitted, which only caused her to blush more, forcing her to turn her attention out the window to hide it.

As the farmlands repeated like the end of old movies flipping through the last slide, Elly wondered if Khalil had felt the pain of being judged for his appearance, relating to the story in the same way that Elly had when she read it. Or was he drawn into the story by the compassion of the king, after all, Elly had never met a person so genuinely nice as Khalil. Although it could be the betrayal of the wife, maybe he had been hurt that deeply before ... Elly was just about to mustard up the courage to ask him, when he spoke first.

"Have you ever been fishing?" Elly's courage to ask her question caught in her chest, as she allowed Khalil to change the subject.

"Oh, uh, no," Elly confessed. "My dad left when I was little." Khalil nodded, feeling an instant need to hug her in that moment. He thought about reaching his arm over the bench, pulling her closer so she didn't feel so alone, but then he remembered how she flinched in the woods that day. He won't cross that line again.

"Well, prepared to be entertained."

"I always thought it would be kind of boring," Elly admitted. In truth, there was little opportunity to fish in the city, so Elly had never thought it interesting.

"Not at all," Khalil assured her, as he turned off the main road down a poorly marked dirt road. Elly jostled in the seat, as the bronco bumped over the roots and rocks crowding the path. Branches slapped at the window, threatening to reach in and latch on to her at any moment. Instinctively, she slid closer to the middle of the seat. Khalil shifted the gear that reached up to the bottom of the seat, his fingers lightly grazing her leg. Elly felt her breath catch in her throat.

They rode in silence until Khalil pulled off the dirt road into an alcove in the trees. Hidden from view, Elly could hear the rushing of the water as she opened up the door. Before she could attempt to get down by herself, Khalil was at the door with his hand outstretched. A part of Elly didn't want to take his hand, but she was sure she wouldn't be able to exit the bronco gracefully without his help and she was not about to fall into his arms, again.

"I've fished this spot for years," Khalil said as he lowered the back of the bronco trunk down. Elly noticed the large metal truck bed seemed to be handmade. Khalil pulled out two fishing poles and a worn, dirty tackle box, leaving a dirt-covered cooler behind. As much as the front of his car was clean, the back was dirty, especially the fishing items.

"I feel underdressed," Elly confessed as Khalil's boot sank into the soft mud.

"Oh, uh, I have some boots in the trunk, if you need them?"

"Uh, I think so."

Regretfully, Elly pulled the oversized black, rubber boots over her jeans, knowing that once again she'd be clumsily walking through the woods with Khalil.

"Here," he offered, pulling a brown leather jacket from the trunk, as well. "This will keep you warm." Kicking the trunk shut, he motioned for Elly to follow him through the woods.

In her rush to leave, she forgot she was only wearing jeans and a light t-shirt. The word *"rockstar"* across her chest so faded that if you didn't know what it said you couldn't read it. She pulled the jacket over her shivering shoulders, the damp, coolness of the leather making it worse at first. But, as they walked through the woods, it warmed to her body.

Elly struggled to pull her feet out of the mud without completely losing the boot, which made it hard to keep up with

Khalil as he seamlessly made his way just a few feet down to the water.

"I thought we were going to a lake?" Elly asked, staring out over a large rock bed that Khalil was effortlessly balancing across, the water a rushing river instead of a placid lake. There was no way she was not going to fall.

"There are rivers that run into the lake. They are the best spots for catching some trout." He waved her down. Elly bit her lower lip, debating the chances of falling if she attempted to cross the rocks in the oversized, mud-covered boots. Khalil saw her hesitation and immediately crossed back over the rocks, leaving the fishing gear perched on the largest rock in the middle of the river.

"Here," he reached out his hand, "I'll help you across."

Tentatively, Elly started to cross the rocks, balancing heavily on Khalil's hand. As she got closer to him her foot slipped on the rock, sending her already unstable body falling towards the rocks. Seamlessly, Khalil caught her, pulling her tightly to his body as he stabilized his footing on the slippery rocks. He held her there, close to him, taking in the smell of her freshly washed hair, as he refused to let her go.

"Uh, thank you," Elly finally said, shifting her eyes away for fear he might try to kiss her again. Reluctantly, Khalil loosened his grip around her body, helping her stabilize on her feet, before assisting her across the rocks again.

Once they reached the large rock, Elly crawled on her hands and knees over to the edge, as Khalil prepared the fishing rods. She gazed down into the clear water, watching the trout as they swam in place amongst the rocks.

"There are so many," she mused.

"Yeah, this is my secret spot." Khalil handed her a rod, but she had no idea what to do with it. He held out a styrofoam cup full of dirt. "Worm?" he asked, pushing the cup towards her face.

"What?" Elly gaped. Khalil saw her face go pale as she realized that he was offering her a live worm in the dirt. He laughed to himself.

"Okay, I'll do it." Khalil dug his fingers into the dirt, as the worms danced around desperately trying to escape. The worm curled and twisted as he pulled it from the cup. Elly winced as he drove the sharp end of the hook through the worm's withering body.

"It's not that bad," he confessed, still slightly laughing at the grimace on her face.

"Do you know how to cast?" he asked before handing it back to Elly.

She shook her head no. He motioned for her to stand up. Uneasy on her feet, she leaned into Khalil as he stood behind her on the rock.

"So you put your finger here," he started, pointing to the top of the reel, then slowly he pulled the line with his finger. He placed it firmly against the pole.

"Flick this."

Effortlessly, he pushed the reel back releasing the line.

"Then you pull back and as you reach your highest point you release your finger." Slowly, he pulled the rod back as Elly held her finger over his own, then he practiced back and forth before he stepped back.

"You try now," he encouraged.

Elly's first throw was a bust, the hook catching and dropping at her feet. Khalil laughed, then showed her a few times with his rod. After a few more practice throws, she finally threw it far enough in the river to have a chance at hooking one of the swimming trout. Within minutes, she felt a strong pull on the line sending a jolt of excitement through her entire body.

"You got one!" Khalil jumped, tossing his rod to the ground, as he rushed to help her reel in her first fish. Elly pulled back hard on the line, never thinking the fish would pull so hard to get away. With Khalil's help, she finally pulled the fish close enough so that Khalil could reach it with the net. It flopped around in the net as Elly burst with pride.

"I caught one, I caught one," she kept saying to no one in particular.

"That was great, it really was," Khalil added, beaming at her as he unhooked the fish.

Afterward, he took a long string from his tackle box and pierced the sharp metal end through the fish's gills. He tossed it back into the water. Elly's heart jumped at first thinking he was throwing it back, but then she realized he was only doing it to keep it alive. It was hooked. It wasn't going anywhere now.

For the next few hours, they stood side by side, catching fish after fish. Elly learned the difference between the fish you keep and the fish you toss based on size. She even started to hook her own worms in the end, not wanting Khalil to think she was squeamish, which she was. By the mid-afternoon, the sun starting to kiss the tops of the trees surrounding the river, they had five large trout tethered to them.

Khalil tossed the fish into the cooler he had in the back of his bronco, as Elly beamed with joy. She had never felt such exhilaration in her life. Fishing was the furthest thing from boring and maybe even her new favorite thing to do, as long as she got to do it with Khalil.

"So, what did you think?" He asked as they perched on the back bumper. Elly was attempting to remove her boots as her jeans and socks had gotten wet while fishing, making it difficult to release the suction they had on her feet.

Khalil slipped his large hands around the heel of Elly's boot, then effortlessly pulled it off her foot. Reaching for the other, gently placing his hand on her calf, he pulled the other boot off.

"You've definitely created another fisherman," she announced, flustered by his touch.

Khalil playfully smiled, his own altruistic reasons verified. Fishing was something he could do every day, the one thing his father had taught him that he enjoyed. For years, he had fished alone, but the moment he met Elly he knew he wanted to share it with her.

"Well, that's great." He playfully nudged her shoulder. "Now, we have to cook them."

"What?" she croaked, shock flooding her face.

"What do you think we are going to do with them?" He laughed.

"Well, I actually hadn't thought about it," she laughed at herself, amazed that the thought hadn't occurred to her at all.

"You don't have to be back for a while, we can go back to my house and have an early dinner before I need to get you home if you want?" Elly bit her lip to hide the smile that was threatening to betray her excitement over the idea of going back to Khalil's house. All she could do was nod yes.

Khalil turned off the road and slowed the bronco to a stop in front of a massive iron gate flanked by the forest. Elly gaped at the ornate golden details, each piece a large wolf on his hind legs, the paws facing each other as if they were about to engage in a boxing match. The yellow, floating eyes flashed across Elly's mind.

"You okay?" Khalil asked, noticing Elly's face going pale.

She nodded but kept her mouth tightly closed for fear a scream would release if she opened her lips. She could feel the rapid beating of her heart as Khalil pushed a button attached to a remote on his visor causing the gate to slowly open. As soon as there was enough room, Khalil shifted the bronco into gear, jolting Elly's body as the car started to weave through the thick woods. Elly could see nothing but woods and the narrow path snaking through the trees. Suddenly, pieces of the home started to come into view.

Elly gawked at the mansion towering before her, as Khalil pulled his bronco to a stop at the enormous, detailed oak front doors. The same set of wolves were carved into the cherry oak of the door, surrounded by spirling detail in all directions. While her grandparent's home was large, this was notably more grand in size and features, with ornate gargoyles peering down from the rafters and polished brick on every surface, giving Khalil's home more the appearance of a stone castle, than the plantation style of her grandparent's house.

"This is home?" Elly questioned, her eyes wide with disbelief. Khalil had seemed rough, rugged even to the point she more pictured him living in a cabin hidden in the woods. This place was the furthest thing from a cabin.

"It is kind of a family heirloom, I guess is what you could call it." Khalil shrugged off the grandeur of the home, as he jumped down from the bronco. Elly glared at him as he walked around the car, unsure of how to interpret his nonchalant attitude.

"So your family is rich then?" She asked as he opened her door. Elly used his hand to brace most of her weight as she jumped down, then followed him around to the back of the bronco.

"Well.. no, I guess -" he hesitated, pulling the cooler from the back of the bronco. "I mean, it is all family money. None of it is technically mine."

"Sure looks that way."

"Come on, I'll show you around," Khalil said, offering his hand. Elly enjoyed holding his hand, feeling the touch of his rough skin against her own, so she took his hand as his fingers instantly wrapped around her own.

With the heavy cooler in one hand and Elly's in the other, Khalil led them away from the ornate front doors towards the sprawling four-car garage. Elly initially thought the piece was connected to the house, but as they got closer she noticed a small iron gate leading to a pathway between the house and the garage. Khalil led her through the gate, as she admired the vines weaving up the brick on either side, making it feel as if she were walking through a tunnel.

"You see my mother never cared much for this house, thought it was ostentatious." Elly nodded in agreement. "So after my father died, she built a more modest home towards the back of the property overlooking the lake."

"Wait, if you live on the lake why didn't you just bring me fishing here?"

"Fish are better at my spot. Trout don't like to work for their food. They prefer to sit and wait for it to come to them," he added, playfully smiling back at Elly, as he continued to lead her down the path.

The brick stopped instantly on both sides, as the pathway ended, opening up to the expansive backyard, dwarfed only by the Olympic size pool built directly in the center of it. In the distance, Elly could see a smaller home on the horizon, almost completely hidden by trees. Never letting go of her hand, Khalil and Elly walked down through the perfectly manicured lawn to the small cottage at the back of the property. Elly gazed at it feeling she had been plucked from the backwoods of Georgia and dropped in the English countryside.

Flowers grew recklessly around the home's brick exterior, mostly just green this time of year, but Elly could imagine the rainbow of colors that would explode in the Spring. Tentatively, Khalil tapped on the door before effortlessly pushing it open. Elly was instantly hit with the smell of cinnamon and lavender, as the warmth of the house reached out and pulled her into its homely embrace.

Elly heard a light humming as they walked through the home towards the kitchen in the back of the house. Khalil held a finger to his lips as they passed by a closed door off to the right. Elly assumed his mother would be in their sleeping. Though, she wasn't particularly familiar with cancer.

"Wait here," Khalil instructed, as he took the cooler into the kitchen. Elly awkwardly tried to make herself comfortable on the couch, the thick abundance of pillows making it difficult. "Okay, come with me," he instructed as he slid the wall of glass apart. The entire wall could fold into itself, giving a full view of the lake glistening in the afternoon sun.

Elly walked out on the patio, the uneven pavers causing her to slightly trip along as she trailed after Khalil. Her cheeks flushed with embarrassment as he turned to help her along. Silently, she cursed her clumsy feet.

"So, I'm going to show you how to fillet a trout." Elly grimaced at the thought, the sour smell of the fish already making her stomach turn. Her eyes caught the gleam of the blade, as Khalil effortlessly pulled it from under the dirty, wooden table. Her heart quickened as he drew the large blade. She could feel each muscle in her body tense. She told herself it was just an instinctive reaction to seeing the large, sharp knife. She trusted Khalil. She knew he would never hurt her.

"Okay, so first you cut off the head." The blade landed hard against the wooden table that was stained with blood and fish scales. Elly was memorized as she watched the blood slowly bleed out from the fish's neck, watching each trail as it crawled through the splintered wood. "Then up its belly." Khalil slid the sharp blade down the smooth underside of the fish, guts immediately bursting out. "Then you just slice off the pieces of meat, of course, you have to be careful. Too close to the bone and you'll be picking out tiny, toothpick pieces of bone while you eat. Too far and you won't really have enough meat to cook without burning it."

Khalil looked up to find Elly's face going pale, as he realized it might have been too much to show her without knowing more about her affinity towards blood and guts.

"Are you okay?" He asked, attempting to clean the board of as much of the guts as he could. "I'm so sorry, I should've -"

"No, it's okay," Elly injected, not wanting Khalil to think she couldn't handle a little guts. It was just that the blood ... as she stared down at it, all she could think about was her mother. There was a way it trailed through the cracks that reminded her of the blood as it ran through the tiles on her kitchen floor. Her mother's blood.

"Whoa, whoa, I got you," Khalil assured her, as he reached out to her. Suddenly, Elly realized she was fainting, her legs slowly giving way to her spinning mind. She felt it happening, but her mind was fixated on the blood, so much so that she didn't even realize what was happening until she was cradled in Khalil's arms. "I'm so sorry, let's get you inside."

Elly allowed Khalil to usher her inside, her feet still struggling to find solid footing. Slowly, he laid her on the couch, tossing the mass of pillows to the floor with one hand as he continued to brace her with the other. He disappeared for only a moment, before returning with a cool glass of water.

"Here, drink this," he offered, cradling her neck with his hands to help her drink. The moment the cool liquid touched her lips it was as if her mind suddenly broke from its trance. Her cheeks flushed as she realized what was happening.

"I'm so sorry," Elly stuttered, as she attempted to support her own weight. Even when she was able to sit up, his fingers lingered on her neck, causing her skin to prickle. "It was just ..."

She couldn't bring herself to say the words for fear she'd start crying.

"It's okay, I understand," Khalil reassured her as he took the empty glass from her clammy hands. "I'm sorry, I just didn't think."

"I'm not sick over the fish," Elly injected, desperate to assure Khalil that she wasn't someone who falls weak over the sight of blood. In fact, it never bothered her until it was her mother's blood. "It just reminded me of my mother."

Elly shifted her eyes down, nervously picking at the sides of her fingers as she waited for Khalil's reaction. She knew if she looked up into his eyes he wouldn't have to say it out loud. She wasn't sure which would be better, so she picked at her fingers as she braced herself for his response.

"Elly, I didn't even think ..." Khalil pulled his fingers tightly through his thick, tangled hair. Shame flushed over his face as he realized what he just did. "I shouldn't have done that, please forgive me?" Khalil held his breath as he waited for Elly to choose between slapping him across the face or forgiving him, unsure of how deeply he offended her by subjecting her to the gore of filleting a fish.

"It was not your fault," Elly whispered, still using all her strength to keep her burning tears at bay. She could feel the heat of Khalil's body, the pressure of his stare, and hear the need in the voice which all made her realize that he did feel something for her, which made her own heart warm to the idea. "You had no way of knowing," she added.

"I should've thought of it though," he confessed, still frustrated with himself. "Okay, I'm going to do all the work, you just rest here."

Before Elly could object, Khalil was gone into the kitchen. An intoxicating aroma of garlic, lemon, and oregano soothed Elly as her mind focused on the meal. Instantly, she realized that the lack of breakfast and lunch had left her famished. Elly hoped that a good meal would settle not only her groaning stomach but also her floundering mind.

Khalil kept focused on Elly, watching her from the kitchen to ensure she wasn't about to have another episode as he quickly sauteed the trout in a buttery, lemon-garlic sauce. It was a familiar meal that Khalil could make blindfolded. He went over the events of the day in his mind, attempting to discern a way to have a conversation with Elly about her mother. It was obvious that the wound was still open, oozing out even, but he wanted to heal it for her, it was all he could think about.

Elly was curled up on the couch when he walked in with a plate in each hand. The smells instantly made her mouth water. He had decided it was best not to ask her to get up, so he perched on the table in front of the couch and slid her the plate.

"It smells delicious." Elly eagerly grasped for the fork as Khalil playful pulled it back from her fingers. "Come on, I'm hungry." Khalil relinquished the fork, smiling at the thought she was feeling more herself now.

Khalil shifted awkwardly on the edge of the table, his weight too much to allow himself to fully sit on it, most of the pressure of his weight being held by his core. Elly seemed to notice and shifted her feet closer to her body. Khalil immediately picked up on the invitation to join her on the couch.

They set there, closely, as they both forked bite after bite of fish. Lemon pierced Elly's taste buds as the butter soothed the sourness. Each bite left her craving more of the fish.

"This is really good," she said between mouthfuls.

"I'm glad you like it," he chuckled, amused by her vigorous hunger. "Sorry, I guess maybe I should've packed a snack or something," he added.

"No, this was worth the wait." Elly blushed as Khalil slid a side smile her way.

As they both finished the meal, Khalil wanted to talk to Elly more about her mother, but a shadow was starting to fall on the room. It was sunset and he needed to return Elly to her home.

"I should get you back home," he announced after he cleaned the plates in the kitchen. Elly was standing by the large windows overlooking the lake, watching as the sun sparkled across the water. She turned at the sound of his voice, casting a yellowish glow against her smooth skin. Khalil's breath caught in his chest as he saw how truly beautiful she was in that moment.

"Is your mother here?" Elly asked, the hum of machines a background to their entire evening.

"Oh, uh ... yeah." Khalil nervously shoved his hands into his pockets, looking down at his feet. He wasn't' sure how Elly felt about it all, mostly because he really hadn't discussed it much with her.

"Can I meet her?" Khalil's eyes grew wide at Elly's request. "I'm sorry, that was too much. I shouldn't have asked," she added quickly seeing how uncomfortable it made him. She only wondered how it felt - to know, or rather watch, your mother dying.

"No, no, it's okay. I'm sure she won't mind." Khalil actually wanted Elly to meet his mother, he knew how precious each moment was and had thought about the fact that he wanted his mother to know Elly. He was surprised by the fact that Elly wanted to meet her, thinking it would be too painful. That was why he didn't ask.

Elly followed him as he gradually opened the door, the low hum suddenly an overwhelming buzzing. The room was dark, only a single ray of dimming light sneaking in through a break in the curtains. Elly could see the lake glistening through the windows. She wanted to open them, show his mother the beauty she was missing, but then her eyes traveled to the woman laying in the bed.

There was a visible slow rise and fall of the lace that gently fluttered against her protruding collarbone. Her delicate face was soft as she slept, air escaping through her cracked, pink lips every few seconds. Elly noticed the cords running from her frail, thin arm to the machines, the bright green and red lights casting an eerie glow over her face.

Khalil moved towards his mother as Elly pulled back on his arm. "She's asleep, don't wake her," Elly said.

"No, I want her to meet you." Elly saw the eagerness in Khalil's eyes and didn't object again. Softly, he placed his large, firm hand on her bone-thin shoulder, brushing her thinned, dark hair from her face with the other. "Mother," he whispered.

Slowly, her eyes fluttered awake. Elly noticed that they were a shocking brilliant shade of almond flecked with gold, a stark contrast to her olive complexion and jet black hair. The moment her eyes focused on Khalil, her lips broke into a strained smile. The movement undoubtedly caused her pain.

"My boy," she whispered, as she labored to lift her hand to his cheek.

"I'd like you to meet someone." On cue, Elly stepped around Khalil's board shoulders, his mother focusing on her. There was a deep, unknown pain in his mother's eyes, not a physical pain, but as if she felt pain over Elly. Immediately, Elly regretted her discussion to meet his mother.

"Elly, this is my mother, Heather."

"Hello, Elly."

Elly wasn't sure what she was supposed to do, not wanting his mother to have the struggle of a handshake, and even talking seemed to take great effort, so she just stood there waiting for his mother to take the lead. Heather shifted her eyes slowly between Elly and Khalil as if somehow she could understand all they were thinking about each other in a single glance. Dropping a dark, painful look at Khalil, Elly suddenly got the feeling that his mother did not approve of their friendship.

"Elly lives just on the other side of the forest," Khalil explained. "She just lost her mother." Elly expected to see a shift in his mother's demeanor but her cold stare stayed trained on Khalil. Elly would've thought his mother could understand their innocent connection, but it only seemed to make things worse.

"I think I'm feeling very tired," Heather finally said to Khalil. Elly could see the fall in Khalil's shoulders as he nodded in agreement. "It was nice meeting you," she offered Elly before she allowed her eyes to flutter closed. Elly knew she was just being polite, as she got the distinct feeling it was not pleasant for his mother.

Elly was silent as they rode back to her house, unsure of how

Khalil was feeling and no idea what she should say. Even though she knew his mother was sick, she had never experienced what it felt like to be so near to someone who was dying, only someone who was already dead. There was a difference.

Her heart swelled with pain at the thought of Khalil having to see his mother like that every day, as one would watch the leaves turning on a tree knowing it's beautiful at that moment in time but the truth is that they are dying. Khalil's mother was beautiful, even Elly could see her beauty under her paled, dry skin and thin, frail body. In the room, Elly saw pictures of Khalil with her when he was a young boy, her long, dark hair cascading over her shoulders as her arms wrapped around him, both with the same, warm smile across their faces.

Glancing at Khalil, Elly sensed a change in his affection towards her that he had earlier that evening. There was a part of Elly that was angry at his mother for seeming to reject her before she even said a single word to her, which filled her with guilt.

"Are you feeling better?" Khalil asked, breaking the silence.

"I am sorry about your mother," Elly whispered, not sure if she should say it at all, but wanting him to know it. She also wanted to defend herself but found that she was at a loss of words, not knowing why his mother seemed to feel that way.

"Sometimes, I wish there was anything I could do to make her better because I would do it," he confessed, a dark sincereness in his voice. "Of course, she'd never let me."

"She seems like a really great mother."

"The best." Elly saw a slight smile on his lips and wished he'd tell her more but thought it'd be too much to ask. "For so long it's just been us, that it's hard to think -" His voice caught in his throat at the thought that his mother's death could come at any moment.

The last year had been the worst, the treatments causing more harm than good. Her body was giving up, no matter how strong her spirit. Now, every minute she spent preparing him for the end, no longer pacifying him by saying she'd be better soon.

Even today, Khalil understood his mother's cold disposition towards Elly. Once his mother died, Khalil would have to disappear, become a lone wolf if he was ever going to survive. His mother saw Elly as an anchor, holding him in place so the pack could surround him.

"Khalil," Elly reached over, taking his hand into her own, desperate to see if the connection was still there or if his mother had completely cut the rope in half.

"What is it like, losing your mother?" Immediately, Khalil regretted that he allowed the words to come out of his mouth as he watched the blood drain from Elly's face and her hand withdraw from his own. "Nevermind," he added quickly.

"No, it's okay." Elly attempted to steal her mind so that she could offer Khalil the only thing she knew she could - *understanding*. It was the one thing that could keep them connected. "It's like a piece of you, the one that matters most is ripped away from you. There is a numbness to it all at first," Elly recalled, the hours her mind stayed locked on a single picture. "A short period of denial for myself anyways. A part of me kept thinking that she was going to walk through the door, claim she had some twin or that it only looked like her, but it wasn't." Elly shook her hand, slightly laughing at her childish wishes she had only a week ago.

"But then it all settles in as you realize you can't just reach out to her, or talk to her, or depend on her because she's gone." Elly quickly wiped a stray tear from her burning cheeks.

"Thank you for that, Elly. I know it can't be easy."

"It can't be easy for you either."

Khalil pulled the bronco around the broken, dry fountain as Elly realized their moment was over. A part of her wanted Khalil to keep driving so they could talk because she realized even though it was painful, she needed to talk about her mother. Her grandparents wouldn't discuss it. She had no contact with her old friends, which she realized was mostly her own fault as she had been completely isolating herself since her mother's death. Khalil was now the only person she had to talk to.

"Back just in time," Khalil announced, putting the bronco in park. Elly saw the last drops of the sun flicking between the trees. "I had fun today."

"I did too."

"Maybe we can hang out again?"

"Yes, I'd like that."

9

Chapter Nine

The woods were uncharacteristically bright, the sun reaching the ground and illuminating all the secrets of the shadows. Elly could distinctly see a spider lying in wait on a thick, white web, a snake curled tightly on the branch like a vine, and a dark, hairy creature moving through the trees, keeping in the shadows. *There are many creatures, dangerous ones,* she could hear her grandmother's voice echoing through the trees as her heart started to quicken. She strained to see the figure in the dark, but it stayed just out of the cone of light.

Suddenly, Khalil materialized before Elly. His bare skin beaming off his dark skin as his sweat glistened in the light. Elly reached out to him, feeling the heat and the damp dew of the forest radiating off his body. His breathing was labored as if he had been running. Before she could ask him, he turned his gaze to the treehouse right in front of them. He reached out his hand, beckoning her to enter, but just as Elly went to take his hand he disappeared. The forest suddenly went dark. She started to scream for Khalil. Fear raised in her chest as she quickly tried to find the path out of the forest, feeling the same panic she had her first time in the woods.

Elly felt something hard hit her across the chest, her back slammed on the forest ground as two yellow eyes burrowed into her own. But it was not the face she expected, this one was covered with fur and she could smell the iron on its breath. She tried to scream, but everything was silent, frozen.

Suddenly, Elly was spiraling down through the darkness. Her body hit something hard, her eyes instantly opening to find herself on the floor in her bedroom tangled within the sheets. Frantically, she tried to free herself, her mind still lost in the nightmare. Finally, as if coming up from drowning, she could breathe again, the sheets and nightmare releasing their hold.

Just as Elly was regaining her composure, she heard a slight knocking on her bedroom door. Then, she heard Jane's voice floating through the cracks, "Are you okay, Elly?" she called.

"I'm fine," Elly called back, knowing that she was the furthest from fine. She had been since she arrived. The nightmares were every night now, each one more terrifying than the last, as they were filled with yellow lights, deafening darkness, and a growing fear that seemed to be getting worse.

"May I come in?" Jane asked through the closed door, her hand on the knob.

"I said I'm fine," Elly retorted.

She could feel the sweat beading on her forehead threatening to drop down the side of her face at any moment. There was a damp fear blanketing her skin causing her to shiver. Feeling the dryness in her throat, Elly knew she had been screaming out loud again. She didn't want Jane to know just how bad it had gotten.

The last three nights had been consumed with nightmares, waking her up at all hours and leaving her body shaking in fear. Jane had not come into the room to hold her again, as she did that first night, but Elly knew she still heard the screams.

"It's early enough, would you like some breakfast?"

Elly didn't feel much like eating, her stomach still in knots, but she didn't want to go back to sleep either.

"Sounds good," Elly called back.

She listened as Jane's footsteps disappeared down the hallway towards the kitchen. Pulling the curtains from the windows, she realized the world was still dark. The moon cast a low, yellow glow across the ground. Straining her eyes she glazed over the forest in the distance but saw nothing.

The logical side of Elly knew that her nightmares were manifestations of losing her mother and meeting Khalil. She figured the woods were the emptiness she felt without her mother, the fear she felt over being alone now that she was gone, and then there was Khalil always floating around in her dreams in some form. She almost considered him a guiding light in the darkness, which is what he felt like to her when he was around.

However, there was another side that felt as if her dreams were connected to someone else who was trying to tell her something. It was unimaginable, but a part of Elly thought her mother was trying to pass her a message of some sort. Of course, she was only getting vague glimpses of what her mother was trying to show her in the dreams. Yet, she sensed her mother was trying to warn her about something in those woods.

Suddenly, Elly saw the first rays of light cascading a pink glow across the sky. She could smell the aroma of bacon waffle through the house, a siren calling her to the kitchen. By the time she shuffled down to the kitchen, Elly could see the sky was now a brilliant mixture of yellows and oranges as the light started to fold out over the sky.

"Good morning," Jane said, as she pushed the sizzling bacon around in the pan.

"Morning."

"How are you feeling?" Jane glanced over her shoulder, as Elly gazed off into the distance.

"Fine." Elly avoided Jane's share.

Jane scooped the bacon from the pan and slid the full plate over in front of Elly, who immediately took a piece and dropped it. The hot grease had burned her fingertips.

"Oh my," Jane called, turning to get Elly a damp cloth. She pulled Elly's hand into her own, delicately dabbing her fingertips with the cool cloth.

"You were screaming again." Jane took the opportunity of being physically close to Elly to see if she could finally open up and discuss the nightmares. For the last few nights, Jane had wanted to talk to Elly. She held back, though, knowing that she wasn't ready to be completely honest with her yet. She kept stalling, hopeful to develop more of a relationship with Elly before she had to tell her the truth. But, that did not seem to be working out too well.

"You are having nightmares. Will you tell me about them?"

Elly pulled her fingers away, cupping them into her lap.

"It's nothing."

"I want you to feel as if you can talk to me," Jane urged, eager to know how much time she had left. The nightmares were every night, which wasn't a good sign.

"Really, I'm fine."

Jane nodded in agreement, defeated in her attempts to once again talk with Elly. She went back over to the stove and continued to cook a full breakfast of scrambled eggs and biscuits. By the time Jane had finished, Elly had eaten most of the bacon, so she just added the eggs to the side of the plate.

The smells pulled at Elly's stomach, as she devoured the bacon and eggs. Elly didn't notice that Jane never ate anything, just drank her coffee as she watched Elly, waiting for the right time.

As Jane finished her first cup of coffee, she watched Elly scrape the last pieces of the egg from the plate. The squeal of the screen door pulled Jane's stare as Austin emerged, returning from the garage. Putting the cup down, Jane braced herself for the conversation she did not want to have with her granddaughter.

"I am glad you seem to be doing better," Jane started. Elly shoved a biscuit into her mouth. "I think it might be a good time to discuss you going back to school."

"What?" Elly stuttered, food exploding from her mouth.

She was more in shock that she had failed to think about school. Her mother's death had dropped a bubble over her world, moving out here didn't help, as she struggled to think of anything beyond the current moment for fear her mind would wander too far away. For some reason, she had the initial thought that at some point she'd finish school virtually. Surely, they didn't have schools out here in the middle of nowhere.

"I was thinking I could do virtual school," Elly confessed, still unsure of how she would make that work, only knowing she didn't want to go to a new school. Not at this point. She was in her junior year but had enough credits to graduate in the Spring, as she had planned. Her mother had agreed to allow her to apply for colleges in New York, only if she continued to live with her that first year. Now, she could go anywhere really.

"I don't think so," Jane started but then caught Austin's glare. She picked up on his signal to soften her tone, as they had discussed this very conversation last night. "We just think that going to school would be good for you right now." Jane glanced at Austin for support.

"Yes, Elly, school starts back tomorrow and you need to go," Austin affirmed. "It will be a good distraction," he added, glancing back at Jane.

Suddenly, Elly realized why they were pushing her to return to school as if going to a new school would make things feel normal again. She felt the tears burning the corners of her eyes and knew she needed to get out of the situation quickly to avoid any conversation over how she was handling everything. In that moment, she found herself desperately wishing Khalil was here.

"Fine, I'll go," Elly conceded as she tried to make her escape.

"I was thinking we could go into town and buy a couple of things you need today?" Jane offered, forcing Elly to stop at the door. "Maybe some new clothes as well?" she added to lure Elly into agreeing.

"I'm not sure what I need," Elly deflected.

"Well, did you bring anything with you from ..." Jane held back saying the word *home*, knowing it would hurt. Jane hoped that school would take Elly's mind off everything changing around her and give her time to adjust to her new life. Of course, she still wasn't sure how long they had but she hoped it was enough.

"I'm not really sure," Elly confessed.

Her mind had been in a haze that day she packed up her entire life in a single duffle bag. Jane had assured her she would have everything else packed away in storage but Elly wasn't quite sure if that was reachable on such short notice.

"Well, then it's settled. We'll go into town today."

10

Chapter Ten

Jane and Austin waited, listening to Elly's footsteps drag up the stairs then down the hallway. It wasn't until they heard the shutting of the door that they spoke in whispered voices.

"Jane, are you sure this is a good idea?"

"Yes, Austin. What else is she going to do around here? Continue to run off into the woods or go on excursions with unknown boys?"

"Oh, come on, he was harmless," Austin retorted hearing the anger in Jane's voice over the fact that he had dared to overrule her decision.

"You don't know that." Jane glanced down the barren hallway, ensuring that Elly was not eavesdropping again. "We can't take any risks."

"So, then why are you sending her to school?"

"Because I don't know what else to do!" Jane snapped,

instantly feeling the heat rise in her cheeks and her heart rate quicken. Austin realized that it took a special level of desperation in Jane for her to admit to him that she didn't know what to do, making him feel compassion for his wife.

"You are doing what you think is best and that is all you can do," Austin offered as comfort.

"It is best," Jane argued.

"I know we've known what her life would become one day but we need to acknowledge that Julianna never wanted that for her daughter."

"I don't need a reminder as to why our own daughter hadn't spoken to us in the past twelve years," Jane snapped. Austin's face appeared as if she had actually, physically slapped him across the face. "I wish it was a choice, I truly do." Jane softened, knowing that Julianna was not wrong for wanting a different life than this for herself and her daughter.

This was not a life anyone would choose.

"But, there is no way around it, Austin. Hunter said she's already got the markers in her blood. Plus, she is already having nightmares. It will happen, it's just a matter of when." Jane affirmed.

Making Elly return home with her was the only choice to make after Julianna's death. Jane knew her daughter wouldn't approve but she assured herself that it was the only way to protect Elly. The change would happen and she would need Jane. Julianna had hoped that she could take Elly away from all of it, protect her. But, Julianna wanted to change history and DNA, which was never going to work.

"I know, Jane," Austin empathized. "It was hard for Julianna when she learned the truth."

"None of us had it easy," Jane added, a sympathetic smile crossing her face as she looked into Austin's eyes. While Austin grew up knowing since a young age, as did Jane, it didn't make it any easier to accept when the time came. They had kept it from Julianna, allowing her to be a child, but Jane regretted that choice.

A heavy, loud knock rang through the hallways, pulling Jane and Austin from their painful memories.

"Who is here?" Jane questioned, as she made her way to the front door. Another loud thud hit against the door.

Elly stood at the top of the stairs, waiting to see who it was at the door. She watched as Jane pulled open the door, seeing only his broad shoulders and dark skin. Elly immediately bolted down the stairs towards the door, not willing to give her grandparents even a second to send him away.

"Morning." Khalil could barely get the word out, as Elly flew at him, pushing him out of the doorway onto the porch. "What's going on?"

Elly quickly pulled the door closed behind her, leaving them both stunned.

"What are you doing here?" Elly blurted out, instantly offending Khalil. "I'm sorry, I mean, why, I guess …" She awkwardly shifted on her feet, pulling a stray hair behind her ear.

"I'm sorry, I had something come up the last couple of days." Elly did not miss the flash of pain across his face and immediately assumed something had happened with his mother. "What are you doing right now?"

"I'm sorry, but apparently I've gotten forced into shopping with Jane today."

"Well, that doesn't sound so bad."

"No, it is. She's making me go back to school tomorrow."

"Oh," Khalil suddenly appeared upset. "Well, that's still not so bad," he added, attempting to hide his disappointment.

All of a sudden, Elly realized that being made to go to school might not be as bad as she thought. As long as Khalil went to the same school.

"I don't want to go, but it doesn't seem like I have much of a choice. What about you?"

"What?" Khalil seemed suddenly very distracted. "Oh, uh, I've been out on medical leave actually."

"Oh, I didn't think about that." Her heart sank.

"So, I guess another time then?"

"Yeah."

They both hesitated on the porch, each needing the friendship of the other in this moment but realizing they lost the time. Elly wondered what had happened the last few days, worried that it was something with his mother. She figured he'd tell her if she had died ... *or would he?*

"Wait," she called, as he started to walk back to the bronco. "Is everything okay?"

Khalil flashed her a forced smile, as he called back, "Yeah." But Elly didn't believe him.

"Are you ready?" Jane called.

Elly reluctantly watched the bronco disappear down the drive. She was suddenly boiling with anger over having to spend time with Jane, wishing she had the time with Khalil.

"Do we have to go?" Elly snapped back, only realizing her tone when she saw the hurt on Jane's face.

"Well, I promise to make this as quick and painless as possible," Jane assured her, walking past her towards the garage realizing that this trip was not going to create the bonding experience she had hoped for this morning.

Elly followed solemnly, knowing she should say something but not sure what would make it better, or take away her anger or hurt. The only person that seemed to make everything feel different, *better*, was Khalil.

It was Elly's first trip into the town and while she didn't expect much, she was still disappointed. A single road ran through the towering, narrow buildings, with cars parked along either side. This truly was a small town with only one traffic light, that was currently dangling in the center blinking yellow. With no other intersecting roads, Elly wondered why it was even there in the first place.

"What would you like to get first?" Jane asked as she pulled the old pick-up truck into an open spot, the engine groaning as she turned it off.

Elly shrugged.

"Well, there is a pretty popular clothing store down that way or a general store this other way -"

"Actually, is there a bookstore?" Elly interjected.

"Uh, yes. Right there." Jane pointed down the street. Elly could see the *Book and Brew Shop* sign a few stores down the street.

"Do you mind if I go there while you get the shopping done?" Elly asked, desperate to not have to shop with Jane.

"Well, I do need to gather a few things at the general store.

I can meet you there when I'm finished. Then, we can go clothes shopping."

Elly nodded.

She could feel Jane watching her as she walked down the street to the bookstore. As she got closer she realized that the building was split into two different shops. One a bookstore and the other a coffee shop, giving Elly more understanding of the name on the sign. The small building was dwarfed by two large office buildings, making it appear cozy, just as a bookstore should in a small town.

Elly smiled at the young clerk behind the desk as she entered the store. Her large black-rimmed glasses fell on her small, round nose that was flanked by millions of freckles and surrounded by wildly curly hair. Browsing down the aisle, not looking for anything particular, Elly scanned the books, her fingers pausing on a book about werewolves. Pulling the book from the shelf, she took it up to the warm-smiled clerk.

"Oh, I like that one," she said, taking the book from Elly's hands. Elly just smiled, not interested in engaging in conversation. "It's fifteen dollars," she added.

"Oh, yeah - uh - well," Elly suddenly realized she didn't have anything on her, including money. "My grandmother is just over -" Elly glanced out the windows seeing Jane walking out of the general store across the street, full bags in hand.

"It's okay," the girl offered, placing the book back down on the counter. "I can wait, not like we are busy." Elly's lips cracked into a smile. "I'm Maddie," she added.

"Elly."

"So, you are new to this place? Why am I asking," she waved a flippant hand in the air, "of course you are."

"What makes you say that?"

"Because, I know everyone in this town," she announced proudly.

"Oh, yeah, I bet you do in a small town like this."

"It's a blessing, but mostly a curse." Again, Elly smiled and even slightly laughed this time. "So you are into fantasy?" Elly gave her a confused look. "The book," she pointed down to the book, a picture of a wolf on the cover.

"Just recently," Elly admitted, thinking of the book Khalil had given her and the nightmare she had the other night. It was silly, but she thought that she saw the wolf in her dreams because of the book Khalil had given her in the treehouse. Or maybe there was something else to both of them.

"This one is good because it's about a girl werewolf, you don't see that much in books," Maddie said. Elly noticed she wasn't a person that was comfortable with silence.

"Do you read a lot of books?"

"Yeah, I mean that's why I work here. We don't see much action in here, so mostly I get to read the books for free."

"That's nice," Elly admitted.

"You know, if you promise to bring it back, I can let you borrow that one," Maddie offered. Elly considered it for a moment, thinking it would be easier than asking Jane for money or explaining her newly acquired taste in reading.

"Yeah, actually that'd be great." Maddie smiled, sliding the book across the counter. Elly tucked it away into the inside pocket of her jacket just as Jane entered the store.

"Elly, did you find anything?" Jane asked looking between Elly and the clerk, recognizing her immediately. "Oh, hello Madeline, how are you doing?"

"I'm doing great," Maddie smiled broadly. "How are things?"

"Good, I see you've met my granddaughter, Elly." Maddie and Elly exchanged tight smiles, as the book burned a hole in her jacket pocket. Elly suddenly worried that her grandmother would see the book and think she was stealing.

"We should get some of your school books," Jane announced. "Do you know what she will need?" Jane asked Maddie.

"Oh, uh, yeah, we have a student book section over there. She'd just need to get the right grade level. It's all marked."

Jane nodded and headed in that direction. She assumed Elly would follow, but she stayed at the desk to talk to Maddie. Jane didn't call her along, hoping that Elly would become friendly with Maddie. She knew her family well and it would do Elly good to have someone to know at school tomorrow. That is when she got the idea.

"So you are going to school here now?"

"I guess so. Didn't seem like I had much of a choice," Elly grimaced.

"It's not so bad really. Kind of classically your small-town high school." Elly internally groaned as Maddie confirmed her fear. That meant that everyone would be talking about Elly's arrival, as she would inevitably hear judgemental whispers and rumors of her life throughout the day. She dreaded having to be the *new girl*.

"Maddie," Jane called, as she returned to the desk with an

armful of textbooks. "I heard you got a car for your birthday a few months ago."

"Why, yes I did." Maddie's smile was filled with pride.

"Would it be too much trouble to give Elly a ride?"

Instantly, Elly flushed and opened her mouth to object, but before she could Maddie was already generously agreeing with Jane.

"Oh, thank you, that would be very helpful."

11

Chapter Eleven

Elly pulled at the sweater her grandmother had forced her to buy yesterday in town. The single clothing store they went into was nothing like Elly's style, which bordered more on athletic wear most days. While she had pulled out of soccer, much to her mother's dismay, to focus on school, she still had an athletic build that allowed her to get away with leggings and t-shirts most days. Even though there was fashion galore in New York City, it was never something Elly found interesting, but she did know enough to realize that everything in that store was at least three seasons behind.

Jane had insisted she purchase a few sweaters, as her winter jacket would be too warm to wear down here in the south. It was hard for Elly to refute her claim as she was sweating in the jacket at that moment. Nor could Elly just wear one of her t-shirts, the wind still a chilling temperature this time of year.

But, this sweater felt too small as it clung tightly to her body. She preferred things to fit big, feeling very uncomfortable in things that showed her growing figure. At least the sweater was longer, so she could wear her standard leggings and black, army-style boots. Jane had tried to get her to purchase a more suitable pair, as she called them, but Elly stood her ground. These boots belonged to her mother.

Elly forcefully pulled the brush through her tangled hair that refused to part right. Finally, she gave up trying and pulled it back into a high ponytail, shorter pieces wisping around her face, but she didn't care. Normally, she would've put makeup on, darkening her eyes with liner and mascara, but that seemed a little overdone for out here in the country. So, she went with just a deep red lip gloss to keep her lips from cracking in the winter cold.

"Are you ready?" Jane called through the door, lightly tapping her fingers on the wood.

"Yes," Elly announced, opening the bedroom door.

"You look great! That sweater fits nicely on you." Jane reached out to adjust the fabric, but Elly stepped away. Immediately, Jane flushed with embarrassment as she realized for a moment she mistook Elly for Julianna. While she had lost her relationship with her daughter in her adult years, when she was younger they were very close. Their relationship only changed when Julianna met him.

"I should go," Elly said quickly, walking around Jane and disappearing from the room.

Elly waited on the front porch step, her fingers threaded into each other as she willed herself to focus her mind on anything else than what was happening. If she thought too much about any of it, she'd cry. Elly always felt as if she was standing on the edge of a cliff about to fall into the depression that is her life.

She watched as a foreign car, with its baby blue color glistening in the rising sunlight and chrome features twinkling like diamonds, pulled down the driveway. It snaked around the fountain and stopped right at Elly's feet. The roar of the engine vibrated the ground as the car idled, waiting for Elly.

"Hi," Maddie called from the window, waving her long jeweled hand for Elly to get into the car.

Maddie's face was bright with a large smile and had much more makeup on than she did the day before at the bookstore. Elly slid across the bench seat of the Chevelle. The white leather was smooth and in immaculate condition for such an older model car.

"This is nice," Elly offered.

"Thanks, it's kind of important to me."

Maddie smiled, her warm, bubbly face a stark opposite to the permit solemn look on Elly's face. Pulling back on the large shifter at her knees, the car jerked forward, as Maddie drove off from the house. Elly watched as the house got smaller in the distance, but just as they turned, she swore she saw Jane watching from her bedroom window.

"Thanks for the ride," Elly offered. "Do you live close?"

"Oh, so it's hard to see the different places, but I live just next door."

Elly considered it was towards the north of their property,

considering Khalil lived to the south through the forest. The north had trees as well but they were thinned, making it more of a grove than a forest. But, Elly had never noticed a house in any direction.

"Of course, it's over five acres so it's not like I can walk over for a cup of sugar," she laughed. The southern expression was lost on Elly's northern upbringing.

"Is that how all the places are out here?" Elly asked.

"Pretty much, I guess," Maddie shrugged. "I assume that is why people move out here."

"For what?"

"Oh, privacy," Maddie responded matter-of-factly. "I'm not sure why else someone would live out on five acres of land without farming it. Closer to school and town there are more traditional neighborhoods, but I've lived out here all my life."

"So your family doesn't farm then?"

"No, not really," Maddie's vague response led to more questions, but Elly wasn't sure she could ask them, Maddie still basically a stranger.

"Have you known my grandparents that whole time?" Elly asked, considering that was the only question out of the many that seemed okay to ask a stranger.

"Not really, I mean my parents know them well enough to say hello in public, as most everyone in this town does, but that's the thing about out here - you don't really get to know your neighbors that well."

"I guess not," Elly agreed, thinking only of how she met Khalil on her first day here. They seemed to become friends rather quickly despite the distance between their homes.

"I'm sure you are used to being on top of everyone, living in a big city like New York," Maddie mused, making conversation. Elly felt a jolt of fear, suddenly realizing that Maddie knew more about her than she was letting on. "Oh sorry, my mother called your grandmother last night, just to make sure everything was worked out okay. She told me about your mother ..." Maddie's voice trailed and her eyes shifted back to the road.

"How long is the drive?" Elly asked, attempting to abruptly change the conversation away from talking about her mother. She did not need to arrive at school with puffy, red eyes to explain or fuel more rumors.

"Oh, uh, about twenty minutes."

Maddie could tell Elly clearly did not want to talk about her mother, so she let a fog of silence fall over the car, as she focused on driving. Her mother had warned her that Elly might be upset and to not mention her mother. Maddie couldn't imagine life without her mother, her heart swelling with sympathy for Elly. She had tried to keep the conversation casual but realized all too late that even talking about her life in the city was painful, so she kept quiet. Which was difficult for Maddie, considering she was a social person, often using conversation to mask her own pain.

"So this car is important?" Elly finally asked, the silence feeling rude.

"Yes, well, because ... it was my dad's car." Maddie stumbled over the words and Elly got the distinct feeling she was leaving out some key information. "He rebuilt it when he *owned* a garage here in town..." Maddie's voice faded away, as she seemed to lose her train of thought, but Elly knew better. Maddie didn't want to talk about it.

Elly gave Maddie a tight smile, knowing the feeling of an absent parent. The fact that Maddie used past tense when speaking of her father was not lost on Elly. However, now she also knew that it was nothing compared to knowing you will never see them again.

"When did it happen?" That was all Elly asked.

"I was two years old."

"I lost my father too - I was four."

Maddie and Elly allowed the silence to fall between them again, both unwilling to talk about their loss as they attempted to hide their personal pain. Elly wasn't sure how Maddie lost her father, only that he was clearly lost to her, just as Elly's father was lost to her as well. Of course, it was different with her father. One day he just never came home and her mother never knew what happened. After a few years, they both started to operate under the assumption that he died. So, that's how she referred to her father now ... and her mother. Tears burned in her eyes as she tried to hold them back with every ounce of her strength.

"Here," Maddie announced ten minutes later, as she pulled the car into the parking lot, a collegial building towering in the distance with a wide, large staircase leading up to the main entranced adorned with an oversized clock.

Maddie's happy disposition seemed to have returned, but Elly was still finding it hard to bury her thoughts. As they drove through the lot, Elly suddenly set up a little taller looking through the window at the explosion of color.

"We all have assigned stops. We even get to paint them, it's kind of a big deal. We all get together, it's a thing," Maddie added, as she watched Elly scanning the parking lot. They were slightly early, most of the spots still empty revealing bright colors of paint all over the gray concrete.

Maddie pulled the old Chevelle into a parking lot with a large, elaborate tree planted over the spot. As Elly got out of the car, she glanced down to see the dark brown strokes of a tree trunk and small pink buds peeking out from under the car.

"It's a cherry tree," Maddie informed, as she joined her.

"I see that," Elly whispered, her mind suddenly pulled into an old memory of her mother. Elly could vividly remember the story of the Asian cherry blossom tree, as her mother told it to her, right after she painted it along with her bedroom wall. *"The tree symbolizes life, the mortality of life specifically. Signifying love and the strength and beauty of women,"* her mother told her each night as she brushed her hair. Elly learned when she was older that her mother painted it to remind her daily of what a strong, independent woman she was born to be. Tears pricked the corner of her eyes.

Maddie noticed the glassy film falling over Elly's eyes and realized that she had touched a sensitive subject. "I'll walk you to the office," she offered, attempting to pull Elly from her painful thoughts.

"Sure," Elly agreed, forcing her thoughts back into the present. Blinking back her tears, she followed Maddie up the large, concrete staircase to the oversized glass doors leading into a wide hallway lined with lockers. Just as they reached the front office, large glass walls surrounding an area filled with desks, a bell rang throughout the school.

"So, I'm going to go to class, but I'll meet you back at the car after the final bell, okay?"

"Yeah." Elly forced a smile. Maddie turned back down the hallway as Elly watched other students trickling into the hallway from various doors. Chatter erupted through the halls, as Elly couldn't make out any of the words. For a moment, she felt completely overwhelmed by the idea of school, but then reminded herself that school is the one thing she is good at. All she had to do was make it six months here, then she'd be free.

"I'm Elly McLeod," she spoke through the hole carved into the glass wall. The woman glanced up at her, thick glasses perched at the tip of her thin, long nose, a questionable look in her eyes. "I'm new here," Elly explained.

"Oh, welcome dear." The woman's pale face effortlessly spread wide as she smiled through the glass at Elly. "Come on in," she added in a thick southern accent. Tapping a buzzer on the wall, Elly heard a click to her right and realized it was a door. Gently, she pushed it open then let it close tight behind her.

"Okay, so let me get your schedule," the woman stated as she clumsily felt around her desk, pushing loose papers all around. Her eyes raised as her fingers found what they were looking for, "ah, here it is," she exclaimed, pulling the small laptop from under a thick stack of files. "Full name?" She asked, pushing her glasses back up on her nose.

"Uh, Elly Ann McLeod." The woman typed frantically on the laptop for the next five minutes as Elly awkwardly waited, noticing the trains of other kids passing by the window, all looking her way. She wanted to crawl under the desk and hide. "Okay, all done," she announced, as the printer sprang to life behind her.

The noise vibrated through the small office. There were a few others in the area, but no one looked up.

Elly looked over her schedule.

"Uh, did you receive my transcripts from my old school?" Elly asked, confused by the classes on her list.

"Oh, uh, yes, your grandmother called a few days ago. We received it yesterday. Is there a problem with your schedule dear?" The woman's light-blond hair, cut into a short bob, glowed like a halo in the bright fluorescent lights around her soft face as she spoke.

"Well, I'm set to graduate at the end of this year, and well," Elly hesitated, not sure she was reading the schedule correctly. "Well, I think I'm in the wrong classes." She handed it back to the woman, who proceeded to skim over it once more.

"I don't see any issues, what classes do you think you should be in?"

"Well, I was taking duel classes at my last school."

"Oh, well we don't have those around these parts," the woman giggled.

"I know, I figured as much," Elly said, annoyed. "But, I was in Calculus. This schedule has me still in Algebra." The woman stared blankly. "Also, I was in creative writing, this has me in basic English."

"Well, dear we have different classes here. But, I think the best we can do is put you in all senior-level courses if you think you can manage that?" Elly flushed as she realized the woman was referring to her mother's death. She cursed her grandmother, who was clearly the messenger yet again.

"That's fine," Elly said through gritted teeth. She feared this was going to ruin her chances of graduating early, which would ruin her plans even further.

She anxiously waited as the woman changed her schedule, eager to get out of the office and away from the woman's judgemental stare. Elly wasn't nervous about taking senior-level classes; she figured what she was doing back in her dual classes in New York was definitely harder than anything this school could throw at her.

"Here you go. Just let me know if they are too hard and we'll move you right back," the woman assured. Elly got the feeling she thought she'd be back by the end of the day. She would not.

"Wait, Elly, don't forget your map," The woman called, folding it and pushing it through the small talk hole in the glass wall. "Have a great day," she added, as Elly unraveled the crinkled map.

It didn't take long for Elly to find her locker, then her first class which she was regrettably late to at this point. She dreaded the idea of being called out in front of every classmate, along with not having any of the materials. She was completely unprepared so she decided it was best to just wait for this period to end. Then, she could talk to the teacher alone.

"Are you lost?"

Elly looked up from her feet, immediately catching her breath as he walked towards her down the narrow, barren hallway. She thought for sure she'd be alone until the bell rang, releasing the waves of students from the classrooms, but here he was as if they were the only two people in the school.

"Uh, no," Elly responded, shifting her eyes back to the floor so he didn't assume she was staring, which she was. Elly was quite sure people often stared at him, with his broad shoulders and light-blonde hair effortless, yet perfectly, pulled to the side.

"I'm Camden," he announced as he approached. Slowly, he came to a stop just a few feet away. He casually slid a hand in his pocket as he leaned against the wall with the other. "You are new?"

"Yep," Elly forced a tight smile, feeling the flush of her cheeks.

"Are you in this class?" He asked, motioning towards the door. There was a sliver of glass revealing three of the five rows of desks, each with a student taking notes. A muffled voice drifted under the door, as the teacher lectured from the front.

"Yes, but I'm late, so I just figured-"

"Figured you'd skip class on the first day," he jeered. "Seems we have a rebel," he flashed a playful, toothy smile. "Just kidding," he added quickly, noticing that Elly didn't seem to enjoy his playful banter.

"Just didn't want to interrupt," Elly shrugged.

"Well, I'm headed out to the courtyard to grab a drink," he quickly looked around, "you want me to show you around?"

Elly thought about this for a moment, wondering if Camden was just being friendly, or if she was about to find herself in a bad situation. She didn't want to miss the bell and not get the chance to talk to the teacher without the other kids present. On the other hand, she had time and a tour would be helpful. She bit her lower lip in contemplation.

"I promise I'll bring you right back," Camden assured.

"Alright," Elly agreed.

Elly followed Camden, his stride slightly longer as he stayed a single step ahead of her, leading her out the door at the end of the hallway. The brisk, cool hair prickled against her skin and her nose instantly turned red with frost. The courtyard was filled with concrete benches and tables, scattered amongst trees and bushes. To the right and left were brick walls lined with windows into various classrooms. Elly worried they'd get busted for not being in class.

"No worries, it's cool," Camden assured her, as if he could read her thoughts. He motioned for Elly to follow her towards the soda machines tucked into a corner against the back wall. "My treat, what would you like?" He asked, pulling change from his pocket.

"Anything is fine." Elly felt odd accepting the drink from a stranger, who in her opinion was being overly nice. Camden shrugged and bought them both a coke. Elly followed him to the benches, anxiously looking around as she realized they were alone.

"So, I didn't actually get your name," Camden confessed, opening his drink.

"Oh, sorry, it's Elly." She smiled, less forced this time around. "Thanks for the drink."

"Really, it's nothing."

Just then Elly heard the large metal doors opening across the courtyard. Her heart stuttered as she noticed other students emerging from the hallways into the courtyard. Camden gave a large wave to a group of boys, ushering them over to the table. Suddenly, Elly felt completely out of place and desperate to get back to the classroom.

"Oh, no don't go," Camden said, seeing her standing up. "Meet my buds." Just then the other boys reached the table, throwing the backpacks under the concrete table and straddling the bench. "This is Logan and Micah, we all play on the soccer team here. This is our practice period." The boys all laughed. "Which just means we all get to come late since we have practice after school," Camden explained.

"Hi, I'm Logan." Elly tentatively took his outstretched hand, noticing that he had the same hairstyle as Camden but his hair a dirty brown-blonde. "This is Micah," he added, motioning to the other boy that seemed more reserved and withdrawn from the group. He set on the third half-circle bench solo, gazing out over the courtyard in thought, only turning once Logan called out to him.

"Oh, hi," he offered, raising his thick, dark eyebrows as a greeting. His hair was shaved short and jet black, which complimented his dark completion.

"Elly."

"Where are you from?" Logan asked.

"Uh, New York City," Elly reluctantly said, not wanting to discuss her life, but knowing the moment she mentioned it they would ask a million questions. She had learned that being from there made you a tourist attraction to others.

"Oh, wow, what the heck are you doing down here?" Logan laughed, completely oblivious to the pale look on Elly's face, but Micah saw it.

"Come on Logan, let her settle in before you ask a million questions." Micah threw a veggie stick at Logan's face, who athletically caught it in his mouth. Camden and Logan both cheered, the question forgotten, as Elly passed an appreciative smile to Micah.

Where Logan and Camden seemed to be playful jocks, Micah seemed different with a more stoic exterior and quiet demeanor. Elly appreciated that more, feeling overwhelmed by the others' outgoing and boisterous personalities. She wished she could sleek away into the background, disappeared unnoticed, but that didn't seem likely.

"How was your break, Logan, where did you go this time?" Camden inquired, flashing a wink at Elly. She wasn't sure if he was changing the subject on her behalf, passing a wink of affection, or thought Logan was about to say something outrageous and winked at her to get ready for a good story.

"Ah, we just went back to Vail this time, same ol' same ol'," Logan boosted.

"Must be hard," Micah jeered.

"Oh, not so much," Camden added, slapping Logan hard on the back. Logan laughed it off, but Elly caught him slightly rubbing his shoulder a few seconds later. "Well, boys, I should get Elly back to her class."

Micah and Logan each gave Elly a slight wave, Logan's smile naturally larger than Micah's, as she followed Camden back into the same hallway. Camden explained that the other doors along the back wall all led to different hallways. All of which led to the main hallway, but Elly struggled to pay attention.

Being around new people made her think of Khalil and how much she'd rather be with him. She didn't feel as if she could talk to any of those boys, but Khalil had been so easy to open up to. She found herself wishing he would return to school, even though she knew he couldn't.

"I'll catch you later," Camden called as he took off down the hallway. A few seconds later the bell rang throughout the school. Within seconds, doors all along the hallway flew open, a sea of kids flowing out bottlenecking into the single narrow hallway. Elly pushed herself up against the wall so she wouldn't get pulled into the stream.

After the class had emptied, she slid into the room, just as the teacher was erasing everything she needed to know from the board.

"Excuse me," she interrupted, as she moved towards his desk at the front of the room. "I'm new." The man stared down at Elly, his eyes squinted and questioning. "Elly McLeod," she offered.

"I wasn't told I was getting a new student," he groaned. He threw his hand out, waving his long, thin fingers, but Elly didn't know what to do. "Your schedule," he prompted, his voice filled with annoyance.

"Oh," Elly fumbled in her pocket for her schedule. "Here." She waited patiently as he pulled his glasses down from his speckled brown hair, glaring at the schedule as he wiped his nose with a tissue. He wore a dark brown plaid sweater vest that gave him a collegiate appearance. He looked back up at Elly, a perplexed look on his face.

"What is this?" He asked, waving the paper in the air.

"You are Mr. Manning, correct?" Elly asked, suddenly worried she had gone into the wrong classroom. "English Lit 4?" He continued to stare at her blankly. "Room 307?"

"You're a junior." His deep brown eyes burrowed into her own, making Elly feel very uncomfortable and wishing she had come into the room when other people were there.

"I know."

"So, this is a senior class."

"I know."

"Well," he tossed the paperback to Elly. "You better keep up."

"I will."

Elly aimlessly walked through the crowd, allowing the current to drag her along, as she lost herself in thought over what just happened. It was clear to her that Mr. Manning had no intentions of giving her time to catch up with the class, nor any slack if she should fall behind because he did not want a junior sitting in his senior class. Her best case was that the class was easy, otherwise, she might actually be in trouble with her GPA.

The rest of the day, Elly made sure to be early for each class, talking with each teacher about her schedule. No one else seemed to give her as much grief as Mr. Manning, all of them pretty much telling her to take a seat anywhere and keep up. While most of the teachers seemed nice, it was a different atmosphere. At her elite, dual enrollment magnet school in New York, Elly participated in college-level and college-taught classes, where students discussed the lesson and talked in groups to achieve understanding. Elly spent most of the day sitting silently in class, listening to lectures. However, so far, she was thankful to find she didn't seem to be in any class in which she felt she was missing any key information that would prevent her from being able to be successful in the class.

Elly didn't see Maddie until the schoolwide lunch hour, at which point she was grateful to see a familiar face after sitting in three different classes speaking to no one. Maddie ushered her over to a table in the large atrium. Elly could smell the fresh aroma of the plants that grew in large groups in various areas of the glassed-in room off the back of the cafeteria.

"Hi, Elly, how is your day going?" Maddie asked as Elly slid her lunch tray onto the metal table. There were pockets of people scattered all over the large atrium, some were eating, others just talking. She had passed tables of students in the cafeteria as well, but they all seemed younger. Out here the kids seemed to all be her age.

"It's okay," Elly confessed.

"I haven't seen you in any classes, I thought for sure we'd have a couple together. Can I see your schedule?"

"Uh, sure." Elly handed her the piece of paper knowing that Maddie would most likely notice that she was in all senior classes.

"Okay, wow. I thought you were a junior?"

"I am." Maddie waited for an explanation. "But I took a lot of advanced duel courses at my old school, so I am supposed to graduate at the end of this year."

"Oh, well then." Maddie handed her the paper and said nothing more about it.

Within a few minutes, the table was suddenly filled with people, all chatting over each other making it difficult for Elly to keep up with any one conversation that all seemed to have started before any of them set down, so she just ate silently.

"Okay, okay, guys, this is Elly," Maddie finally interjected into all the random conversations to introduce Elly. "She just moved in next door to me." Everyone nodded, but then most returned to their own conversations.

"I'm Lauren," the girl next to her introduced. Elly gaped at the beauty Lauren naturally possessed, with her crystal blue eyes that were almost clear and straight golden blond hair, all made more beautiful by her soft, bubbly exterior.

"Lauren and I have been friends since we were babies," Maddie explained.

"Our mothers were besties," Lauren added. Elly thought they could be sisters, both with blonde hair and blue eyes, if not for the mass of freckles Maddie had sprinkled all over her face and wildly curly hair, they were almost identical.

"They were sorority sisters at UGA," Maddie started.

"Then my mother met Maddie's uncle when she came home for a visit with Maddie's mother," Lauren explained.

"Much to my mother's dismay, at first anyway, they fell in love," Maddie dramatically batted her long, dark lashes. "Of course, now that they are best friends, so it's the best thing."

"So you are cousins?" Elly confirmed as she realized that explained why they appeared so similar.

"Yep," they said in unison. They both laughed.

"Oh gosh, Lauren," called a girl across the table."Here comes Camden." She rolled her eyes, as Elly attempted to hide her face.

"Sis!" He called, opening his arms as he approached the table.

"Did I mention Lauren is a twin," Maddie whispered to Elly.

"Oh, hello, Elly." Camden pushed his way in between Elly and Lauren.

"Cam, stop it," Lauren whined. "What is wrong with you, why are you sitting with us?"

"How's your day so far, Elly?" Camden asked, ignoring his sister completely, as Lauren realized the reason he was sitting at their table.

"How do you know my brother," Lauren asked, leaning around his body block.

"We met this morning in the hallway," Camden explained, taking great pleasure in ruffling his sister's feathers. "How do you know her?" He asked without taking his eyes off of Elly, giving her another awkward, unknowing wink.

"She's my neighbor," Maddie interjected.

"Cam, leave the girls alone," the girl called from across the table, a sly smile crossing her dark, pursed lips. Elly could tell she didn't care for him much by the dark, contemptuous look in her eyes as she glared across the table.

"As you wish." Camden flashed Elly another smile before he retreated from the table, much to Elly's astonishment. She wasn't sure who this girl was, but she immediately envied her confidence.

Elly watched as Camden joined another table filled with boys, including Logan and Micah, who glanced her way. Catching her eye, Micah gave her a slight smile. Elly assumed by the look of the group, all of them athletically built, that it was the entire soccer team.

"Don't let him bother you." The girl motioned towards Camden. "I'm Niyanna, by the way," she added. "All the boys here are so juvenile."

"And my brother is leading the pack," Lauren laughed.

"Just stick close with us girls, we'll help you survive," Niyanna assured, her dark brown eyes wide with excitement. Her smooth dark skin melted into her slick, long black hair that slightly curled at her shoulders. Her beauty was more exotic, Elly thought. Elly felt plain compared to them all at the table, as she noticed they all had their own level of fashion that seemed to play into their personalities.

Maddie was more laid back, her clothes a simple pair of jeans and a t-shirt, while Lauren's bubbly personality translated to her bright, overly monochromatic clothing choices. Then there was Niyanna, who carried herself as sophisticated as she acted and looked, with her hair professionally styled and paired with a tight, expensive black top. Her look was completed with gold buckled black boots. Elly hadn't seen anything like that in any of the stores in this town, leaving her to wonder just where these girls were going to get fashionable clothes.

Elly found herself lost again as they all started to talk in various conversations. She tried to listen to a few of the conversations, attempting to pick up on something she could talk about, but her mind was in a fog, so much so she could barely focus. So when Niyanna stopped all conversation with her next question, Elly didn't even hear it.

"Elly, I asked why did you move here?" Niyanna repeated, ensuring that everyone at the table was now staring at Elly. Her cheeks burned. Out of the corner of her eye, she could see Maddie slightly shaking her head no towards Niyanna. Elly realized this was the moment she had dreaded.

"My mother died." Elly heard the echoing gasps of each girl.

"I'm so incredibly sorry to hear that," Niyanna offered, a sympathetic hand over her presumably aching heart. "That must be so hard for you." Elly just returned her empathy with a tight smile and silence.

"Elly, we should –" Maddie started, but Niyanna abruptly cut her off.

"What about your father?" Maddie glared at Niyanna again.

"Oh, uh, I don't know my father - so..." Elly shrugged.

"That's so tragic."

"Okay, we have to go," Maddie announced, mouthing something at Niyanna as she grabbed her things and Elly's bag forcing her to get up as well. Niyanna gave a small wave to Elly, as she followed Maddie out of the atrium and into the main hallway.

"I'm really sorry about that," Maddie offered. "Niyanna can be ... well ... it's just she ... I'm sure she didn't mean," Maddi stuttered over her words, unable to give any justice to how she would describe Niyanna, who had only been at their school for the last few months, a *new girl* herself. Maddie thought she would've shown a little bit more compassion, but then again Niyanna never struck her as a compassionate person.

"So, I'll see you after last period," Maddie confirmed as she stood at the top of the large hallway that ran like a main river down the middle of the school. "We have to pick up my sister from girl scouts, but then we'll be right home," she assured. Elly nodded in agreement as she started down the mostly empty hallway.

Elly heard a bell in the distance signaling the end of lunchtime. Within a few minutes, the hallway started to flood with other students. Elly wasn't quite sure where she was going but didn't dare stop to pull out her map now, so she just kept walking until she got to the next small hallway off to the right. Feeling less claustrophobic, Elly pulled out the crumpled map.

"Hi, Elly," Niyanna called from down the hallway. Elly groaned as she quickly made her way to Elly. "I'm sorry about lunch, I hope you are not upset?"

"No, it's fine," Elly brushed off.

"Okay, good, because I would like for us to be friends." Elly glanced up from her map, perplexed by Niyanna's statement. She only just met this person, why would she be so concerned with their friendship. "I am new here too, so I just thought ..." Niyanna shrugged, attempting to keep her request for friendship casual, but Elly got the feeling it meant a lot to her to be friends. Only it didn't to Elly.

"What is your next class?" Niyanna asked, looking down at the still opened map.

"Oh, it's Physics, I think Mr. Rock, room 312," she added, secretly hoping Niyanna's class was in the opposite direction.

"Oh cool, I'm going to 313, so we can walk together."

Elly followed Niyanna back out into the main hallway and for a brief moment they were surrounded by a crowd of students swimming through the river. Elly followed as Niyanna naturally flowed through the crowd, as everyone just instinctively stepped out of her way. As they turned into a secondary hallway, they found themselves alone.

"Wow, it seems as if there are a lot of kids at this school."

"Well, the main hallway feeds into all the other mini hallways that house all the different classrooms. Right now we are in the science hall. All the math classes are on another one, and then English and so on," Niyanna easily explained.

"Oh, good to know. Well, this is me," Elly motioned towards the open door. Inside she could see the high, black marbled tables but no one seemed to be there yet.

"So," Niyanna glanced around and lowered her voice. "Don't be fooled by Mr. Rock's nice demeanor, I hear he's one of the hardest teachers here. Most people never pass his class the first time," Niyanna revealed. Then she winked and walked across the hallway into her classroom. Elly wasn't sure how she felt about Niyanna's tidbit or the fact that she would now most likely spend every day walking from lunch to Physics with her having forced conversations.

"Ah, you must be the new student going around posing as a senior," Mr. Rock jeered as Elly entered the room, her face instantly burning red. "I'm just kidding," he added, laughing to himself. "No, no, come in, find a seat. Have you taken physics before?"

"Actually, no," Elly confessed, taking a stool at the front table, putting her directly in front of his desk. He walked around the desk, casually leaning back on the front, putting him only a couple of feet from Elly.

"So why are you in this class?" He questioned, folding his arms across his chest. Elly started to get the feeling that getting a blanket "all senior classes" was a bad idea.

"I'm not sure the woman in the front office knew what to do with me," Elly shrugged.

Mr. Rock laughed to himself, nodding in understanding at the same time. "Yep, that sounds about right," he agreed. "Well," he clapped his hands together, making Elly jump slightly in her seat, as he made his way back around the large lab table. "I guess you are going to need some help then." He shifted through some papers, gathering a stack of them together.

"Here," he handed her the stack, as other students started to trickle into the room. "Study guides from last semester." He looked around the room. "Oh, Micah, come over here," he motioned. "Micah is my star student," Mr. Rock confessed, putting an arm around his broad shoulders. Micah awkwardly smiled. "Micah, can you assist Elly here in class, possibly some tutoring?" He dramatically winced, waiting for the answer he already knew was coming.

"Sure," Micah shrugged, throwing his backpack down across the table from Elly. Mr. Rock smiled triumphantly, satisfied with himself that he solved the problem of Elly knowing absolutely nothing about Physics.

"So, you are a senior?" Micah asked as they waited for the class to get started.

"No, actually. I was in dual classes at my previous school though." Elly felt exhausted having to repeat that singular fact so many times in a single day. "I was Biology though, not Physics."

"Why not get it changed then?"

"Well, seemed more trouble than it might be worth honestly," Elly grimaced at the thought of having to go back to the office to ask for another class change. Even though it was due to the fact the classes were completely different, she hated the idea that the woman would assume she was correct that Elly couldn't handle the senior classes.

"I can share my notebook with you if that helps?" He offered.

"Yeah, that'd be great," Elly whispered, as Mr. Rock called for attention in the class. After the lesson, Micah passed his notebook to Elly before they parted ways to the next class.

Elly easily found Maddie leaning against her car at the end of the day. Lauren and Camden were also there, much to Elly's dismay. The day had been overwhelming, her mind fried, as she realized for the first time she just wanted to be back at her grandparent's house.

"Oh, hey, Elly and I have to get going. I've got to go pick up Lily," Maddie explained as Elly reached the car. Camden immediately jumped in front of her and opened the door, shooting her another awkward feeling wink. Elly didn't respond, quickly looking away.

"Sorry, Camden can be a little extra," Maddie explained as they started to pull out of the parking lot. Elly turned to see Camden and Lauren walking to a rather high off-the-ground white jeep wrangler with large floodlights, making the car appear more like a giant insect than a vehicle. "Don't worry he'll settle down in a few days. He's just all about some new blood," Maddie jeered.

"New blood?"

"Oh, so Camden has literally dated like every girl in the school and botched it each time," Maddie laughed, thinking about all the times Camden has ruined a relationship, mostly because he is incapable of staying focused on one person at a time. "He actually is a really great person, just easily excited."

"Yeah, I can see that."

Elly was thankful that Maddie allowed them to ride in silence to her sister's school where she was just finishing her girl scout meeting. Maddie pulled up to the curb, allowing the car to noisily idle as Elly felt the vibrations of the muffler through her entire body.

"There she is," Maddie motioned, as a group of little girls bounced down the sidewalk, led by a tall, slender woman with dramatically long, dark hair.

A single girl broke away from the crowd, waving wildly as

she walked towards the car. Her dark curls were pulled back into two puffballs on the top of her head, her face consumed with a wide smile.

"Hey, Lily," Maddie greeted as she opened the car door. Elly tried to hide her shocked reaction. "Lily, this is Elly."

"Oh, hi Elly!" she squealed, bouncing in the back seat as if it were a trampoline.

"Now, buckle up," Maddie instructed. Lily rolled her eyes as she calmed down and pulled the belt over her shoulder. It barely hit her shoulder, her eyes not even above the window.

"Elly, I'm eight years old," Lily announced, as they started to drive. "How old are you?"

"Well, I'm fifteen –" Elly paused realizing her mistake. "No, sixteen now." Her eyes prickled and burned over the memory of her last birthday just days before her mother's death.

"Maddie is sixteen too because she gets to drive. I'm such a long way off from being able to drive," Lily mused, pouting in the back seat. Instantly, as if the thought left as quickly as it came she said, "So you are from New York, right?"

"Uh, yeah."

"My daddy and I are from California," Lily offered, "but we had to move away." Lily looked sad for a brief moment but quickly pushed the painful memory aside. "But now we live with Maddie and her mother and it's the best," she smiled real big and Maddie smiled back at her from the rearview mirror. Elly had assumed with Lily's dark complexion, curly jet black hair, and deep brown eyes that she wasn't biologically related to Maddie in any way.

"They've been together now for two years," Maddie added. "My mother was selling her artwork -"

"Oh, she's an amazing artist," Lily interjected.

"Well, she is very good but she just sells at the local market. That is when she met Lily's dad." Maddie explained. "*They* would say it was love at first sight."

Maddie didn't seem too convinced, which she wasn't.

While she adored having a father and little sister, she wasn't one to romanticize love to the point of believing in such silly things as love at first sight. She was a self-proclaimed realist. She had never dated a single person in her short life. Her mother always told her she got her analytical brain from her father. What her mother never understood was that it wasn't her analytical brain that stopped her, it was the fact that she never wanted to feel unwanted again - ever.

Elly assumed that Maddie had lost her father, but it was her father who lost her all those years ago. It was her father who decided that he didn't want to be a father anymore, so he just left. All Maddie had now was a few photos and this car. Maddie masked her feelings of insecurity and being unwanted with her happy disposition and focus on sports, but deep down she was desperate to talk to someone who could understand what she was going through. The moment Elly told her about her father, Maddie thought that Elly could be that person. She just wasn't sure if or when Elly would be ready to talk.

"My daddy is a writer, what does your daddy do?" Lily asked. Elly knew it was the innocent question of a child, but it still made her catch her breath and her chest burn.

"I don't really *know* my Daddy," Elly admitted through broken gasps, the pain of not knowing what happened to him almost - almost - worse than her mother actually being dead. Maddie immediately saw the tears start to well in Elly's eyes.

"Lily, not everybody has a daddy, kind of like how you didn't have a mommy for a few years." Instantly, Maddie regretted her words seeing the tears pooling in Elly's eyes.

"Oh, yeah," Lily awkwardly glanced at Maddie, "sorry, Elly."

"So, tell us about your day," Maddie asked, changing the subject before Elly started to cry. Elly turned away, gazing out the window. The fields were a blur through her tears, as she tried to hide them.

Lily proceeded to recount every single second of her day in shocking detail the rest of the way home. Maddie knew that her little sister would talk for hours about her life when given the chance and figured it would be a good way to give Elly a much-needed break.

There was something about losing her mother, finding her dead, that held a finality that suddenly had her rethinking her notions over her father's death because she wasn't actually sure he was dead. Elly hadn't realized it, but the moment she found her mother dead it called into question everything she thought about her father. The thoughts forming and festering in a dark, unknown place in her mind. But, the moment Maddie brought up her father it seemed to bring those thoughts to the front of her mind.

"So, you still want a ride after all that," Maddie asked, motioning to Lily who was up on her knees frantically waving goodbye to Elly from the back seat of the car. Maddie had taken the time to get out of the car to walk with Elly to her front door, hoping she might find an opening to connect with her about their fathers.

"Yeah, it's okay, she's a sweet kid." Elly waved back, which caused Lily's smile to grow if that was even possible.

"Okay." Maddie paused, trying to think of just the right words, but couldn't bring herself to say anything but, "Alright, bye."

12

Chapter Twelve

Elly immediately abandoned her studies to go down by the tree, hoping that Khalil would be roaming around waiting for her to return from school. Taking Micah's physics notes she nestled into the large embrace of the oak tree, prepared to wait until nightfall.

Her eyes felt heavy as she tried to understand Micah's scribbled notes on things she had no base knowledge on. She found herself re-reading various parts of his notes as she attempted to put the jumbled up puzzle pieces together. Finally, her mind couldn't even understand what the picture was supposed to be, so she pushed the notes away and resolved to change out of the course in the morning.

The sun was floating on the tops of the trees, the warmth of its rays blanketed her body, as she found herself drifting off to sleep. In the last moments, before her eyes fluttered closed for the last time, she recalled the immense amount of heat she felt throughout her entire body. It lulled her into a deep sleep.

She drifted through the dream, as it came to life before her closed eyes. Elly danced in the warmth of the sun as she gazed at the bright colors of the forest in the daylight. It was her first pleasant dream since she had arrived. Suddenly, the dream turned as she saw movement at her bare feet. Slowly looking down, realizing her feet were bare only at that moment, did she see the black snake twisting and slithering towards her, hissing as it approached. Just before it was about to strike, Elly screamed. Suddenly, Khalil was there. She could see his face, hear his voice, but he seemed too far away.

"Elly, Elly, are you okay?" Khalil stared into Elly's deep hazel-colored eyes, but they stared blankly back at him. "Elly, wake up," he urged. Recognition sprang to life in her eyes.

"Khalil?" He could tell she needed support, still dazed from the dream, so he gently wrapped his arm around her waist, pulling her closer to the tree so she could sit up. "What happened?"

"I think you were sleeping."

"Oh, yeah, I guess I was." Elly quickly glanced around the ground, the fear of the snake still fresh on her mind. But, it was just Khalil.

"What's this?" He asked, picking up Micah's physics notes.

"Oh, I was just trying to learn Physics, but it wasn't working."

"Physics?" He gave her a questionable look. "Isn't' that a senior-level course?"

"Well, actually yes."

"You are a senior?" He raised a disbelieving eyebrow.

"No, well, technically yes I am. I was taking dual classes to graduate early. Unfortunately, things are a little different here." Elly snatched the notebook back from Khalil. "I know nothing about Physics."

"It's not so hard," he shrugged. "Want some help?"

"I was going to just withdraw from the class tomorrow."

"Is that going to mess you up?"

"No ... maybe... I don't know." Elly was still noticeably flustered from the dream.

"Okay, so why don't you give me one afternoon, and if you still don't understand, then at least you tried, right?"

"Well, okay, that is really nice." Elly suddenly felt awful for being short and irritated with him about it, knowing it had nothing to do with him and everything to do with the immense amount of fear she felt over a snake springing from the ground. "I'm sorry, it was a long day," she confessed, as she remembered just how much she needed to lean into him for support and how much she just needed to talk to Khalil.

"I can imagine. First day at a new school after everything you have been through." Elly knew Khalil would understand, in a way that no one else really could, not even her grandparents. After all, they were the ones that made her go in the first place. "Okay, so let's start at the beginning."

For the next two hours, Khalil combed through Micah's notes filling in all the gaps so that Elly started to understand the simplicity of physics. As Khalil explained each law, relating and correlating the most basic things to help her remember, Elly realized just how brilliant Khalil was at it all. By the time they reached the final page, Elly thought she could stay in the class after all.

"I appreciate it," Elly offered. Dusk started to fall over the fields. The last rays of light were fading quickly, as Elly regretted spending so much time studying. She wished they had more time to talk. "I really wish you were at school with me." Elly's eyes grew wide as she heard the words pushing themselves from her mouth. She thought it, but never intended to say it out loud.

Before Khalil could say anything, Elly quickly gathered her things and started back towards the house, not wanting Khalil to see how embarrassed she was for blurting out. Elly knew full well why Khalil wasn't at school and knew her words would be received as judgment, which she never intended them to be.

"Elly, wait," Khalil called, but Elly quickened her pace. "Hey," he said, effortlessly reaching her, pulling softly on her arm to make her stop running away.

"I'm sorry, I shouldn't have mentioned it. That was insensitive."

"No, no, it's okay." Khalil could see that Elly was about to cry, the green in her eyes glistening as the light caught the drops of water. Slowly, he pulled her into his chest, unsure if she'd be receptive to his affection. The moment she wrapped her arms around his waist, he pulled her in tighter. He could feel the slight lift of her shoulder as his own started to feel damp from her tears.

"It's going to get better," he whispered into her ear.

"Elly!" Jane's voice cut through the dark silence. Elly immediately pulled away from Khalil, frantically brushing away her tears. "Elly," she called again.

"I should go."

Khalil watched as Elly ran back up to the house, Jane glaring, piecing his gaze through the darkness of the fallen night. For a moment, he thought she knew but then assured himself that it was impossible. No one would believe his secret, because it was too dark. At least that is what he told himself every day.

13

Chapter Thirteen

The next morning, Maddie and Elly drove in silence. Maddie bit her lip as she tried not to bring up the subject of Elly's father, along with her own. Elly's eyes were puffy this morning, so Maddie assumed she had been crying. As much as Maddie wanted to connect with Elly, she knew it wasn't the best time. Elly already seemed overwhelmed, which she could only imagine after losing her mother in such a violent way. Maddie was resolved to let the conversation happen naturally or not at all.

"So, is Niyanna from here?" Elly asked. They were about halfway to school and Elly finally broke the silence. Elly had allowed her mind to wander and it seemed to stop right on an image of Niyanna each and every time. Elly recalled how out of place she seemed and her eagerness for Elly's friendship.

"Oh, yeah, you noticed," Maddie laughed. "She just transferred here a few months ago from some big-time boarding school in Atlanta. She told everyone she got bored with the city life and needed to slow down, but we all think she got kicked out," Maddie gossiped.

"Do her parents live here then?"

"Well, yes and no. She tells it as they travel a lot for work. Her parents, I think, are lawyers, as Niyanna is always saying they are always working some case in the city." Maddie shrugged as if the matter didn't concern her much at all.

"You are friends?" Elly asked. While they sat at the same table during lunch, Elly had gotten the impression that Maddie didn't care for Niyanna.

"Well, not really. I mean Lauren is... so by proximity I guess I am." Elly got the feeling there was more to the reason than that.

"So, she's just home alone all the time?"

"Yeah, I guess so," Maddie shrugged. "She's always throwing these *events*, as she calls them, at her house," Maddie added. "I try to stay focused on soccer, so I don't go. But..." she bit her lower lip, unsure if she should tell Elly the truth. "Well, let's just say if you get invited, I'd stay clear of it."

Before Elly could ask any more questions, Maddie pulled the car into a crowded parking lot. Camden's bright white jeep caught her eye. It was surrounded by other boys and a few girls, as his music blared through the parking lot. Lauren saw Maddie pulling in and immediately started walking towards them.

"Hey," she called, waving her hands, as Maddie got out of the car. They both returned her wave, as Elly reached back inside to gather her backpack. If not, maybe she would've seen what all the commotion was about.

"Oh my gosh," exclaimed Lauren, as Elly hit the back of her head on the door frame, trying to quickly get out of the car.

"What is he doing back at school?" Maddie questioned.

Elly raised her head just in time to see Khalil's unmistakable bronco pulling into the parking lot. Her breath caught in her chest, her cheeks instantly flushed, as she realized that he was coming to school. She couldn't help but think about what she had said to him yesterday and if that was the reason he was now here.

"I thought his mother was like dying?" Lauren said as Maddie jabbed her in the ribs. Lauren instantly covered her lips realizing her blunder. *Sorry*, she mouthed to Maddie, as they both stared at Elly waiting for her reaction. But, Elly had not heard them, as she was completely focused on Khalil as he leaped down from the car. Without looking around, as if he already knew her direction, he started to walk towards Elly.

"Elly, Elly," Maddie shook her shoulders to get her attention. "Do you know him?" All three girls stared at Khalil. He was obviously walking directly towards Elly.

"Uh, yeah, he's my neighbor," Elly forced out, not taking her eyes away from Khalil.

"What?" Lauren slapped Maddie's arm. "You didn't tell me he lived that close to you."

"I didn't know," Maddie defended. "Heck, out there no one really knows what's behind their woods."

"Hi, Elly," Khalil greeted, as Maddie and Lauren were rendered speechless.

"What are you doing here?"

Khalil glanced at Maddie and Lauren, girls he knew but never spoke to, as they stared up at him as if he were the star of a popular movie.

"Well, I couldn't let you face another day alone," he admitted, as the other girls swooned. Elly noticed the way they were acting and felt uncomfortable. "What's your first class?"

"Uh, English Lit."

"Shall we?" He offered his elbow much to Elly's disbelief. She refused to take it, as she just started walking in the direction of the school, completely embarrassed. Khalil nodded to the other girls, then turned on his heels easily catching up to Elly. "You okay?"

"Yes, I'm fine." Elly glanced back over her shoulders, noticing Maddie and Lauren in whispered conversation. She knew they were talking about her. "Just really surprised to see you here."

"Well, my grades were starting to slip," he lied. "So, I had been thinking of coming back. Just needed a push I guess," he shrugged, attempting to sound casual but Elly was the singular reason he returned. "I figured we'd have a couple of classes together considering you are taking all senior-level courses," he jeered, lightly pushing his shoulder against her own.

"Oh." Elly stumbled slightly, his playful nudge pushing her off balance.

"No, but really, let me see your schedule."

Elly stopped, pulling her schedule from her backpack and handing it to Khalil, who immediately scanned it memorizing every class, period, and teacher. She was the only reason he was back, so he planned to make sure he got into as many of her classes as he could.

"Thanks." Khalil handed the paper back to Elly. "I have to go check-in at the office, but I'll see you around."

Elly watched as Khalil effortlessly made his way through the crowds of people now starting to swarm the hallway. Through the sea of people, Elly could see Khalil as he was practically a head taller than most of the students here. Only when he turned the corner, did she release the breath she had been holding.

After their rude introduction yesterday, Elly was not looking forward to her first class with Mr. Manning, which filled her with resentment as literature was her favorite subject by far. Walking into the room, avoiding all eye contact with him as he seemed enthralled with a book at his desk, she slipped into the back of the classroom unnoticed.

Elly busied herself with unpacking her backpack, hopeful, that Mr. Manning wouldn't notice her in the classroom. There were a few other early arrivals in the class as well, but everyone preoccupied themselves with reading. Elly stole a glance at Mr. Manning, noticing he was wearing another sweater vest over a plaid shirt, topped off with a decorative bow tie, none of which matched in the least. She could see his eyes shifting quickly side to side as he read the tattered, old book perched between his fingers.

Suddenly, a bell rang throughout the room, but Mr. Manning didn't even flinch. Students filed into the room, each taking a seat and pulling out their supplies as they shared in casual chatter. Mr. Manning still didn't seem to notice anything, until the second bell when he instantly dropped his feet from his desk, slammed his book, and jumped right into the lesson. He babbled on about the popular parodies in English literature, writing frantically on the chalkboard until he was interrupted by the door opening.

"Oh, you are back?" Mr. Manning stuttered, looking utterly bewildered, as Khalil stood in the doorway.

"Uh, yes sir." Khalil scanned the room, catching Elly's shocked gaze. Scoffing at Khalil's broad smile, clearly annoyed by his return, Mr. Manning flippantly motioned for Khalil to find a seat.

"Okay, well, take a seat." Mr. Manning turned back to the board continuing with his lesson, as Khalil made his way through the rows of desks, taking the empty one right next to Elly.

"Fancy seeing you here," he smiled. Elly got the impression it was no accident.

"Did you copy my schedule?" Elly asked.

"No, no ... well, maybe a few classes," Khalil admitted, his smile growing so wide that his dimples showed.

"Okay, so something you want to share with the class?" Mr. Manning cut through the daze of the class, as Elly realized suddenly everyone was looking at them. She quickly shifted away from Khalil.

"Actually, Mr. Manning, I was just discussing with Elly here how I wouldn't consider that a Parody at all."

"Oh, really?" Mr. Manning glared at Khalil, challenging him to retort.

"Yes, it's a satire."

"And how do you figure?"

"Because it isn't funny," Khalil jeered.

Elly sank in her seat, mortified that Khalil was debating with a teacher and in the same breath drawing more attention onto her by the one teacher who seemed to already hate her enough.

"Well, then, I challenge the entire class to write their own parody. Homework, compliments of your classmate here," Mr. Manning announced as the entire class groaned, launching glares in their direction.

Just then the bell rang, as everyone stood, dispersing out of the class quickly.

"Khalil, stay for a minute," Mr. Manning beckoned as they reached the door. Khalil gave Elly a slight smile, as she disappeared out the door.

Elly was assured that Khalil was getting into trouble for his behavior in the classroom. As his friend, she should've waited outside the door, but she was immediately washed away with the crowds of people flooding out to the courtyard. In the few minutes between each class, students seemed to find the time to congregate in that area.

Elly was just passing through to her next class when suddenly Niyanna was right next to her.

14

Chapter Fourteen

Khalil stood in front of Mr. Manning, waiting for him to divulge why he kept him after class, as he read over a note on his desk. Removing his glasses, tossing them on the table, he met Khalil's stare.

"What are you doing back?" Khalil shrugged. "Is your brother still in town?" A flash of fear passed over Mr. Manning's face.

"No, he left the other day." Khalil saw a noticeable shift in Mr. Manning's demeanor.

"Well, so what do you hope to accomplish by returning to school?"

"I don't think that is your business, Mr. Manning."

Mr. Manning scoffed at Khalil, realizing that he had no plans to be honest with him about what was happening. Mr. Manning had been shunned by his family many years ago. He held Khalil after class because there had to be a reason for him returning at this time and he needed to know why.

"I just need to make sure that this has nothing to do with me," Mr. Manning confessed.

"I assure you, Mr. Manning, this has nothing to do with you."

Khalil turned to walk away, but Mr. Manning still had one more question.

"How is your mother doing?"

"Again, how is that your business?" Khalil could feel his anger rising, as he glared at Mr. Manning, who had no right to ask about his mother.

"I can still care for my cousin, even if I-"

"She's fine," Khalil interjected. "Now may I go, please?"

"Yeah - yeah," Mr. Manning waved his hand. "Just be careful, Khalil. I get the feeling you are getting very close to the fire."

Khalil pushed through the classroom door, ignoring Mr. Manning's words of caution. Looking around, he expected to see Elly but the hallway was mostly emptied by this point. He could feel the heat of his anger over Mr. Manning pulling him after class for many reasons. While he was technically family, a second cousin to his mother, he had chosen a life without them a long time ago. Khalil didn't blame him, he envied him.

Niyanna effortlessly slid her arm through Elly's elbow and dragged her along beside her as they walked through the courtyard. Elly could smell the intoxicating mixture of perfume and hair products that made her stomach turn.

"I missed you after Physics yesterday," she was saying, as Elly was trying to shake the shock of what was happening. "So, I wanted to see if you could hang after school? Just a few of us getting together at my house, cool?" Elly just stared at her, Maddie's words of caution echoing in her mind.

"I - uh - I should really just go home."

"Oh, come on, it'll be so fun," Niyanna insisted, tightening her arm. While Elly wasn't sure what happened at Niyanna's home, by the look on Maddie's face this morning, she didn't want to find out.

Just as Elly was attempting to think of an excuse, wiggling her arm to try to loosen Niyanna's grip, Khalil appeared right in front of her, glaring down at Niyanna.

"Elly?" Khalil questioned without taking his eyes off Niyanna. "Everything okay?"

"Do you know him?" Niyanna asked, holding tightly to her elbow. Elly wished she could disappear, the building negative tension causing her anxiety to raise. She could feel the convergence of two tides and did not want to be caught in the rip current.

"Actually, Niyanna," Elly forcefully removed her arm, as Niyanna stayed locked on Khalil. "I do, and we have the next period together, so I should go."

"You really should think more cautiously about who you want to be friends with, Elly," Niyanna jeered, still glaring at Khalil.

"I couldn't agree more," Khalil retorted.

Elly pulled against Khalil's sleeved arm, as she attempted to get out of the water before they both got pulled under by Niyanna. She could feel Niyanna's glare on their backs as they walked away, but she refused to turn around or look at Khalil. She kept her eyes trained on the pathway in front of her, ignoring everything else until she found herself alone in the sterile hallway with Khalil.

Elly already didn't care for Niyanna, her sophisticated presence bordered on pretentious in Elly's opinion. She still had no idea why Khalil would glare at Niyanna, or anyone for that matter, with such blind hatred.

"Okay, what was that?" Khalil kept walking, ignoring her question, so Elly completely stopped. Khalil realized she wasn't next to him and turned, noticing Elly standing, hands crossed over her chest, as she waited for an explanation.

"Okay, but can we do this somewhere else," Khalil scanned the hallways. A few students appeared from a classroom, walking with purpose in the opposite direction. The first bell would ring in three minutes, at which time the halls would flood again as everyone made their way to the next class.

"No one is listening," Elly assured him, confused why he hesitated to tell her considering it was very obvious that they both hated each other. Elly doubted it was a big secret.

"She's just not a good person. You shouldn't hang out with her," Khalil demanded. Elly stared at Khalil, not satisfied with his explanation. "Look, she has people over at her house and you don't want to be associated with what they do, trust me," he affirmed.

"Oh, come on, I don't need you telling me who I can be friends with or what I can do," Elly snapped, suddenly feeling very defensive of herself as Khalil was showing a possessive nature she didn't care for at all.

"It's not like that ..." Khalil was frustrated as he pulled his fingers through his thick hair. "Okay, I'm sorry. That came across wrong. I'm not trying to tell you what to do."

"What are you trying to tell me?" Elly demanded.

"Niyanna doesn't like people like me," Khalil confessed. Confusion flashed over Elly's face, as she thought about the kind of person Khalil was, which was a person who seemed nothing but empathetic and decent, making it hard for her to believe that Niyanna would think any differently.

"Let's just say it's a class thing."

"You're rich," Elly blurted out.

"Not that kind of class. Can we just drop this for now? We really should get to class," he urged, desperate to change the conversation. He knew there was no way to be honest about the reason they hated each other. It was in their blood and Elly would never understand.

"Fine," Elly reluctantly agreed, not wanting to be late for class.

As it turns out, Elly and Khalil discovered that they did not have the next class together, so they parted ways in the main hallway. Elly could feel Khalil watching her until she turned down what was known as the Math hallway. Even though she was already slightly behind, she found it hard to focus on anything in the class. Her mind wondered about Khalil and what happened with Niyanna. It was not as simple as a class difference, or not liking him as a person. It was clear to Elly that something had happened between them. You didn't get that look of hate for nothing.

Elly didn't see Khalil again in her next period either but then found Maddie in the lunchroom. Pausing briefly, wanting to make sure that Niyanna didn't hold a seat at the table, Elly glanced around the atrium. She noticed Niyanna perched on a bench at the other end of the atrium talking to Camden and the other boys. Letting out a sigh of relief, she headed towards the table. Sliding her tray down next to Maddie, Elly scanned the lunchroom again but this time looking for Khalil.

"He's not here," Lauren said, knowing who she was looking for without asking.

"What do you mean?" Elly asked, attempting to cover her tracks.

"He doesn't eat lunch here with us," Lauren reiterated.

"Khalil," Maddie added as if Elly didn't already know. "He's a senior, they eat off-campus every day or in the courtyard. Just as Juniors are allowed in the atrium and sophomore and freshman eat in the cafeteria," Maddie explained.

"That's not where he goes though," Lauren giggled.

"Well, where does he go?"

Maddie and Lauren both exchanged an awkward look, unsure if they should tell Elly. It was obvious by the way Elly gazed at him she thought, as every other person did in the school, that Khalil was beyond good looking. Khalil didn't have a common beauty, but it was more the unique features that made him stand out. But, Maddie and Lauren weren't sure if Elly wanted to know the true person behind the gorgeous mask.

"What are you not telling me?"

"So, obviously, Khalil is hot, but he's kind of a loner," Lauren explained.

"I don't think he's that much of a loner, he just likes to do his own thing," Maddie added defensively, often feeling separated from the group because she wouldn't join them at Niyanna's house.

"Oh, please, he never comes to anything. He has no friends," Lauren added justifying her opinion. "When was the last time you even saw him talk to someone?"

"This morning." Lauren rolled her eyes. "And Elly is his friend," Maddie added, smiling at Elly.

"Okay, I think I understand," Elly said, just wanting to stop the conversation. Elly had intended on asking Maddie about what happened between Khalil and Niyanna, but now she realized all too well what Khalil meant by class.

"You've got to be kidding me," Lauren gaped. Elly looked up just in time to see Khalil walking through the main doors in the atrium.

They were not the only ones who noticed Khalil, everyone seemed to stare at him as he walked through the tables headed straight for Elly, who was suddenly even more grateful that Niyanna had not sat at their table today.

"Hi, Elly," Khalil greeted, standing over the table appearing to be waiting for an invitation to join them. Elly wasn't sure she should invite him though after the way Lauren spoke about him. She didn't want her to say anything to him that would hurt his feelings or worse something that would cause him never to come back again.

"Take a seat," Lauren offered, kicking the chair out across from her that almost hit Khalil right in the knees.

"No thanks," He smirked at Lauren. "Elly, can we talk?"

"Uh, sure, yeah," Elly said, quickly gathering her stuff, shoving the apple she had left into her backpack.

"I'll see you after school," Maddie called as Elly followed Khalil from the atrium feeling as if she were on the runway at New York Fashion week with everyone staring at them.

"I am sorry about earlier, I hope you don't think," Khalil said as they reached the courtyard.

"No, no, I don't," Elly assured him, suddenly feeling awful for the way she treated him earlier. It was clear to her now that Niyanna was judging him because she thought he was a loser. It was the class of high school that he was referring to.

"I wanted to talk to you, but not with everyone around. I hope you don't mind?"

"Of course not."

The courtyard, normally filled with students between classes, was particularly empty this time of the day, only a few huddled groups of students sprinkled through the tables. With the sun directly overhead, Elly noticed the flickers of light dancing throughout the courtyard, giving it an illusion of movement. Elly followed Khalil to a bench set off to the side far away from the other scattered seniors who didn't go off campus for lunch.

"Should I be out here?" Elly asked.

"You are with me, it's fine," Khalil assured, glancing around taking inventory of who was in the courtyard. He recognized everyone, none of them were friends, nor would any of them care that he brought a junior into the area. "Technically, you are kind of a senior. After all, you are in all senior classes."

"Yeah, I guess so." Elly still felt slightly uncomfortable. "So, what did Mr. Manning want?"

"Oh, uh, nothing really. He was just catching me up on what I missed being out."

"Well that was oddly helpful of him, when I joined the class all he said was *keep up*," Elly scoffed, annoyed to find out that it was her that the teacher apparently didn't care for, not the fact that he didn't want the problem of helping.

"I had him earlier this year before I went out on medical leave," Khalil explained.

"I thought for sure you were getting into trouble," Elly affirmed. "He seemed so upset."

"Why? He was wrong."

"I don't think teachers like it when you tell them they are wrong."

"No, they don't really like that much, I guess." They both laughed.

"So, you said you wanted to talk to me about something?" Elly asked.

"Oh, yes, well ..." he hesitated, desperate to talk to Elly as they did under the tree, but feeling as if something was different between them at school. "Just really wanted to see how you are doing with everything?"

"It's hard," Elly confessed, feeling the rolling pressure of sorrow on the horizon, building like a dark thunderstorm. "I think my grandmother told absolutely every person about my mother, which makes it all worse. On top of the fact, that despite my higher education, I am behind in every class here, as if I just picked up a book and had to start reading in the middle - no going back, sorry." Elly froze, suddenly realizing she could feel herself losing control. Internally, she cursed herself as she willed her mind to calm down before she completely exploded.

"I can help you," Khalil offered.

"Thanks, really. Everything yesterday was really helpful."

In truth, Elly knew she could catch up, she just needed to get out of the water to get a break from the waves constantly bashing against her, then she'd be able to focus.

"How's your mom?" Elly wasn't sure about asking Khalil while they were here at school, unsure of how open he'd be talking about it here, but she didn't want to keep talking about herself.

"She had a rough couple of days," he admitted, Elly remembering the days he disappeared. "It's hard for her when my brother is in town but she seems better now if that's possible." Khalil winced at the thought, knowing his mother never truly felt better at any point, but he could see a difference in a good day versus a bad day.

On a good day, she'd talk to him, sit up for a few hours throughout the day and eat. But, it seemed to exhaust her more, the next few days followed by sleeping all day, not eating, and Khalil worrying endlessly that her death would be any minute.

"You know, I just feel awful some days thinking that'd it be better - for her of course, not me - if she moved on for all this pain." Elly saw the redness in his eyes, causing her to instantly reach out to him. Seamlessly, Khalil and Elly's fingers wrapped around each other, empathy flooding Elly's eyes. "I'm an awful, selfish person," he confessed.

"No, you are not," Elly assured him, squeezing his hand as tightly as she could. "You love your mother, of course you don't want to let her go, I get that. You shouldn't beat yourself up about that."

"Thanks, but her death means a lot more ..." His mind trailed off, Elly watched as Khalil became deep in thought, knowing the changes that came with losing a parent - twice over. However, Khalil seemed to be alluding to more than what she was thinking.

He was standing on the precipice of the cliff knowing his mother's death would be the final push into the darkness, but he couldn't be honest with Elly. It was the one secret he could never tell her - *ever*.

"I think we should get to the next period," Khalil announced, breaking free from his thoughts and her hands.

Elly wanted to assure Khalil that she was here for him as his friend, be the stable tree he could cling to in the storm, but deep down she knew her roots were not strong enough. In the end, they would both blow away in sorrow.

As Elly and Khalil approached Physics, she caught Niyanna's staring gaze. Leaning up against her own classroom door, as if waiting for them, she gave a tight smile to Elly. She took it as a warning, as Niaynna flipped her long, curled hair and disappeared into the classroom as they reached the door. She didn't bother looking at Khalil's reaction, knowing that would only increase the tension.

"Elly," Micah called from his seat, beckoning Elly to join across from him where she set yesterday. Elly waved and took her seat, as Khalil followed closely behind, sliding into the stool right beside her. "Uh, hey, so did the notes help?" Micah asked awkwardly, shifting on his seat as he stole a look at Khalil.

"Oh, yes, thank you." Elly pulled the notebook from her backpack and slid it across the counter.

"Well, you know, anytime." Micah glanced at Khalil, who appeared to be ignoring them as he riffled through his backpack.

"I was going to see if you had time after school, we could - uh - go over it, if you need to, that is." Micah was definitely uncomfortable in Khalil's presence.

"Well, actually, Khalil walked me through it yesterday." At the sound of his name, Khalil flashed a smile across the table, as Micah's face fell into solemn retreat.

"Yeah, sure, just you know," he shrugged. Micah saw that he was beaten, unable to compete for Elly's attention when she was already focused completely on Khalil.

Before Elly could respond, the class started. Even though Elly barely knew Micah, he seemed the kind of friend someone always wanted. He had helped her when he didn't have to and called off Logan yesterday when he picked up on the fact she was upset. She appreciated it more than he realized, so she felt guilty as she saw his face accept that she did not intend to return his friendship in the same way. Even though she couldn't change her feelings, Khalil being the person she needed the most right now, she still couldn't get over the feeling that she was losing out on a friendship with Micah because of it.

15

Chapter Fifteen

The moment Elly walked out the doors to the parking lot her heart stopped. There leaning against Maddie's car was Niyanna forcing a conversation with Maddie. Quickly, Elly scanned the parking lot hoping to see Khalil. She figured if Niyanna saw Khalil she'd back off, but he was nowhere to be seen. Reluctantly, she made her way to Maddie's car, really not wanting to have any conversation with her after what Khalil told her during lunch.

"Oh, Elly," Maddie called, eager to end her conversation with Niyanna. "Are you ready to go?" Elly picked up on Maddie's body language, her eyes burrowing into her own, sending a secret SOS message.

"Oh, please, Maddie, I was really hoping you gals would join me," Niyanna insisted. "My treat," she added, attempting to sweeten some deal Elly was unaware of. She knew Maddie wouldn't agree to go to Niyanna's house, so she wasn't worried.

"Well, I guess so," Maddie conceded. Elly's eyes bugged with surprise. "Just for a minute though," she added.

"Great!" Niyanna practically jumped with excitement.

"Where are we going?" Elly asked before Niyanna was out of earshot, which was a mistake because Niyanna whipped back around.

"Well," Niyanna interjected, "I am treating you girls to a smoothie at Wild Lemon. They are by far the best smoothies you will ever have," Niyanna assured Elly. Maddie gave Elly a tight *"I'm sorry"* smile.

Elly did one last look around for Khalil, but he was still missing in action, the Bronco left untouched in the parking spot. Running out of options and with no excuse or other ride home, Elly reluctantly got into the car with Maddie.

"Are you okay with going?" Maddie asked as they belted up. "I'm sorry I didn't ask you, but Niyanna was pretty persistent."

"Yeah, I picked up on that."

"It really shouldn't be that bad, a lot of students go there after school just to hang out. I promise we won't be long. Normally, I'd have soccer practice, but that won't start for another few weeks. Oh, yeah, I won't be able to take you home then."

"It's fine …" Elly figured she didn't have a choice about going to get smoothies, only hoping that it would in fact not be too long. "I'm sure I can get another ride home then, no worries," she added, thinking it would be a good excuse to ask Khalil for a ride, assuming he didn't disappear after school every day. As much as he seemed to interject himself in her school day, she found it odd that he wasn't there at the end waiting for her to come out.

Khalil rolled his shoulders as he waited in the small, cramped office. Diplomas and certificates adorn the walls, ensuring that everyone in the office knew just how qualified Ms. Simmons was to be the high school guidance counselor. Her desk was cluttered with pictures of her family and stacks of files, not only on her desk but all over the room on chairs and the floor. It gave Khalil a claustrophobic feeling as he waited in the guidance counselor's office. Anxiously, he glanced at his watch, knowing that any moment the final bell would ring and he wanted to be waiting for Elly.

As he dozed off in his final class of the day, Khalil was jolted by his name being called over the intercom. Annoyed he presented at the guidance office, assured that she would once again want to discuss his future since this was his last semester. At the beginning of the year, Ms. Simmons had urged him to apply to various Ivy League Schools, his brilliance and hardship making him a shoo-in, but Khalil knew he could never go to college. His life would be forced down another path.

"Ah, Khalil," Ms. Simmons greeted as she walked into the room, her glasses perched on her nose and a file opened in her hands. She attempted to keep reading as she crossed the few feet to her desk, but stumbled over the various stacks of files. Righting herself quickly, she fell into the chair behind her desk, slapping the file down on the wood. "I was glad to hear of your return today."

Leaning back in the office chair, Ms. Simmons cupped her hands together over her stomach as she stared down her nose at Khalil. He knew she was waiting for a response, but Khalil had no intentions of dragging out this meeting by opening up the conversation as to why he returned or never applied to colleges.

"How are things going at home?" She probed.

"Fine."

Ms. Simmons's eyes narrowed at his short remark. "Your mother?"

"As well as to be expected." Khalil wasn't rude, but he wasn't forthcoming either, which irritated Ms. Simmons.

"So, why did you return?"

For a moment, Khalil thought about just getting up and walking out. While Ms. Simmons was a nice woman and seemed to care for her students, Khalil knew she could never begin to understand his situation. His life would never be normal. He was not normal. But, there was something about her chopped off, gray peppered hair that framed her stern blue eyes and a soft smile that gave Khalil pause. He wasn't used to others caring for him, aside from his mother, and no matter how much he wanted to walk away, he couldn't bring himself to do it.

"Just to finish out the year." Again, Ms. Simmons glared at him through her glasses, annoyed with his vague reason.

"Well, then, I assume you have a plan for after graduation then?" Khalil shook his head no. "It's a little late, Khalil. If you had been here at school, I could've ..." Khalil knew exactly what her unspoken words were going to be, as she allowed her voice to trail, her shoulders shrugging. It was a very parental way of saying he had to accept the consequences of his actions now.

"It'll be okay, Ms. Simmons," Khalil assured. Just then, he heard the bell echoing throughout the school, increasing his anxiety to get out of this conversation. "No need to worry about me," he added, reaching down for his back.

"No, not so fast," Ms. Simmons stalled, pointing her finger back at the chair. Khalil fell back into the dirt-stained chair. "We need to discuss your credits to graduate and these classes you somehow registered yourself into today." She opened the file on her desk and pulled out a single sheet of paper. Khalil could see through the thin sheet, as he realized it was his class schedule.

"Physics?" She raised a questioning eyebrow. "You've already taken that course."

"I was told it was the only course open," Khalil lied, as he had to the secretary that morning about what classes he needed to be placed into.

"Well, let me see–"

"No, really, Ms. Simmons, I don't need any help. I'm sure my schedule is enough to allow me to graduate." She glared at him across the desk, knowing that he was factually correct, he did have enough to graduate, but not enough for him, which is what she cared about at this moment. Ms. Simmons knew what a bright, intelligent person Khalil was, along with how much money his family had in this town. She slightly envied the fact that he could do anything, be anyone, yet somehow he didn't seem to care. She took him for a spoiled, complacent rich kid.

"Khalil, you can do better," she urged, folding her hands over her desk and leaning in with a stern look of disappointment.

"Trust me, I know."

With that Khalil quickly pulled his backpack up on his shoulder and left the room, leaving Ms. Simmons completely deflated by his last comment.

Regrettably, Elly got out of the car across the street from where Niyanna and Lauren were entering a shop that was covered in bright yellow lemons. They were all over the large windows to the street, only slightly obstructing her view of the brightly colored shop. Elly could see the mass of people in the shop, wondering if that would make it worse or better in her efforts to avoid Niyanna. In a single moment, she had learned that she didn't care for Niyanna, and by the end of the day that had festered into a full-on deep feeling of dislike.

A bell chimed throughout the store, as Elly and Maddie entered the shop. Most people didn't even turn around, engrossed in conversation, while others waited in the line that ran the length of the glass wall giving everyone a first-hand view of their smoothie being made.

Maddie saw Lauren and Niyanna already at a table in the front, right under the lemon-covered windows. Maddie and Elly slid into the booth beside each other, as Niyanna flashed her a satisfied smile.

"Hey gals, what do you want?"

Lauren and Maddie instantly provided their orders to Niyanna, leaving Elly completely in the dark as to what she even remotely could want at the store.

"I'm not really sure," Elly confessed. Smoothies weren't a thing up in New York ... coffee shops and bookstores were her typical after-school socialization spots.

"Well, come up to the counter with me and check it out." Elly got the feeling this was Niyanna's plan all along to get her alone. She feared Niyanna would want to talk about Khalil, revealing some damning information that would change Elly's mind. But,

Elly was sure there was nothing Niyanna could say to change the way she felt about Khalil. "I love pineapple, so anything with that, I pick. What about you?"

"Oh, uh, I guess mangos."

"Well, you should try the Sunrise Smoothie," Niyanna recommended, keeping the conversation casual. Elly felt she was about to receive a sneak attack at any moment.

Niyanna ordered for them both, paid for all four, then they started the arduous trek down the glass wall as they waited for the smoothies to be made. It gave Niyanna plenty of time to have an unwanted conversation with Elly.

"So," Niyanna started, leaning against the glass, her body language casual, but Elly knew her words were not. "So, your mother died and that's why you moved here?" Elly thought it was more of a statement than a question, so she didn't answer. "My parents are always gone, not the same thing of course, but I mean relatable in a way," she shrugged.

It only made Elly hate her more, as it was in no way the same or relatable. She would've said it to her, but then bit her lip, knowing she did not want to go toe to toe with Niyanna on the subject. She decided it would be best to just ignore her and get this over with as soon as possible.

"I want you to know you can talk to me, I'd like for us to be friends."

"Why?" The word jumped from Elly's mouth.

"Oh, uh, because, like I said, I can relate." Niyanna appeared honestly confused over the fact that Elly had no interest in being her friend, then realization washed over her face. "Is this because of Khalil? What did he tell you?" she demanded.

"He didn't tell me anything," Elly lied. Niyanna narrowed her eyes in disbelief. "It was clear to me though you don't like him - why?"

"Oh, it's nothing really," she shrugged, attempting to push Elly off the subject by making it seem as if there was nothing between them, when in fact there was everything between them both. Niyanna knew Khalil would never tell Elly, he couldn't. But, Niyanna gave a sly smile, because she knew something neither of them did. "Really, though, it's nothing actually between the two of us, we just have different lifestyles," Niyanna continued. "I'm sure you'll understand that one day."

"No, I don't. What is that even supposed to mean?"

"Order up!" The boy behind the counter called.

Niyanna jumped on the interruption, grabbing Lauren and her smoothie, then immediately returning to the table. Elly was left bewildered and agitated.

"Your order," the boy probed, pulling Elly back to life.

"Uh, yeah, thanks." Elly carried the smoothies slowly back to the table, her mind fogged with confusion. There was something about her words that made Elly feel as if she was missing a valuable piece of information.

Niyanna intentionally left the conversation on the edge of the cliff, dangling Elly over the edge and she wasn't sure if she ever planned to pull Elly back. As Elly approached the table, she realized that all three girls were already deep in conversation. Annoyed, Elly decided she'd have to continue the conversation with Niyanna another time.

"Hey sis," Camden called, entering the shop a few minutes later with Logan and Micah. "Fancy seeing you ladies here."

Camden effortlessly pulled a chair around from another table and set it close to Niyanna. Pulling his legs around he leaned over the back of the chair as he said, "Are we having another *gathering* at your house this weekend?" He winked at Elly as if she knew what the word *gathering* meant. Awkwardly, she shifted her eyes away already knowing she had no intentions of going.

"Well, that depends," Niyanna smirked. "Are your annoying friends going to trash it again?"

"Hey, hey," Camden raised his hands in defense. "That was not us."

"Oh, please, I know it was."

"Look, we promise we'll stick around this time and help clean it all up," Logan interjected. Niyanna gave him a sly smile, a secret compliance with his offer. "Yes!" He slapped his hands together in triumph.

"You ladies joining us?" Camden asked looking right at Elly.

"Oh, uh, I don't know," Elly deflected.

"Maddie, what's your excuse this time?" Camden jeered.

"Oh, back off, Cam," Lauren interjected. "You know her mother would never allow her to go."

"Seems Maddie is smart enough to get around that one," Logan offered.

"She's not a deviant like the rest of you," Lauren jeered.

"Oh, come on, it's just a couple of people having a fun time," Logan defended. "Harmless fun," he added holding his hands up.

"Maddie, you and Elly should come, it'll be fun," Niyanna urged.

"Yeah, we'll think about it," Maddie conceded, just wanting

the conversation to shift to something else. "We should get going."

Maddie shoved against Elly, glaring at Camden, as he refused to get out of the way. Just when Elly thought she was about to have to literally push him out of the way, he moved, slowly pushing the chair back to allow Elly and Maddie to escape. Just as Elly slipped out the door behind Maddie, her eye caught Micah's stare. Instantly, he smiled and gave her a slight wave. Elly waved back.

"I'm really sorry about that," Maddie offered as they stepped out of the store into the street. "Those guys can be a lot sometimes."

"Oh, it's okay. Do you think you will go this weekend?"

"Oh, gosh no," Maddie confessed. "I just said that to get them to stop."

"What do they do over there anyway?" Elly asked.

She had her assumptions but honestly felt slightly naive to the after-school weekend activities, assured that what she used to do with her friends in New York was very different. Her evenings were mostly filled with watching movies and the occasional concert with Makiyah and their mothers.

"Oh, well -"

"Elly." She heard his familiar voice over the crowds of people in the streets. Turning, Khalil was right behind them.

"Hey," Maddie and Elly said in unison as he stopped at their feet.

"Sorry, I was hoping to grab you after school for some tutoring," Khalil explained, "But, I got held up in the guidance office."

Maddie glanced at Elly, noticing her flushed cheeks.

"Oh, it's okay."

"Well, is now good?"

"For what?" Elly was visibly flustered.

"Tutoring?"

"Oh, uh -" Elly turned to Maddie for approval to ditch her for Khalil.

"Yeah, sure, I'll just see you tomorrow morning." Elly nodded in agreement.

Maddie glanced back into the smoothie shop, seeing Lauren and Niyanna talking in the same booth, Camden and Logan now sitting across from them. For a moment, she thought about joining them again, but then considered they may be talking about their plans for this weekend and decided against it.

"So tutoring?" Elly asked once Maddie was out of earshot, knowing full well they had not made plans.

"Well, you know," he shrugged, a sly smile crossing his face. "Figured you could use the help."

"You're probably right." Elly bit the side of her lip but couldn't stop the smile from spreading across her face.

Elly followed Khalil down the street towards the bronco parked at the end. Just as she passed the smoothie place she turned to catch Niyanna glaring at them through the lemons.

The next morning, Elly anxiously waited on the porch for Maddie, eager to get to school to see Khalil. She stood quickly when she saw Maddie's car turning into the driveway. She waved, as the car roared to a stop, seeming to be angry for the stalemate.

"So..." Maddie glanced at Elly as she got into the car, desperate to know what happened with Khalil yesterday. Elly saw the large smile on her face and knew what she was asking.

"Nothing really, we have some classes together."

"No really, though, I know that whole tutoring thing was bogus," Maddie giggled.

It was clear that Maddie had picked up on Khalil's affections for Elly, which she found intriguing considering both of them didn't seem to talk much or seem to even want to be around other people. Maddie had finally concluded that there had to be something else between them that pulled them together as friends.

"No, we actually studied. I'm really behind in all my classes and he's in most of them," Elly explained nervously. She didn't want to have the conversation with Maddie, because she honestly didn't know what was happening.

At the end of the day, Elly made her way to Maddie's car, thankful that she seemed to avoid Niyanna for the entire day. Looking up, she realized that her luck had run out, as Niyanna was leaned up against Maddie's car.

Elly dreaded the idea of being dragged to Wild Lemon or some other place today in an effort for Niyanna to force a friendship. She still wasn't sure what Niyanna meant by different lifestyles but she had also come to the understanding that it didn't matter anymore. She chose Khalil as her friend.

"Hey." As if her thoughts conjured him up, Khalil was right beside her.

"Oh, hey. No after-school meetings today?" Elly joked.

"No, in fact, I was going to see if you needed a ride?"

"Well," Elly glanced back at Niyanna, who was still leaning up against Maddie's car. "Yeah, let me just tell Maddie."

Maddie saw Elly approaching, as Khalil made his way to his

car. Before Elly could say the words, Maddie knew she was being ditched. Of course, she just thought it'd be today. But, as the days passed, Maddie learned that Elly had found another ride home in the afternoons. Maddie couldn't shake the feeling that it had something to do with Niyanna.

16

Chapter Sixteen

A blanket of darkness fell over the forest, so deep and so thick that Jane could barely see the hand holding the bow only inches from her body. Closing her eyes, allowing her other senses to guide her, Jane listened to the sounds of the forest. Each rustle of a leaf, crack of a twig, and howl of an animal flooded her senses, as she attempted to identify and place each individual sound.

Slowly, pulling the bow and arrow to the bridge of her nose, opening a single eye, and glaring out into the distant darkness. Jane aimed her arrow. Her eyes glowed in the darkness, so she could see the figure in the distance. Her finger could feel the softness of the feathers as she waited for just the right moment. The crack of a twig, this time it was so close Jane could feel the vibration of sound on her fingers. She released the arrow.

The crunch of the leaves, followed by a reverberating *thud* confirmed Jane's success. Making her way through the thick brush of the forest, her eyes now trained to the darkness, Jane found the animal laying on the ground. Wrapping her fingers around the squirrel's tail, Jane lifted it, blood slowly dripping from the arrow that was still buried deep into its side. She pulled out the arrow and stuffed the animal into her pouch.

I still got it, Jane thought proudly.

Just as Jane entered the kitchen, pulling her heavy, muddy boots from her sore feet the phone started to scream for attention. Bracing herself on the wall beside the door, she answered the phone with one hand tucking it under her chin, while she continued to get her boot off with the other hand.

"Yes, hello."

"Mother, how are things?"

"Ah, Trace, I have been waiting to hear from you. It's been over a week - any news?" Jane had grown accustomed to waiting for news over the last years, her days of hunting long over except for the occasional squirrel.

"Yes, but I will need to tell you in person," Trace explained.

"Any more news from Hunter?"

"Yes, in fact, I am here with him now." Jane waited as she heard the ruffling through the phone as Trace passed the phone to Hunter.

"Hunter, I assume you have good news for me."

"Oh, uh, yes ma'am, well... I mean I guess." Although he had known Jane for most of his life, she still scared him to his core. He often thought that maybe the fact that he did *know* Jane so well was why she scared him so deeply.

"Oh come on with it Hunter, just tell me, does she have the gene or not?" Jane demanded, her patience already nonexistent as she would've preferred this information years ago, but was denied it by Julianna.

"Elly has the mutation, of that I am sure." Jane found herself less relieved than she assumed she would be, suddenly realizing there had been a part of her that had hoped it skipped Elly. Of course, Jane was unsure of what that would mean for the family if Elly did not have it.

"The same one?"

"Yes, she has the genetic mutation as do you," Hunter confirmed confidently. It had taken some extra time to be sure. Hunter wanted to be sure, fearful that any false information given to Jane would lead to his death. He was assured that Elly was Jane's granddaughter, her blood relative in every way possible.

"But…" Hunter braced himself, glancing nervously at Trace who stood solemnly in the corner of his tight, dark, underground lab.

"Well?" Jane probed.

"The genes are changing," Hunter confessed, anxiously twisting back and forth on the metal stool as he stared at the computer screen that cast an eerily green glow on his pale face.

"What do you mean changing?"

"Well, see, when I was testing for the OCA-G2, which we found, don't get me wrong it is there for sure," Hunter affirmed again, "but just as some forms of cancer can be ignited per se by the sun, it seems as if Elly's mutation has been ignited as well." Hunter braced himself for Jane's anger.

"So it's happening then?" Jane asked calmly. Hunter shot

Trace a shocked look over the millions of beakers and lab equipment that cluttered up the small lab.

"Yes, I believe so and quickly, more quickly than I've ever seen."

"I was afraid of that." Jane sighed into the phone, her worst fears confirmed. While she needed Elly to have the mutation, otherwise she feared a war she was not prepared to fight anymore, in her heart, she wished Elly had more time to adjust to the change. Time to understand it and accept it. If Julianna hadn't taken her away she would've had that time years ago, but now it was too late.

"There is something else as well... but I'm just not sure."

"Tell me, Hunter."

"Elly also carries another mutation."

"What kind of mutation?"

This was the part he did not want to tell Jane.

"It's affecting the MSRA gene, it's dramatically overexpressing, making it appear, and I mean it's crazy, but as if it's expanding her lifespan, and then MAPK 14 is highly unexpressed, suggesting that Elly's cell will age at a much slower rate than most. Her MC4R is off the chart, literally increasing daily."

"What does that mean?" Jane asked, halting Hunter's babbling.

"Well, that's her metabolism which affects everything really - how fast she can run, how strong she is ..." Hunter trailed off, as Jane stopped listening attempting to digest all that Hunter was saying.

"Wait, Hunter, so this single gene is affecting all these other genes?"

"Well, it's not so much a gene as more of a genetic parasite.

Except, this parasite is doing the opposite, in that it's improving the genes."

"Okay, so what does all this mean for Elly?" Jane pressed.

"Well, the only other place I've seen anything like this... well, you know how you gave me those blood samples-"

"Are you saying that this genetic parasite is in those samples?" Jane's voice cracked as realization started to bleed into her mind.

The other end of the phone fell silent, as Jane took in a deep breath attempting to calm her growing fear.

"Uh, yes, I'm afraid so."

The phone fell to the tiled floor, the darkness of the night encircled Jane, pulling tighter as it started to strangle her from the inside out. Her mind swirled as she considered the implications of Hunter's discovery. If he was right, Elly would be different from them all. She would change in a way none of them could ever truly understand. She could even be the start of a new species or the death of them all.

"Mom, mom ..." Jane vaguely heard his words through the phone. "I'm coming home. It'll be okay. I'm coming..."

17

Chapter Seventeen

    Jane watched Elly from her bedroom window, still wrapped tightly in her robe, her eyes bagged and tired from lack of sleep last night. Elly rode off with Maddie, disappearing behind the trees as she turned on to the street. Reluctantly, Jane determined that she would not be able to lay in bed all day. No, Trace would be arriving soon and they would have to tell Elly the truth. A truth Jane wasn't even sure of herself anymore.

    With that thought, Jane couldn't help herself and curled back into her bed, nestling in the comfort of the warm embrace of the blankets. Austin emerged from the hallway, pausing in the doorway. It was clear to him that something was wrong, but Jane had not been forthcoming last night after her phone conversation with Trace. Austin simmered, not liking the fact that she was shutting him out. He had gotten used to it with matters of business, but this was his granddaughter.

"Jane," Austin whispered, gently touching her shoulder. Jane flinched. "What's wrong."

"I'm tired. I didn't sleep well." Jane pulled her shoulders tighter together.

"What's wrong?" Austin probed, this time his tone no longer suggesting a question but demanding of an answer.

"Austin, I just don't think I can talk about it right now," Jane confessed, desperately wanting him to leave her alone. It wasn't that she wouldn't discuss it with him, only that she didn't feel as if she had the mental energy, or more so, the understanding to discuss it with him now. Austin heard the strain in her voice.

"You know I am always here for you, Jane. All you need to do is ask." With that, Jane rolled over and smiled up at the man that had never wavered in her life. She was grateful for Austin's loyalty and his ability to ground her in the most difficult of times. Jane understood Austin's reserve all those years ago when they married. Their life was never going to be easy or equal, but still, he accepted his calling with grace and dignity, which can not always be said with these matters. Austin knew that Jane would always be the leader, it was in her blood ... and now it was in Elly's.

Elly slid across the bronco's bench seat, as Khalil climbed into the driver's side of the car. Elly gazed out across the parking lot, watching Niyanna as she once again occupied Maddie and Lauren in conversation. Each day, Niyanna continued to engage Elly in friendship by always being around when she was with Maddie. It annoyed Elly.

"Can we do something else today?" Elly asked, not really in the mood to study as they had been for the last week.

"Like what?"

"I don't know."

"We could go fishing?" Khalil offered.

"Yes, that'd be great."

"Is something bothering you?" Khalil asked as he pulled back into the slow-moving traffic through the parking lot. Elly blinked blankly as she pushed Niyanna from her mind.

"Just distracted, I guess." Elly glanced back as she saw Maddie leaving with Niyanna and Lauren in her car.

A few minutes later, Khalil turned the bronco off onto the familiar dirt road heading to his spot at the lake, Khalil glanced over at Elly who was now staring out the window at the passing trees. Rays of sun cascaded down illuminating the path through the thick woods. Khalil could see the puddle of light just a few feet ahead, where the trees cleared and the river rushed by.

Khalil pulled the fishing gear from the bed of the trunk, passing Elly the same rubber boots as before. She pulled them over her jeans, then took the pole Khalil handed to her to carry. Following Khalil through the brush of trees before the rocks, Elly ducked and swayed to avoid the reaching branches.

As they reached the rocks, Khalil went first, taking all the gear effortlessly over to the large rock. Then he returned, extending his hand for Elly. Slowly, he guided her across the slippery rocks, her feet only losing their footing a handful of times. Each time, Khalil was ready, holding tightly to Elly's hand and bracing all her weight with just his forearm. Elly envied how easy it all seemed for him to manage his larger frame, while she always felt so clumsy.

There was a calmness to fishing, Khalil knew it well, often escaping to his spot alone to let go of all the stress and anxiety he faced at home. Now, he watched as Elly learned to allow that calmness to wash over her own body. It was hard for him to focus on the fish, as he watched Elly casting and reeling effortlessly as if she'd been doing it for years. Within fifteen minutes she caught her first trout.

By the end of the hour, they had caught over five decently sized trout. Putting the poles aside, Elly and Khalil naturally found themselves sitting across from each other on the rock to take a break.

"So your grandmother - sorry, Jane," Khalil corrected, "won't even talk to you about it?"

They had fallen into a conversation about her mother, as Elly vented to Khalil about her growing feeling of uneasiness and her grandmother's avoidance of the topic. In the last weeks, each time Elly attempted a conversation with Jane on the subject of her mother, she was told that the investigation was not over and she had no new information. But, Elly couldn't stop the nightmares or the memories from haunting her every day.

"No, she just told me she's not ready to talk about it, or that I don't seem ready to talk about it, but really, it's all I think about," Elly confessed, knowing it was a lie, as she also thought about him most of the time.

"Maybe you should try talking to her again," Khalil offered, attempting to be helpful, but Elly knew if she brought it up they would probably just lie to her again.

"You know that first time we met, well... I had just," Elly bit her lip, unsure if she could tell Khalil what she heard that day. While she didn't worry about telling him, she worried that he wouldn't believe her and that would be worse than Jane lying.

"What is it?" he probed, knowing that when she bit her lip she was holding back, just like she slightly lifted her left eyebrow when she lied.

"It's just that my mother's death ... well... I think she was murdered."

Elly allowed the words to sink in as Khalil seemed to be methodically processing the information. Her mother dying accidentally was very different from her getting murdered.

"Why do you think that?"

"Well, that first time we met I had just overheard Jane saying my mother had been killed, of course when I confronted her she denied it. They both did, saying that I misunderstood what they were saying, but how could I?" Khalil could visibly see the anxiety building in Elly's body. "And now that she said it out loud, that is all I can think about and I keep going over every detail again and again."

He could tell she was about to explode, the whites of her eyes turning red as she tried to hold back the tears, her fingers fidgeting in the air as she spoke. Gently, he reached out to her, taking her hands into his own and folding them into his lap.

Staring into her eyes, he softly said, "I believe you."

Elly had failed to realize how much she needed to hear those words, instantly her body releasing the anxiety as a wave of relief washed over her mind.

"*Can* you tell me what happened?"

"I just remember all the blood," Elly admitted, the scene flashing before her eyes. She pushed it away, determined to focus on the facts. If anyone could help her make sense of all the chaos in her mind it would be Khalil.

"I think I remember the detectives said it was an accident, that she fell, hit her head on the counter of the bar, and just died. But ..." The scene flashed in Elly's mind again. The blood all over the counter, the smears of blood on the kitchen floor, the trails of red through the white tiles, her mother's blank stare, the bloody knife ... "it just doesn't add up."

"How so?"

"Well, for starters if she hit her head on the corner, why was there blood all over the counter?" Khalil nodded in agreement, propelling Elly forward in her theory. "The blood was everywhere."

"The head bleeds a lot."

"No, I mean the blood wasn't just from her head. It was all over her. Everywhere. Don't you think it'd only be from her head?"

"Did the police seem to have a reason why she just hit her head?"

"Yeah, actually, there was water all over the floor. She had been boiling water," the memory was suddenly coming back in more detail. "The stove was on when I found her, the heat radiating through the small kitchen making it so warm and the red light." Elly was shocked by the amount of detail she was recalling. She'd never given any thought to what happened right before, only the final scene, but of course, she realized, knowing what happened right before was crucial.

"Maybe someone attacked her from behind, while she was cooking, and she threw the water at them," Khalil mused.

"Yes... yes! That's it!" Elly exploded, her mind finally seeing the entire scene. "Someone had to attack her and they made it look like an accident."

"But, Elly," Khalil forced Elly's attention to meet his gaze. "Who would do that?"

"I have no idea."

18

Chapter Eighteen

Jane could feel the tightness in her bones and the growing heat on her back, as she pulled a rake through the dirt. Her gloved hands dug into the cold soil, as she pulled at the dead vines. It would be another few months before she would plant, but maintaining her garden kept her mind busy, which she needed right now.

Just as her bones could feel the rain coming, Jane could sense danger on the horizon. Hunter only confirmed what she was already feeling about Elly, that Julianna's death only accelerated the process. But she never expected ... Not only would it be different for Elly, finding out this way, this early, but she had no idea how different it could become if what Hunter said is true.

She dug harder, deeper, the loss of control bursting from her arms. She couldn't imagine how she would begin to approach the subject, or how Elly would handle it all on the heels of losing her mother. The entire thing had become unpredictable to Jane, and she hated unpredictability.

"Mother." Jane's hand froze in the dirt at the sound of his voice, a smile breaking her lips apart.

"Hello, dear," she responded, pulling the dirt-covered gloves from her hands, and bracing them on her knees to stand. "It's good to have you back home." Jane rose and reached out to her son, embracing him in a rare hug.

"Good to be home, mom."

"Trace, it's been too long," Jane admitted as she stepped back to admire her son, bracing either side of his broad shoulders in pride.

"Yes, it has." Empathy flushed his face, as the unspoken loss of Julianna flooded both their eyes. "I am sorry," He began to say, but Jane held up a steady hand.

"No, son, you need not explain. I understand more than anyone." Jane softly placed her hand on his bristled cheek. "Come inside, so we can talk."

Trace followed his mother up to the back door of the house, trailing her footsteps as he did as a little boy toggling after her all those years growing up in this place. While his father taught him many things, such as hunting, fishing, and all the typical things a father and son bond over, it was his mother that he felt closer to all those years. His mother was a nurturing person but there was another side to his mother. One that taught him how to survive.

"Welcome home," Austin greeted his son as they entered the kitchen, slapping him firmly on the back. "Good to have you home."

"Good to be home, dad." Austin handed Trace a steaming cup of freshly made afternoon coffee - Trace's favorite time to drink it.

Jane made her way to the sink, washing her hands as Trace and Austin made simple chatter as they caught up. She waited impatiently as Austin procrastinated the conversation they needed to have before Elly returned from school. Jane knew they had an extra hour, Elly taking up some tutoring hours after school to catch up to the new curriculum the last couple of days. But, they had much to talk about and she was anxious for Trace's news.

"Okay, boys," Jane glared at Austin, "We need to talk business."

"Oh, well that's my cue to leave then," Austin announced. "Maybe we can do some fishing later, son?" Trace nodded in agreement, as his father retreated from the kitchen.

"So, tell me what you found out?" Jane asked, taking the seat across from Trace at the small round breakfast table tucked away in the bay windows that overlooked the side of the yard. From here, Trace could see the drive leading to the garage, and a partial view of the driveway from the road, otherwise it was mostly trees.

"I followed the trace, but you are not going to like what I found," Trace admitted.

"Did you find who did this to Julianna?" Jane demanded, bracing herself for the answer she had been waiting for the last few weeks.

"Yes, I did, but, as I said, you are not going to like it-"

"Tell me, Trace."

"It was them, as we had feared. I traced the killer back to the den," Trace confessed. "But, mother, I implore you, this is not going to end well if you go to war."

"They started it," Jane flared, her anger palpable as her worst fears were confirmed.

"Mother, right now we need to focus on Elly," Trace affirmed, wrapping his firm steady hands around her shaking, tense ones. "Let us handle one situation at a time. Elly will need to leave with me, I will take her to the camp."

"No, no I don't think," Jane protested.

"Mother, please, this is the best for Elly. She will need to go, that is the only way she will learn."

"I will teach her," Jane offered.

"You know that will not work. She already doesn't trust you, what do you think will happen when we tell her?"

"I don't know," Jane admitted, the lack of control burning in the back of her throat.

"That is hard for you, I know. But, I am here to help. Elly trusts me, we all know this is for the best." Jane could hear the satisfaction in his voice, the feeling of control intoxicating to him as she knew it would be since he was a little boy. Trace would crave it, but it could never belong to him, which would only ruin him one day.

"I am still in charge, Trace, don't forget," Jane warned.

"I am well aware of that fact, mother." Trace glanced through the open doorway at his father reading in the den, cast out by his mother who could never relinquish even an ounce of her power. "Hunter will be there," Trace revealed, knowing this would be the singular thing to change his mother's mind. "He can run some more tests, monitor her -uh - situation."

Jane was about to launch into another protest, but just then, Trace noticed a car turning into the driveway, a flash in the corner of his eye. "Elly is home," he announced, rising from the table. Jane stayed behind as Trace made his way outside to greet his niece, unsure of how the next few hours would go.

Trace stood on the last step of the porch, leaning against the large ornate, flaking columns as he watched the bronco bounce down the gravel drive. Squinting through the sun, he could see Elly's dark hair and her bright green eyes catching the glow of the sun. It had been too long since he had last seen his niece. Last he saw her, she was more a little girl skipping through Central Park, less a teenager riding down the drive in a boy's car.

Elly saw him the minute the house came into view. His distinctive all-black attire, adorned with a large black-rimmed hat, could not be anyone else than her uncle. In all the years he'd visit them in New York, Uncle Trace had yet to change his gothic appearance, as Elly considered it. She could remember when she was younger asking about the black oval emerald encased with gold that he wore all the time on his left pinky finger. All she got was that it was a family heirloom before her mother shut down the conversation.

As the car drew near to the house, Elly caught a ray of light flickering off that pinky ring. Knowing that her uncle was still the same comforted Elly, as a fossil from the past that was still intact leaving no questions as to what it was before. He could shed light on the past.

"That's my uncle," Elly explained to Khalil, who was staring directly at him as he drove. "I haven't seen him in years," she mused. "He'll be able to help me figure out what happened to my mother, I just know it," Elly said more to herself than Khalil.

"Oh, well, that is good then." Khalil broke away from his trance and smiled at Elly. It was clear she needed her uncle, so no matter how much Khalil did not want to let Elly get out of the car, he didn't dare to stop her from jumping from the bronco the moment he cruised to a slow stop.

Elly ran the distance between them and wrapped her arms around Uncle Trace. He could feel the soft heave of her shoulders as she started to cry. Trace gently stroked her hair, as he glared at the young man stepping out of the bronco. His height matched his own, as his long legs covered the distance between them in only a few wide steps. Instantly, Trace knew his secret, he could smell it, as he held tightly to his niece.

"Who is this?" He asked her, keeping a protective arm on her shoulders.

"This is Khalil, he offered me a ride home today. Uh, Maddie went out with some friends," Elly lied. Trace could see the lie in her eyes, the slight flick of her eyebrow as she spoke. But, he didn't bother to mention it was hours past the last bell, the fresh mud on the bronco's tires, or the smell of fish on her hands.

"Well, that was *nice* of you." Trace narrowed his eyes as he surveyed Khalil attempting to find the telling signs that would confirm what Trace already suspected. There was nothing, but Trace was sure he wasn't wrong.

"I live just across the river, it was no big deal," Khalil added, a slight, casual smile on his lips that revealed nothing to Trace.

"I see," Trace nodded.

If Trace was right, Khalil should show some signs of nervous anxiety, because if he realized Trace knew his secret then he would know Trace's secret as well. Yet, Khalil seemed completely oblivious, which didn't mean Trace was wrong, but it did mean something.

"So, I guess I'll go. See you at school."

Trace watched as Khalil turned back towards his car, but he caught the slight affectionate gaze he passed to his niece before he jumped back into his bronco. Trace waited until the car disappeared into the street, still holding Elly close to him as he questioned his instincts, which were never wrong.

"How do you know him?" Trace asked as Elly started to empty her backpack at the desk in her room. The room was familiar to Trace, a distant memory of it from his childhood. It still smelled the same. He could remember hiding from Julianna in the closet for hours one time, the smell of mothballs all-consuming.

"Who, Khalil?"

"Yes, Elly, the boy that drove you home after only being here for two weeks," Trace sneered. He stood possessively in the doorway, his black boots still caked with mud, hands resting on his hips, as he took in all the changes his niece seemed to have made in the last years. She was taller, thinner, and her hair was longer, less wildly curly which took away from her childlike demeanor.

"Just someone I met at school, which Jane forced me to go to by the way."

"You mean your grandmother?" Trace corrected.

"I don't even know her," Elly protested. "I still don't understand why I had to come here in the first place."

"As I told you on the phone, I had things to take care of."

"More important than me?" Trace heard the pain in her voice, regretting that he couldn't take her after Julianna's death, but Jane wouldn't allow him. He was her hunter and she needed him to hunt down her killer. Elly would understand soon, but not now. Right now, he just wanted to have a few more moments with his niece before she most likely hated him forever. He knew Julianna would.

"Nothing is more important than you, of course, you know that. But yes, I had something important to do that needed to be done quickly otherwise ..." Trace stopped before he opened more doors than he was willing to walk through at this moment.

"Well, are you finished now?" Elly asked.

"Yes, I am."

"Are you going to stay here?"

"For a while."

Elly smiled. Trace knew it wouldn't be long, the green flecks growing in her eyes and the nightly nightmares. "So, how are you sleeping these days?"

"Did she tell you?" Elly asked annoyed. Trace shrugged, the black chains around his neck slightly clinking together. "Just a few nightmares," Elly lied. Trace knew they were every night. He even knew what they were. He had the same ones at one time.

"Well," Trace raised his eyebrows, conceding that Elly needed some space right now. "See you down there for dinner." Elly nodded in agreement, as Trace retreated from the room.

"I'm not wrong," Trace assured Jane, as he paced the kitchen while she boiled the noodles. The cooking chicken sizzled on the stovetop, forcing Trace to talk louder than he preferred.

"No, I met him myself," Jane assured, unwilling to accept

that she missed it. Of course, Trace knew why she couldn't see it anymore, but Jane just wasn't willing to admit it.

Trace had noticed his mother's aging in the years since Julianna abandoned them with Elly. Ever since that time, Jane started to age significantly quicker. Now, Trace could see the physical changes in her protruding knuckles, the first signs of arthritis taking its toll on her hands, the once dark hair now had specks of gray, and the wrinkles pulling at his mother's mouth and eyes. She was getting old, much too old for a woman in her position. While Jane refused to admit her aging mind and body, Trace was well aware that his mother no longer had the same keen sense she used to have when he was younger.

"Mother, please, it has been some time for you."

"What is that supposed to mean?" Jane snapped.

"Nothing," Trace sighed, holding his hands up in surrender. Jane started to strain the noodles. Trace assisted by coming to her side to lift the pot, another sign he was right.

"I got it," Jane snapped again, pushing him aside as she drained the water herself. He could see the labor in her weak muscles as she held the heavy pot. Even though she refused to accept that she was getting older, weakening with the passage of time, Trace could see it in everything she did.

"Mom, I think you should trust me. Tell Elly to stay away from that boy," Trace urged. "He might not even know it yet, but he is one of them. It will only complicate things when we tell her."

"Tell me what?" Elly stood in the doorway. Trace's shoulders fell, knowing she had heard the conversation.

"I was just telling your grandmother here that it might be best if she starts to take and pick you up from school." Trace stood firm, fatherly even, as he said it. Elly pursed her lips in annoyance. Trace could tell she wanted to say something in protest but held back, which made him realize she had come down with an agenda.

"Let's go eat," Jane interjected, carrying the large pot of pasta into the dining room.

For the first few minutes, they all sat around the table in silence, each slowly eating their dinner contemplating their own agendas. Trace and Jane stole looks at Elly, as they each attempted to read how she was feeling. To Trace, his niece seemed to be handling it all rather well, after all, she just lost her mother, the single person in her life she trusted and loved. Trace knew that feeling all too well.

Trace mindlessly turned the black and gold ring on his finger, watching the M pass around and around, as he waited for someone to break the silence. His mother was very clear about her intentions for him upon his arrival, but he would have to wait for her to start the conversation.

"I want to know what was more important?" Elly asked, breaking the silence. Jane glared at Trace, given him an unspoken reprimand should he say something to Elly before she had approved.

"What do you mean?" Jane asked naively.

"Uncle Trace said he had something important to do after my mother died. I want to know what it was?" Elly demanded. Trace raised a knowing eyebrow towards Jane, letting her take responsibility for her orders. If it had been up to him, he would have stayed. He would've sent someone else. But, his mother would not have anyone else do it.

"Your uncle had something very important to take care of. Your mother would've approved with you coming home with us," Jane assured, but Elly obviously did not believe her lie. "It didn't matter though either way, you needed to come home."

"This isn't my home," Elly retorted.

"It was your mother's home," Jane affirmed.

"That means nothing to me."

"Now, this is becoming too much," Austin interrupted. Jane narrowed her eyes at Austin from across the table. "Elly, we understand losing your mother was hard and that you'd have preferred your Uncle Trace here, but the fact of the matter is, whether you like it or not, you are our granddaughter and you might not think so, but your mother would've wanted you with us."

"My mother also would've wanted me to know the truth," Elly affirmed. All three of them paled as if a ghost had just joined them for dinner. Trace could see the satisfaction on Elly's face as he realized this was her agenda. She knew. He must have told her already.

"I know something happened to her, I know it wasn't an accident," Elly blurted out, cutting through the unspoken tension with a sharp, dull knife.

Trace realized she knew a single truth, but not *the* truth.

"Elly, I am not sure what you mean," Jane said, her demeanor posed in a way Trace only knew to happen under certain circumstances.

"Mom, Elly was there, I don't think-"

"Stop right there," Jane warned, a heavy hand slamming on the table causing their silverware to rattle in their bowls.

"I want the truth."

"And what truth is that?" Jane snapped, her nerves taking over for a brief moment. Taking a deep breath, she stilled her shaking hands as she attempted to regain control over the situation.

"The truth about my mother's death."

Trace could see the burn in Elly's eyes, her need to find understanding over her mother's death. He saw what she saw, the blood smeared over the counter, the small round curves of fingerprints ... the fading red of dried blood all over his sister as she lay on the kitchen floor.

"The truth is your mother, my sister, was killed." Jane threw her hands up at Trace's words.

"Really, Trace, why put that in her head."

"She deserves that truth, mother."

"We do not know-" Austin injected.

"Yes, we do. We do know," Trace affirmed, glaring at his father. For a moment, he thought his father would've been on his side, but as he stared into his eyes he saw his father's fear.

"Trace, now that's enough," Austin affirmed. Trace was dumbfounded by his father's complete denial of the truth. A truth Elly needed to know in order to accept what she was about to learn.

"No, I'm done with all of this," Elly screamed, pushing back from the table. "I'm tired of being lied to. I know what I saw. I know what I feel. Why can't you all just be honest with me?"

"It's not that, Elly," Jane said, standing and attempting to reach out to her, but she pulled away. "Please, just trust us-"

"Why would I trust you?" Elly screamed again, pushing around Jane. "I know she was killed and if you can't be honest with me then I'll figure it out myself!" Elly ran from the dining room, through the kitchen, and slammed through the back screen door.

"Now look at what you've done." Jane glared at Trace. "It was not the time to bring up Julianna. We have more important things to address with Elly."

"No, actually, I don't think we do," Trace retorted. He believed that Elly needed to hear the truth about her mother's death, then she would understand everything else more clearly. This truth was the first in a long line of truths that Elly would need to understand in a very short amount of time.

"You think by telling her about her mother she'll somehow agree to go to the camp," Jane affirmed.

"She has no other choice, you of all people know this." Trace was shocked by his mother's sudden reluctance to accept Elly for what she would need to become.

"Just calm down, Trace," Austin injected, but Jane held up a firm hand in his direction, an unspoken gesture for him to back down.

"While Elly might not have a choice on when she goes through the change, she will have a choice to stay here with us. We will protect her until she is old enough."

"That is never going to work, mother. She needs to learn now." Trace dragged an exasperated hand through this thick, dark hair frustrated with his mother's refusal to see the truth that was staring her directly in the face. "You can't protect her."

"Yes, I can."

19

Chapter Nineteen

Elly took off running through the night, no longer afraid of its shadows, her mind exploding with anger at the entire world. She was so driven by her anger that she didn't even pause as she disappeared into the woods. She knew they would follow her, track her down, so she had to go someplace they'd never find her but *he* would.

It was harder in the dark, the trees reaching out to her in the shadows, moving and morphing into tall demon-like creatures as she desperately tried to find it. The faster she ran, the harder her tears poured down her face. At one point, she heard screaming not realizing it was her own as she ran in circles.

Finally, it emerged in the distance, a beacon of light guiding her to salvation. Quickly, without fear this time, she climbed the boards to the treehouse. Pulling herself into the cold, empty room, she only then realized that Khalil was not here. Elly cursed herself knowing that he wouldn't be here and angry with herself for thinking that he would be here. As if somehow he would magically know she was there.

Shaking, a deeper, bone-chilling cold settling in the night air, she crawled into the far corner of the treehouse. She pulled her knees tightly to her chest and cried. She cried feeling as if she would never stop, the only thing she saw when she closed her eyes was her mother's blood-covered face. She wasn't sure how long she cried, or when it happened, but eventually she fell asleep.

As the cold night air surrounded her body, Elly's breathing slowed to only a small mist of smoke in the darkness. Even in the numbing cold, he could still smell her as he ran through the forest. Quickly, Khalil climbed the boards, two at a time, as he raced to save Elly. When he entered the treehouse, he saw her cold, shaking body in the corner. Pulling the shirt from his own body, he curled up close to her allowing his own body heat to warm her frozen body.

"Come on," he whispered into the silence, "come back to me."

It had been hours since Elly first disappeared into the woods. The echoes of her grandparents' voices rode in like a wave straight to Khalil's ears. At first, he wasn't sure what happened, but as he lurked in the shadows, he heard the frantic calls for Elly. The moment he knew she was gone, *lost*, he knew where to find her.

Khalil's warmth leaked over Elly's body, the cold of the air having caused the tips of her fingers and her lips to turn blue. As his warmth consumed her, the shaking lessened, and color flooded back into her red lips. Gently, he pulled her into his arms, then jumped from the hole in the treehouse. Effortlessly he landed on the ground, Elly safely in his arms. Following a familiar path, he carried her back to the edge of the forest.

"Elly," he whispered, beckoning her awake. He pushed her hair from her face as her cheeks flushed with heat from his body. Khalil knew that he couldn't take Elly all the way to the house. There was something about the way her uncle glared at him as if he knew his secret. Even if he only suspected this morning, the moment he returned with Elly he would know. He would smell the familiar stench on his skin. Trace had his own familiar scent.

Khalil had picked up on it the moment they turned into the drive. He had only encountered a hunter once before and only from a distance, but he would never forget that smell. That smell came before death, that was what Khalil knew. But, he didn't smell it on Elly. She had to be different.

Elly moaned slightly, her eyes refusing to lift, their weight insurmountable. She curled into the heat that was racing through her body. Her mind was still frozen in that treehouse, unable to understand what was happening around her at that moment.

Khalil pulled her tighter, resolving that he'd have to return her to the house, it was the only way to keep her safe. His body heat was the only thing keeping her frozen body alive. If he put her down, left her here for them to find her, she would surely freeze to death.

"Elly," he whispered into her ear again, trying to wake her, but she just moaned, making it all the more clear to Khalil that he had no other choice. He had to take her back. He had to risk everything.

Slowly, he crossed the field, Elly's uncle a statue in the

distance, unmoving, but he knew they could see them. He could feel the cold stare prickling the hairs on the back of his neck. As he moved in the dark, their eyes locked onto each other, Khalil's survival instinct started to take over. He could feel his heart quicken, the rush of adrenaline, and the painful shift of his bones. Gathering all his strength, Khalil forced his body to calm down, to accept its fate without protest.

Khalil knew that if his suspicions were right, that Trace could very easily kill him right now.

"Just what do you think you are doing?"

He stopped in his tracks, keeping Elly safely and protectively in his arms.

"I found her in the woods," Khalil explained.

"Give her to me," Austin demanded, just as he barreled through the screen door, the sound of a stuck pig ringing through the night air.

"Sir, I just found her out there. She was cold, shivering in fact," Khalil tried to explain, but he could see the anger in Austin's eyes as he rushed towards them.

Suddenly, Khalil realized just how dangerous of a situation he had put himself in to save her as Trace's eyes flared a bright green color in the darkness. He could only hope that her uncle hadn't quite put all the pieces together yet, giving him time to disappear. But, as Trace approached, Khalil instantly knew that they all knew his secret.

Willingly, Khalil released Elly into Austin's arms, who immediately pulled her away. Khalil felt as if Austin had ripped out a piece of his heart.

He felt a hard pressure on his chest pushing him away. Caught off guard, his mind solely focused on Elly, Khalil had failed to notice Trace's blitz attack. Trace was now inches from his face, pushing Khalil back with all his might.

"You keep your hands off of her," Trace warned. "I know what you are," he growled, his eyes flashing with anger.

"I saved her," Khalil retorted, digging his feet into the ground to prevent Trace from pushing him back any further.

"Stay away from my niece, understand?" Trace relinquished his hands from Khalil's chest. He wanted to kill him, but he stopped himself knowing that if he did it would make things that more dangerous for Elly.

Turning back to Elly to ensure she wasn't dead, Trace softly brushed her face, flickers of life exploding at his touch. Trace sighed in relief.

Khalil continued to stand there, his feet planted in the ground, needing to ensure that Elly was going to live before he disappeared. He couldn't leave without knowing for sure. So, no matter how much his instinct to survive screamed at him to run or fight, his will to protect Elly was greater.

Trace whipped around, glaring at Khalil who seemed to refuse to move. In any other situation, Trace would have shot him the moment he emerged from the woods, but this was different. He had saved her. There was no reason for him to save her, in fact, he should've killed her for who she is, for who they all are, but he didn't.

Suddenly, Elly started to cough, her eyes flickering opening as she called out a single word.

"Khalil."

"You are safe now," Austin whispered down at Elly.

At that moment, Khalil knew that Elly would survive. Now, he needed to survive.

"Why did you do that?" Trace asked as Khalil started to walk away. "Why did you save her?"

Khalil turned, unsure of how to answer his question. Now that he knew he could never see Elly again because of her uncle, he wasn't sure if being honest was the best choice. If they knew how much Elly meant to him, they could use it to hurt him, after all, that's all they did was hurt people like him.

"Because ..." he paused, glancing at Elly. "It was the right thing to do."

Trace gave him a tight smile and nodded. Khalil turned, walking away from the single person that had seemed to care for him as a person, without judgment or prejudice.

20

Chapter Twenty

Elly could feel the cold surrounding her in the darkness, causing her body to shake. For a moment, she turned to ice, her entire body crystallizing in the blank space that surrounded her body. Then, the ground gave way behind her as she fell through the darkness. Elly tried to scream, but her mouth was frozen. She feared she would shatter when she hit the ground, but before she crashed to the floor, she froze in mid-air. Slowly a heat started to grow around her, pieces of her body started to melt falling into a puddle underneath her levitating body.

She realized she was no longer surrounded by the cold, but an indescribable warmth that made her body feel as if it were entirely on fire. Looking into the distance, she could see the yellow lights as they started to swarm around her body. She reached out to catch the fireflies, but they were too far away even though they seemed to be right in front of her face.

Then, the fire inside her burst through, a beacon of light, illuminating the entire forest. She could see through the trees into every corner of it. The yellow lights disappeared, along with the shadowy figures. She could see them now, clearly in the light. They were all around her, a low hum coming from the pit of their stomachs as they glared at her in the center of the trees. She was surrounded by wolves.

Gasping for air, Elly pulled herself violently from the nightmare. At first, the room was dark, empty, but then as her eyes adjusted she could see her Uncle Trace asleep in an armchair across the room, his large black hat pulled over his face. His snores filled the silent room.

It was only a dream, Elly told herself, but her mind refused to believe it. The cold was too real, her fingers still tingling, coupled with the fact that last she remembered she was in the treehouse waiting for Khalil to psychically know to meet her there. He had to have arrived because she could smell his familiar musty, natural scent on her own skin. *It wasn't a dream, it had to be real,* she determined.

Elly could feel the dampness of her sheets, the sweat still sticky on her body, so she silently pulled her body from the bed. She wasn't sure what time it was, but she knew she couldn't go back to sleep. Quietly, she tip-toed to the bathroom.

The sun was just starting to peek into the window as she emerged, noticing that Uncle Trace was now awake as well.

"How are you feeling?"

"I'm fine," Elly deflected, still unsure of how she ended up in her bed. "What happened?"

"Well, you ran off into the woods and got lost for one," Trace scolded. "You got lucky though," he softened.

"How?"

"That guy, the one you don't know but gave you a ride home," Trace and Elly exchanged a knowing glance, as her lie was revealed. "Well, he found you out there." Elly's breath caught in her throat. "He saved you. Any idea why he'd do that?"

Her suspicions, or intuition, were right. But if *parts of the dream were real, were they all real*, she wondered.

"I'm not sure, the last thing I remember -" The words caught in Elly's throat, as she realized what she was about to say. Her lie was quickly unraveling.

"What - what do you remember?" Trace pressured her for answers, for the truth that he already knew. He just needed to know if Elly knew the whole truth.

"I was in the treehouse." Elly winced, preparing herself for what was surely to come next.

"The what?"

"The treehouse," Elly sighed, resolved in the fact that now she would have to be honest about their relationship. "It was a place he showed me in the woods. I just wanted to be alone and I guess I fell asleep."

"So, when did he show you that? I thought you didn't know this boy?"

"No, I lied. Khalil and I are friends." Elly instantly saw the disappointment mixed with anger on her uncle's face, as his fears were almost confirmed - *had Khalil told her the truth*? "It's not a big deal," she assured him.

"That's the thing, Elly, it is."

"Why?"

"What do you really know about this boy?"

"I know enough." Trace's heart stopped. "I know he's a good person, a good friend. I know he's been there for me these last couple of days when I had no else to talk to because you abandoned me." Suddenly, Elly realized she was screaming and crying all at the same time.

Trace wrapped his arms around his hysterical niece, allowing her to break down on him as he provided her the support she needed the most. He regretted following his mother's orders and leaving without even talking to Elly after her mother died. If he had stayed, none of this would be happening, or at least that was how Trace felt.

Even if Elly didn't know the truth about Khalil already, it was only a matter of time. Trace's heart swelled for his niece as he realized that he just banished the only friend she seemed to have right now, even if he was an animal.

"It's going to be okay?" Trace whispered in her ear.

"Tell me the truth," Elly pleaded into her uncle's strong, protective shoulders. "Please, I need to know." Elly pulled back, her eyes red with pain as she begged her uncle to say the words.

"Yes, it is true. Julianna was murdered. That is what was more important. I had to found out the truth for all of us."

Elly opened her mouth to ask the millions of questions that now flooded her mind, but her uncle stopped her before she could spiral out of control.

"Elly, please, there is a lot we need to discuss," Trace admitted. "Let's just take it one thing at a time, okay?"

Elly nodded. There was empathy in his voice, compassion

in his eyes, that affirmed to Elly that her uncle did have every intention of being honest with her, so she held her questions at bay.

"Let's get some breakfast first, I'm starving."

Trace and Elly were the only ones up at this early hour, so Trace toasted some bread and smeared peanut butter on each one. Sliding one towards Elly, they both ate in silence at the kitchen counter.

"So, Jane-" Trace glared at her, "Okay, grandmother," Elly changed, rolling her eyes. "So, grandmother said not to go into the woods when I got here, that there are dangerous things in there."

"Yeah, I mean they are woods," Trace deflected, shoving another bite in his mouth.

"No, like, are their wolves?"

Elly noticed Trace's eye twitch, his mouth freezing mid-bite. It was quick, but she didn't miss it. She was right. It only confirmed that her nightmare was more than likely a memory.

"Uh, I'm not sure really. I would guess so," Trace lied.

Elly took a bite of her breakfast toast, contemplating how everything fit together in her world. The moment her mother died, her world exploded, pieces scattered all over the place. She had recovered a major piece in learning her mother was murdered, but there was more, Elly could feel it.

"Is that why she told me to stay out of the woods?"

"Amongst other things," Trace blurted out.

"Uncle Trace," Elly said, pulling his attention from his breakfast. They stared at each other for a second before she asked, "Am I in danger?"

21

Chapter Twenty-One

Reluctantly, Elly waited on the front porch for Maddie. While her uncle had assured her over and over again that she was safe here, Elly knew he was lying. Elly couldn't let go of the pit in her stomach that something horrible was about to happen.

Someone had killed her mother and Elly was almost positive that person wanted to kill her as well. She had put together the pieces of her removal from New York. Her grandparents forced her to leave in order to hide her away in the middle of nowhere. The obvious reason was to shield her from the truth and to protect her from whoever killed her mother. But, she still just wasn't quite sure why they had to lie about it all.

As much as Elly didn't want to deal with going to school after everything that happened, she also knew it was the only way to see Khalil. She needed to talk to him about what happened and why she went to the treehouse that night.

Anxiously, she waited by Maddie's car in the parking lot at school, waiting to see the bronco. Maddie had already disappeared behind the glass doors, but Elly cared more about talking to Khalil today than she did being on time for her first class. Only when the warning bell echoed through the parking lot did Elly finally concede that he was either late or worse, not coming at all.

Throughout the day, Elly was solely focused on watching the doors and looking in the hallways for Khalil. With each passing period, the bell ringing the finality of each class, Elly's heart sank as she realized the worst - *he wasn't coming at all.*

Elly tossed her backpack across her room, pacing back and forth as she pushed her mind to find the missing pieces. Her life felt like a giant puzzle, the pieces all scattered about, but instead of finding pieces to build it, she just kept adding new pieces that didn't even seem to fit together with any of the other ones.

Presently, her current frustrations were focused on Khalil's absence from school. Even though Trace told her that Khalil was the one that found her, she still had so many questions. Elly wasn't sure what part of her dream had been real. She wasn't sure if she really saw the wolves.

She heard his footsteps on the stairs before he knocked on the door. Elly immediately opened it, eye to eye with her uncle.

"Bad day?"

"You could say that," Elly snapped, walking away from the open door. Trace followed her into the room. "I'm just so-" Elly stopped, not quite sure what she was feeling.

"Elly, I know it's hard right now," Trace offered.

"It's only hard because no one will just be honest with me."

Trace wanted to tell Elly the truth and if he had it his way he would've told her the moment he arrived after Julianna was murdered. But, Jane was in control. Trace couldn't understand why she kept putting off the inevitable. The longer Elly was in the dark about the world, the more danger she was in.

"How did she really die?"

Trace chewed on his lower lip, debating with himself just how much he could get away with telling his niece before he'd have to reveal the truth.

"It appears as if there was some sort of fight." Elly nodded, validated in her theory. "The police thought maybe she slipped on the water, fell by accident, but-"

"She was attacked," Elly affirmed. Trace nodded. "Who would do that?"

Trace had to pick his next word carefully.

"I'm not entirely sure."

"Well, can you tell me why?"

Elly saw it in his eyes that he knew why someone attacked her mother, but he refused to tell her. It was possibly one of the biggest pieces of her puzzle and he refused to even show it to her.

Without any other way to release her frustration, anger, and sorrow, Elly took off running. She wasn't sure how far she'd run or where she was going, only that she suddenly had the urge to be moving. Nothing else seemed to matter.

Having never been a runner, Elly was shocked at how easily her feet fell into a rhythmic pattern as she ran without direction. For a person that had always felt out of place, clumsy even, Elly was surprised how comfortable she felt as she mindlessly ran towards the ever-moving horizon.

Suddenly she found herself standing at the gate, straining her eyes to see if Khalil was in the drive or standing outside his house, but nothing. For a moment, she considered jumping the fence and knocking on his door, but then felt a heavy, invisible hand holding her back. As she gazed through the metal bars, beyond the swaying trees, Elly saw an ominous fog that seemed to have fallen over this place.

Returning home, Elly could feel the beads of sweat starting to puddle and slide down her temples and back, as her breathing labored to catch up. She had not felt any strain to breathe or the ache of her muscles during the run, but now that she had stopped it was hitting her all at once. Bending over, she felt as if she might vomit.

"Here," Trace called, tossing her a water bottle. "Drink."

Elly immediately drank half the bottle of water as her lungs started to calm down and her muscles relinquished their tightening hold.

"Thanks."

"How far did you run?"

"Oh, I don't know."

"Where did you go?" Suddenly, Elly realized what her uncle was asking.

"I just ran." Elly's vague answer was a strategic response to his invasive and vague answers about her mother.

"I'm going down to Atlanta today," Trace explained. "But, I'll be back tomorrow before you get home from school," he added quickly so Elly did not have a moment to assume he was leaving again. No, he wouldn't do that this time until she was ready to go with him.

"Okay."

"You sure you'll be okay?"

"I'm fine."

Elly knew her uncle was lying to her about her mother. But, there was something else. She almost thought that Khalil's disappearance today was his fault, but she had yet to gain the courage to ask him outright. She kept telling herself she felt this way because he was not forthcoming with her about her mother's murder, but still, she couldn't shake this feeling that there was more to all of this. Somehow it all had to be connected.

"Okay, I'll see you tomorrow."

Her uncle was not home when Elly returned home from school, yet another day without Khalil. Immediately, Elly retreated up to her room to do her homework. She thought she had escaped everyone for the day when there was a slight knock at her door.

Groaning, Elly called, "I'm working."

"Well," Trace pushed the door open slightly. "I thought maybe you'd want this visitor." Instantly, Elly's heart jumped as she thought for sure it was Khalil.

Turning, Trace opened the door wider revealing a familiar face, but it was not Khalil.

"Makiyah?" Elly questioned, unable to believe that her best friend from New York would be in backwoods Georgia.

"In the flesh," she announced, opening her arms wide. Elly ran to her arms, falling into her warm embrace, instantly forgetting all the anger she had built up towards her friend. Makiyah was at least a head taller than Elly, wrapping her long, muscular arms around Elly's neck. Even though she was touching her, Elly still couldn't believe she was still here.

"What are you doing here?" Elly asked, glancing to her uncle for more of an explanation. He smiled proudly as if he had just presented Elly with the most coveted gift.

"Your uncle thought you could use a friend right now," Makiyah confessed. "I'm only here for the weekend and we have a lot to catch up on." Makiyah tossed her duffle bag on the bed and looked around. "Nice place out here. It's definitely bigger."

Elly and her mother had lived in a small two-bedroom, one-bath apartment that was the size of the living room in this place. Her bedroom alone was the size of their entire kitchen and living space back at the apartment. Even though she had more space, Elly would still go back to that apartment in a heartbeat.

"It's a little pink for you," Makiyah jeered, walking around the room.

"Yeah, I guess so," Elly blushed.

Elly turned to find her uncle, but he had disappeared, leaving them alone to catch up. As much as Elly was happy to see her friend, now she had to face the reality that she had not called her since she left. Deep down, Elly was still hurt and angry. She knew Makiyah felt the same as well, Elly had not been kind when she last talked to her friend, which is why she was so surprised to see her.

Seeing Makiyah standing before her, the same girl she remembered spending every day with, Elly's heart softened. She regretted how she treated her friend, realizing recently that it had nothing to do with her mother not wanting or being willing and everything to do with her grandmother.

"Makiyah - I just need -"

"No, Elly, it's okay," Makiyah assured her, accepting her unspoken apology as friends so often do in these situations.

"I'm really glad you are here."

"Yeah, me too."

22

Chapter Twenty-Two

Trace faded into the background of Elly's life, knowing that Elly needed more than he could give his niece. Trace had called Makiyah the day before expressing his concern to her mother, Ava, that Elly would need Makiyah to help her through everything she was about to go through in the next few days.

Just days before Makiyah's arrival, Trace had watched his niece spiral into a depression that could cause catastrophic damage. Khalil had held true to his word and was gone from Elly's life, but what Trace didn't realize is that it would open a gaping wound that would fester. Her thoughts seeming to be consumed with either Khalil or her mother's murder. Trace continued to urge Jane to tell Elly the truth, but Jane was waiting on Hunter. Jane needed to be sure what was happening before she talked to Elly. But, Trace didn't agree.

Unsure of what to do, Trace decided that Elly needed a

confidant to support her and talk to her - *a best friend*. Learning the truth at the same time as she would change would be overwhelming. Elly could use all the support she could get. Trace, reluctantly, reached out to Makiyah's mother.

"Ava, it's Trace," he announced into the phone. He heard a deep sigh on the other end, then silence. For a moment, he thought she hung up on him, which would not surprise him considering their last conversation. "I need your help," he admitted.

"What is it this time?"

Trace could hear the anger in her voice and know without seeing her that her eyebrows were raised and her lips pursed tightly together - *her angry look*. Trace knew all of Ava's looks, having spent years studying each look in great detail as they spent their lives together. Of course, that was another lifetime ago, long before Makiyah was born. Back then they were just a couple of kids, blissfully unaware of the truth in life.

"Please, Ava, I am sorry for how things ended -" Trace couldn't say the words.

"At my best friend's funeral," Ava blurted out.

"Really, I am sorry, you have to believe me. Everything was just so …" Trace couldn't finish his thought about the way Jane treated her at the funeral as if she was a pariah that caused her daughter to abandon the family.

"Trace, just tell me what you want," Ava demanded.

"Things are not going well," Trace admitted. "I was calling to see if - well, I wasn't sure if - can Makiyah come down?" He finally blurted out.

"No, no Trace, I will not send my daughter down there to that woman's house."

"Please, Ava, she needs her best friend."

"Ah!" Ava scoffed through the phone. "She hasn't even called or messaged her once."

"As I said, things aren't going well-"

"How do you think they are going for me?" Trace froze as if they were in high school all over again and he was leaving her behind. "I lost my best friend, not to mention the constant fear we are now living in. Any moment -" she paused, taking a deep breath. "It's been hard here too," she calmly added, attempting to quell her fear and anger.

"I promise you, Makiyah will be safe here."

"You don't know that."

"I do, actually. This is probably the safest place right now."

"Even so, I will not allow my daughter to become your puppet."

"Please," Trace breathed into the phone. "I'm desperate."

"I'll give you two days."

"That's not enough-"

"Two days," Ava affirmed and Trace knew not to ask again. "And tell that mother of yours this means that she leaves her alone after this, you hear me?"

"Ava, you know -"

"No, Trace!" She screamed into the phone. Trace could hear the crack in her voice, the pain in her cry. "This is my only - I have nothing else," she managed to say before Trace could hear her start to cry. "Please, you can't -"

"Ava, I give you *my* word," Trace promised. "I will keep Makiyah safe. I will not let anything hurt her - ever."

"Why don't I believe you?" Ava sighed again into the phone,

knowing that no matter how much she didn't want to release her daughter into the clutches of his family, she had no other choice. If she didn't agree, they would force her to rejoin or kill them both. At least this way, maybe she would be able to protect her daughter from a life that Julianna and she had vowed to protect them from the moment they moved away.

Squeezing Makiyah at the terminal, Ava forced the tears back knowing she needed to show strength to her only daughter. Ava took a moment to take in all that was her beautifully bold daughter as she now met her eye to eye in height. Makiyah was lean as was her mother, their muscles defined by daily exercise and a passion for Taekwondo.

"Mom, I am going to be fine," Makiyah assured Ava.

"You make sure to call me every night."

"I know Mom, I will make sure to do everything they say and as soon as I'm done I will leave. I promise."

"Just be careful, these people - this family - has a way of sucking you in."

"I know that too."

Ava watched as her daughter walked through security and down the hallway until she was out of her sight. Only then did she allow the tears to flow down her smooth, dark face. She could taste the salt on her lips as she stood frozen in place.

There was a time she trusted Trace with her entire life, vowed to love him forever, but in the end, he left her alone and scared. Julianna was the one who picked up the pieces her brother shattered all over the ground.

Julianna and Ava became best friends. When Julianna refused to live the life Jane dedicated for her, she begged Ava to follow her to New York. But, is was only when Ava got pregnant that she gained the courage to follow Julianna. At the time, Ava thought it was the only way to keep Makiyah away from the family, knowing that they would never come after Julianna, who became pregnant with Elly a year later. But, the moment she died, she knew the family would come for her ... and Makiyah.

She couldn't shake the feeling that she was never going to see her daughter again.

Chapter Twenty-Three

Elly pulled Makiyah to the window seat, where they sat only inches from each other, their legs crossed as Elly started to tell her all about moving in with her grandparents. For the next hour, Elly told Makiyah everything about her grandparents, school, Khalil, and even her theory of her mother's murder.

"Elly, I'm so sorry I haven't called," Makiyah confessed, the guilt turning over in her stomach. "I had no idea what you were going through down here."

Makiyah was starting to grasp the true depth of what Elly had been going through since her mother died. Initially, Makiyah was angry with her friend for shutting her out that day she left. Anger that she harbored for weeks as Elly didn't call. Makiyah could understand the hurtful words she spoke at her mother's funeral, she was distraught. But, it hurt more that she never called. But now, she understood.

"It's okay, I had-" she paused, the knot growing in her throat at the thought of Khalil's sudden absence in her life.

"Well, now you have me," Makiyah assured. "I think we should get out of here," she announced. "Show me this town."

"Well, I've literally only been to the smoothie shop - oh, except when I went shopping with my grandmother, which was awful. They are literally years behind in this place." They both laughed, as Elly realized how much she truly missed her friend and how quickly her anger melted away.

An hour later, Elly and Makiyah were walking arm in arm down the main street. Makiyah was mesmerized by the hometown feel, frequently saying she felt as if she had been transplanted onto a movie set. Every other store, she pulled back on Elly's arm gaping at the shop window, making comments such as "how quaint" and "so charming". Elly didn't notice any of it, as her eyes constantly scanned the pockets of people for Khalil.

"Okay, so is this the smoothie shop?" Makiyah asked. Elly pulled herself from a daze, glancing into the shop to see Maddie and Lauren squeezed into a round table with too many other people in the center of the store.

"Oh, yeah." Just then Maddie started to wave at Elly.

"Do you know them?"

"Yes, that is Maddie, remember?" Makiyah nodded, pulling on Elly's arm.

"Let's go meet the new friends then," she insisted.

Reluctantly, Elly followed Makiyah into the shop. She quickly scanned the shop, letting out a sigh of relief that Niyanna didn't seem to be socializing today. They went over to the table, which could not even attempt to house two more seats, as all the chairs from the surrounding tables had already been pulled up to it. Lauren and Maddie seemed to be the only people to notice them walk up.

"Hi, Maddie and Lauren, this is my friend, Makiyah," Elly introduced.

"From New York City?" Lauren's eyes were wide, taking in Makiyah's grunge-chic style, with her torn, faded black jeans, black combat boots, and a loose-fitting tank top that advertised a local band. She had a brilliantly wild fro that was like a halo around her smooth, dark-skinned face all in deep contrast with her bright green eyes. Makiyah took in their stares as that first cup of rejuvenating coffee in the morning.

"Yes, I am," she confirmed, the table falling silent as they stared at Makiyah. Elly stifled a laugh, as everyone stared, knowing that Makiyah was nothing like they were used to around here. Her tall stature held a commanding presences, but it was her striking beauty that held people's attention. Her endless supply of confidence didn't hurt either, something Elly lacked in most social situations.

"How long are you in town for?" Maddie asked.

"Oh, just a few days."

"Yeah, we should get going," Elly interjected, not wanting to share her friend's time with anyone.

"Oh, please join us, we were just about to go bowling," Lauren pleaded, pushing her hands together and pouting out her lower lip.

"That could be fun," Makiyah offered, looking at Elly for approval.

Elly had little desire to go bowling with a bunch of people she didn't know well. Plus, she was worried Niyanna would show up to bowling. After some attempts to debate with Makiyah, Elly conceded that she had lost the battle before it even started. They were going bowling.

Makiyah and Elly followed the crowd from the smoothie store three blocks to the bowling alley, positioned right next to the only movie theater in town. Makiyah gushed over both of them.

Maddie and Lauren joined them on one team, while the others broke off into various teams. Elly was grateful she at least got to play with them instead of the others, who she didn't even know by name. But, she quickly regretted that.

"Hey, Sis!" Camden called as he entered the bowling alley with Logan and Micah. They all three joined them in the lane right next to them. "A little boys versus girls," he jeered, winking at Elly. It was not missed by Makiyah, much to her dismay. Elly gave an internal groan.

"Who is this?" Logan asked, sliding close to Makiyah and offering a gentlemanly hand. Makiyah glared at his hand, a true feminist to her core she had no intentions of taking his formal hand. "I'm Logan," he offered, shoving his hand into his pocket.

"This is my friend from back home, Makiyah," Elly introduced. "This is Camden, Lauren's brother, and then Logan and Micah." Logan gave a tight smile, accepting defeat, while Micah gave a stoic nod.

"We have an extra player," Lauren was protesting to her brother.

"No worries, we'll still beat you," Camden jeered.

"Come on, Cam. It's no fun this way, let's just play," Lauren retorted.

"I bet you my share at Niyanna's house tonight?" Camden offered. Lauren glared at him.

"Fine," she conceded. Makiyah gave Elly a questionable look, but Elly just shrugged. She still had no idea what happened at Niyanna's but she was too scared to ask. She was quite sure she wouldn't like the answer.

Camden clapped his hands together, as he eyed Maddie in challenge, who returned his challenge with a smirk. It was clear to Elly that Lauren did not have the competitive gene as her brother had, but she suspected that Maddie did.

"Oh, it's game on," Makiyah added, narrowing her eyes as Camden, who was taken back by her aggressive stance. She raised her two fingers pointing them to her eyes first then to Camden in a challenge. Judging by the smile on his face, he accepted.

Elly watched as Camden and Makiyah slammed the pins over and over again, keeping their scores neck and neck. Maddie tried to keep up, but bowling was definitely not her sport, as for Lauren and Elly, they both held the bottom two positions mostly bowling gutter balls. Logan and Micah were decent players, but after the fifth round, it was clear to everyone that this was a game between Camden and Makiyah.

"Anyone want another drink?" Elly asked, her throat growing dry from cheering on Makiyah.

"Yeah, I'll go with," Micah offered, effortlessly jumping over the back of the seats and landing at Elly's feet.

"Oh, okay." Elly nervously pulled at the stray hairs around her ears.

Despite Khalil's absence in Physics class, Micah had continued to maintain his distance. It was as if they both felt he was going to return at any moment. For Elly, she didn't intentionally ignore Micah, she was just preoccupied with thoughts that would not quell no matter how much she tried to bury them in the dirt. But now, in this moment, it felt as if Micah was reaching out to her again.

"How have things been?" He asked, pulling out his wallet to buy the drinks.

"Uh, fine, I guess." Elly tried to hand him a dollar, but he waved it away. Elly gave a tight smile, unsure of what it meant to let him buy her a soda. It was just a dollar, she told herself, but it was the gesture that held the meaning she was trying to ignore.

"Keeping up in Physics?"

"I guess so," she shrugged. A part of Elly felt quilty that Micah was suppose to be her tutor but she picked Khalil instead.

"So are you going to Niyanna's house tonight?" he asked.

"Who's Niyanna?" Makiyah interjected. Elly jumped at the sound of her voice, unaware her friend had come over.

"Oh, uh, another friend from school. She has these events at her house on Friday nights," Micah explained. "We are going by after this. You should come," he directed at Elly, who immediately blushed. Makiyah noticed.

"Yeah, sounds fun," Makiyah agreed, nudging Elly's shoulder. Micah gave them both a tight smile before heading back to the lanes. "Okay, so why didn't you tell me about him?"

"What?"

"Oh, really, you don't see that?" she jeered. "He completely likes you," Makiyah announced, overly loud in Elly's opinion.

"Stop, no he doesn't," Elly insisted, hoping that he didn't hear. She quickly glanced around to see if anyone else might have heard, but most people were bowling and the building was filled with sounds of crashing pins. "Look, I don't think we should go to this party," Elly confessed.

"Why not? Sounds fun."

"No, really, I'm not sure what they do there, but I don't think it's something we want to be involved in," Elly assured her, but again, Makiyah had already made up her mind that they were going. Elly could see it on her smirky face.

"It'll be fine," Makiyah brushed off Elly's concerns. "We will go, see what happens, then you will know. We can totally leave if you don't want to stay, okay?"

"I already want to leave," confessed Elly, as Makiyah pulled her into a side hug forcing her to walk beside her on the way back to the group.

"Anyways, I am crushing this Camden guy." Elly and she both laughed.

Lauren beamed as Camden hung his head in defeat, Makiyah and Elly slapping hands as the final score flashed across the screen.

"Pay up," Lauren probed, holding out her hand.

"Oh, come on, you totally set me up with that one," he protested flapping his hand towards Makiyah.

"Yeah right! I had no idea she was so good, I only just met her," Lauren retorted.

"Whatever, I'll give it to you at the party. Anyways, we need to go so we aren't late." Camden motioned to Logan and Micah to join him.

"I'll see you there," Micah offered Elly, at which point Maddie turned beat red.

"You are going?" She asked Elly, who sheepishly nodded. "I told you-"

"Oh don't worry about it," Makiyah interrupted. "She'll be fine."

Maddie glared at Makiyah, then turned back to Elly for reassurance she was okay with going. Elly shrugged, knowing that she didn't want to go, but she didn't think she should allow her friend to go alone. A part of her wished Maddie would agree to go as well, but she hugged Lauren goodbye and left.

"I'll drive," offered Lauren, turning to Makiyah and Elly.

The sky was already dark when they exited the bowling alley, following Lauren as she led them back to her car. As they approached the parking lot, Elly saw Camden's lifted jeep wrangler pulling out into the darkness, the blaring music fading as they got further away.

Lauren drove a more modest car, low to the ground, with no extra embellishments as her brother's jeep had, only a simple white BMW. Elly had considered the fact they had money, but now she was assured as they slid into the tan, leather interior seats and noticed the fully loaded dashboard. Lauren had all the tech the car had to offer. They were undoubtedly rich.

"Nice car," Makiyah offered, getting into the backseat, shoving Elly into the front.

Makiyah and Lauren chatted the entire drive, as Elly pretended to listen. But, really she was staring out into the night sky as the twinkling stars fluttered and the dark trees wisped by as Lauren effortlessly drove the car down the dark road. Niyanna's house was like most of the homes in this town, out in the middle of nowhere surrounded by acres of forest.

Lauren slowed as they approached a flickering light in the distance. It was the entrance to a long drive through a tunnel of trees that broke revealing a German-style cottage home so large that seemed as if they had fallen into Alice in Wonderland's world. Cars were randomly parked along the circular drive, upon the grass, and blocking one another, as Lauren pulled in right behind her brother's jeep.

"Now he can't leave without me again," she snickered, tossing her long blond hair as she turned the car off. Elly got a fearful feeling in the pit of her stomach that she too was not going to be able to leave.

Just before they made it to the front steps. Lauren at least three steps ahead, Elly pulled back on Makiyah's arm. "I really don't think we should go in," Elly urged, suddenly feeling an overwhelming sensation that something awful was going to happen.

"It's okay," Makiyah assured, wrapping Elly's arm around her own. "I got you."

Reluctantly, Elly dragged her feet alongside Makiyah feeling slightly bulldozed by her best friend, who seemed to be completely ignoring the fact that Elly was feeling uncomfortable. Makiyah was known for pushing Elly out of her comfort zone, but in this particular instance, she was starting to get very annoyed with her friend. While she had a way of getting Elly to do things she didn't want to do, this felt different. She felt as if Makiyah was pressuring her to do something wrong and she didn't like it.

But, Elly didn't understand. It was Makiyah's mission and she couldn't afford to fail.

Instantly, the music pulsated through Elly's entire body as they entered the house. The ceiling stretched to the highest point of the house, a large, wooden staircase weaving up the wall. Elly gazed around at all the people moving between the endless tables positioned in every room. In the distance, she watched Lauren disappear into the crowds of people.

"Oh, wow, Elly, welcome," Niyanna sneered, suddenly appearing before Elly and Makiyah. She glared at Makiyah taking in her entire presence, before turning her attention back to Elly, a large smile breaking her lips apart. "I'm so glad you came. Follow me," she motioned them both deeper into the house.

Makiyah took in every part of the house, mentally counting her steps to each place, memorizing each face she saw in the flashing, colored lights as Niyanna led them to the enormous, open kitchen. From the kitchen, Elly could see the glistening pool just on the other side of the large floor-to-ceiling windows that spanned the length of the back wall. Beyond that it was black.

"Okay, so what's your game of choice?"

"Excuse me?" Elly asked, still slightly stunned by Niyanna's house.

"We have poker, blackjack ..." She waited for Elly to answer as realization set in. The tables were scattered throughout the house, people standing in front of the chairs they had been assigned, and cards placed in the center of each table. *They were gambling.*

"Poker for me," Makiyah chimed in before Elly could scream it was time to go.

"No, Makiyah, we should go," Elly urged, pulling on her arm. Makiyah shrugged her off, handing Niyanna a clipped stack of money. Elly glared at Makiyah wondering where she got that amount of money. It did not pass by Elly that her friend didn't seem shocked by what was going on here. In fact, she seemed prepared.

"Oh, come on, let's just have a little fun," Makiyah insisted glaring at Niyanna, an unspoken challenge hanging in the air between them.

"Sure thing," Niyanna said, changing out her money for chips. "Elly, you don't have to play. Lots of people watch." Elly nodded, knowing that even watching felt wrong.

Elly saw Makiyah take her seat at a table in the living room, Camden glaring at her from only a few tables away. She didn't see Lauren anymore, nor did she see Micah or Logan through the crowd. Not only did she feel alone, but she was deeply disappointed in her friend, to the point that she found herself wishing she had never come to visit. The guilt churned in her stomach, making her feel as if she was about to vomit.

Quickly, Elly raced from the kitchen out to the pool. The cool night air slapped her across the face, bringing the nauseous feeling down as she allowed the cold to rest on her skin. Suddenly, her mind flashed back to the treehouse. It was so cold, she could remember the feeling. Then, a new memory of Khalil's warm body against her own.

"Elly?" Niyanna called from the sliding glass doors. "Are you okay?" she asked, seeing the paleness of her skin, which seemed to glow against the black background of the night sky.

"Yes, I'm fine. It was just really loud inside," Elly lied.

"Well, I'm glad you are here. I've been wanting to talk to you." Elly groaned under her breath. "See, I think we got off on the wrong foot," Niyanna explained, stepping closer. "You see, I've been waiting for you," she confessed, a devilish smile crossing her lips. Suddenly, Elly could feel the fear rising in the hairs on her skin.

Inside, Makiyah pulled the cards into her long, slender fingers, peeking over the top at the other players. Everyone seemed focused on their cards, glancing from their hand to the cards in the run, as Makiyah took advantage. She stole a glance around the room, looking for a particular person.

During the two-hour drive from Atlanta to the house, Trace had made it very clear of Makiyah's purpose for visiting. As much as she hated to force Elly to attend this party at Niyanna's house, something she very clearly did not want to do, Makiyah had to find a way inside the house.

Over the last week that Trace had been home, he had been doing some of his own research. Growing up and living in a small town had its advantages. While Hartsville was a vast landscape of mostly forest and small farms, people in the town made it their business to know everyone, especially the newcomers to the area. It didn't take long to learn about a new young girl who seemed to have no parents.

Angrily folding her cards onto the table, claiming to be over the game, Makiyah made her way out into the foyer. After another scan, assured no one was watching her, she climbed the staircase to the second floor and slipped away into the first bedroom. The faint glow of the moon cast an eerily glow over the room, the canopy bed appearing to stretch across almost the entire room, reaching out to the vanity on the opposite wall. The mirror reflected Makiyah's tall, lean body as she walked towards it.

Gently, without sound, she pulled open the drawers of the vanity, carefully running her fingers over the items looking for anything that would confirm the truth. When she didn't find anything on the desk, she moved to the bookcase on the other wall, dragging her fingertips over the leather-bound books. Her fingers paused on a book, the leather felt different than the others. Pulling the book down, she thumbed through the pages until a loose paper fell out.

Picking up the paper, Makiyah realized it was a handwritten note, the pen blurred as the author put pressure on each letter that they wrote in perfect cursive. Suddenly, Makiyah heard footsteps and laughter outside the door. Quickly, she slid the book back into its place and tucked the letter into her back pocket.

As she stepped out of the room, she saw two people disappearing into another room down at the end of the dark hallway. Taking a moment, she pulled the letter from her pocket to read. Her lips moved, her voice only a whispered as she read the entire letter. Her eyes grew wide as she realized the letter confirmed her worst nightmares about Niyanna.

Suddenly, her head shot up - *Elly*.

"What do you mean?" Elly asked, stepping back away from Niyanna. But, she just stepped closer still, matching each step Elly took to bridge the gap.

"It's been absolutely pathetic having to act like any of these people are my friends," Niyanna mused, twisting a single, gold ring on her middle finger. "I mean all this for you," she laughed. "It's really ridiculous in my opinion."

"What are you talking about?" Elly quickly looked around, trying to think of a way to get out of this situation, as the fear spread to every nerve. Niyanna had her trapped, her only option to run out into the darkness, which almost seemed worse - almost.

"I was elated when I finally heard the news that your mother was killed."

"What?" Elly could feel the anger burst through her skin, the cold melting instantly as she burned with hatred towards Niyanna. "How dare you."

"Oh, please," Niyanna shrugged as if her mother's death was nothing.

"How do you know she was killed?"

"Oh, wow, you really don't know do you?" Niyanna sneered.

"Know what? Tell me!"

"Awe, if I tell you, I'll have to kill you. Oh wait, I have to do that anyway." Niyanna's eyes flared, as Elly realized that she was not joking. In a split second, Elly realized that the dark woods were better than standing here.

Turning quickly, Elly didn't even see him coming as she started to run, the fear blinding her eyes as her mind screamed at her to escape. His arms snaked around her as she fought to get away, her mind completely focused on survival.

"Elly, Elly," he called to her, holding her tightening as he tried to calm her down. "It's just me." Suddenly she looked up, the familiar sound of his voice, the feel of his skin - It was Khalil.

Seamlessly, he quickly moved her behind him, putting his body between her and Niyanna, who suddenly appeared very different than just a second ago. Elly could see her own fear reflected back in Niyanna's eyes as she stared up at Khalil.

"You stay away from her," he threatened.

"You know," Niyanna stepped back, regaining her composer, "this isn't going to work. Your little trick here," she motioned towards Khalil and Elly, "is going to backfire, just you wait."

"You should go," Khalil warned. Elly could feel the tension in his muscles as she clutched onto his protective arm.

"You'll do my job for me anyways," Niyanna jeered, smirking as she turned to go back inside. Just as Niyanna disappeared back into the house, Makiyah rushed out of the living room doors towards Elly.

"Elly," she screamed, stopping short at the sight of Khalil. "Elly, are you okay?"

"Yes, I'm fine," Elly assured, coming out from behind Khalil. "This is Khalil," she explained.

"That is Khalil?" Makiyah's eyes were wide with shock. "Okay, girl, we can talk about that one later, right now we need to go."

"Yeah, I know."

"I'll give you both a ride home," Khalil offered.

"No, I can't go home. I need to talk to you," Elly affirmed.

"Okay," Khalil agreed. "But, please let's just get to my car and get out of here. I promise I'll answer all your questions once you are safe."

Makiyah opened her mouth in protest, but Elly glared in her

direction. They were in this mess because of her and Elly had no intentions of following along with her friend again. She needed answers and Khalil was going to give them to her tonight.

24

Chapter Twenty-Four

Elly reluctantly followed Khalil to his bronco, parked off into the woods at the top of Niyanna's driveway. She was never more sure that Khalil's explanation of the tension between him and Niyanna was, in fact, a complete lie. There was no time for her to dwell on the betrayal of the lie, not after Niyanna just threatened her life. It was truly the only reason Elly had agreed to go with Khalil.

While she was desperate to understand his absence or what happened that night she fell asleep in the treehouse, pressingly she had to deal with the most recent death threat by her classmate, who Elly was starting to think was not who she claimed to be.

As they approached the bronco, Khalil pulled open the passenger side door, but Elly refused to get into the car. Standing her ground, she was resolved to get answers.

"What did Niyanna mean you will do the job for her... what job?" Elly demanded, glaring at Khalil, feeling a mix of emotions. She couldn't figure out if she was more relieved he had returned or angry that he was lying.

"What did she say to you?" Makiyah demanded. Elly flustered with annoyance, wishing she could be alone to discuss this with Khalil and wanting her friend to leave.

"She said she was going to kill me," Elly announced. "Wait a minute, did you know?"

Elly wasn't sure what it was about Makiyah's stare, if it was her unflinching lips that should've gaped into an oval, but instead remained tightly drawn together across her face or her glistening green eyes that didn't even register an ounce of fear over learning someone threaten to kill her best friend. But, instantly, Elly knew that she already had time to adjust to the information.

"No, I mean, yes, but I didn't know until just now. I never would've taken you to her house if I knew that," Makiyah affirmed.

"What, how did *you* know?" Khalil asked, stepping towards Makiyah which put him physically between Elly and her friend.

"I found a letter." Makiyah pulled the tattered envelope from her back pocket. Before she realized it, Khalil snatched the letter from her fingers and vigorously started to tear it open.

"What is going on?" Elly demanded, suddenly feeling pushed out of the conversation that she started.

"Elly, I think we should go home," Makiyah urged, as Khalil became enthralled with the letter.

"No, you are welcome to go, but I'm not leaving until I get some answers."

"You found this tonight?" Khalil confirmed. Makiyah nodded.

Khalil stared at Elly, dumbfounded by the letter between his fingers. The moment he met Niyanna, he knew what she was inside. He knew she was dangerous. But, he never knew how dangerous or the reason Elly would become her next target.

"I mean I knew that ..." Khalil whispered, reading over the letter again, just to make sure he understood correctly.

"Know what?" Elly screamed, only realizing afterward that she had lost control. "I mean, please, someone tell me what is going on."

"Niyanna was not lying to you. She wants to kill you," Khalil affirmed, flipping the letter in the air just out of Elly's reach.

"What? Why?"

"Because of who you are."

"That doesn't make any sense," Elly confessed, growing increasingly frustrated by the minute. It didn't make sense to Khalil either.

"We need to go now," Khalil demanded, ushering Elly into the car. Elly was forced into the middle seat, as Makiyah slid in beside her, their shoulders pressed into each other.

As Khalil quickly walked around the car, Elly took a brief moment to whisper to Makiyah. "What is going on?"

"It's all your uncle," Makiyah confessed, her eyes filling with tears. It was only in this moment that she saw the true betrayal in Elly's eyes and realized the consequences of her actions. Everything had gone so horribly wrong.

"What do you-" The door swung open, as Khalil effortlessly pulled his large frame into the bronco. The words caught in Elly's throat. Elly could feel the warmth of his body close to her own.

His fingers grazed her leg as he reached for the shifter, pulling back hard and hitting her straight in the knee. Elly winced but didn't say anything.

Khalil spun the tires of the bronco as he pulled it out of the woods, speeding through the encroaching trees, as he made his way to the main road. Elly could feel her heart rate rising as Khalil raced down the barren, dark road. Each time she thought about speaking, the words would not come out, her body overtaken with anxiety as she feared any moment Khail's bronco would slide off the road into a tree.

It was only when he slowed to turn the bronco into her driveway that she felt her heart rate slow and her body release the tension in her muscles.

"I want to read the letter," Elly demanded, as Khalil pulled the bronco to stop in the driveway. The house was dark at this hour and Elly knew they were home too late, but she didn't care anymore. She needed answers.

"Elly, I need you to know this was never some trick for me," Khalil confessed, turning to Elly, their faces so close she could feel the heat of his breath and smell the mint on his tongue. He never would've done anything if he knew the truth, but he was still having a hard time wrapping his mind around the idea.

"This was real for me, always remember that." He pulled her hands into his own, but Elly didn't feel the normal rush of emotion, only her fear growing as she saw the fear in Khalil's eyes.

"I want to read the letter." Elly pulled her hands away.

"Niyanna would fill your mind with dark thoughts of me, but she is wrong. I am not that person. I am not like the others."

"The others - wait, what?" Elly held up her hands so Khalil

could not reach for them again. "I'm so confused, please just tell me the truth."

Suddenly, the lights from the front porch cut through the night, illuminating Elly and Makiyah in the front seat of Khalil's bronco. Trace stood as an ominous statue, the light casting dark shadows over his face, but Elly could still meet his gaze as his green eyes seemed to glow in the darkness.

"We should go," Makiyah urged, pulling on Elly's arm, but she didn't move.

"What do you mean you are not like the others?"

"Please, just -" Khalil paused, the pain flooding his face. "You will be safe here, you really should go."

Elly felt as if she was just hit by a truck, the pressure immediate as she no longer felt as if she could breathe. Suddenly, she realized that Khalil had chosen to stay away, that he didn't want to be her friend anymore. She had told herself he just missed a day, convinced herself that something probably happened with her mother, but now she understood. He had avoided her on purpose, and that hurt more than anything.

"Elly," Trace called from the porch, Jane appearing in his shadow. For a moment, Elly swore she was holding a gun, but then pushed the ridiculous thought away.

"We really should go," Makiyah affirmed, pulling harder on Elly's arm as she now forced her to slide out of the bronco. Falling from the bronco, Elly stumbled to gain her footing as Makiyah continued to pull her along to the house. Glancing back at Khalil, Elly grasped for one more look that would change her mind.

Then, suddenly, Elly remembered that Khalil had the letter.

Just as Elly stepped to go back to the car she felt the firm, paralyzing hands of her uncle on her shoulder. All Elly could do was just stand there as Khalil drove away, that pit in her stomach growing stronger.

As the headlights disappeared, leaving behind a dark void, Elly could feel her uncle release his grip on her shoulders.

"Inside," he demanded. Elly and Makiyah both followed him inside. Just as Elly walked through the door, she saw a large shotgun slightly hidden behind the curtain of the window by the door.

"What happened?" Trace asked his gaze directly on Makiyah, which confused Elly.

"We are okay," Makiyah assured him, as Jane entered the foyer.

Elly saw an instant change in Makiyah's demeanor around her grandmother. Makiyah never had a subservient attitude towards anyone, but now Elly watched as she appeared to be physically bowing her head towards her grandmother.

"Nothing happened," Elly affirmed, assuming Trace was upset that they were home later than she would've been allowed out if, in fact, she had even informed them they were going out. "I just want to go to bed."

Trace glared at Makiyah, who avoided eye contact with everyone. As much as he wanted to question Makiyah, he knew he couldn't do it in front of Elly, so letting her go to bed was the best option. "We will discuss this later," he eyed Makiyah directly, who nodded slightly, as she followed Elly up the staircase.

The moment Elly closed the door she turned on Makiyah.

"What was in that letter, Makiyah?"

"Elly, I - I -" Makiyah stuttered, wringing her fingers together.

For the first time, Makiyah wasn't the confident, commanding person that Elly knew her entire life. Even as little girls, she still managed to capture the room with her presence. "I'm sorry," she whispered, a single tear falling down her cheek.

"Makiyah, what is going on here?"

"I wish I could tell you but -" Makiyah nervously shifted her eyes towards the door, fearful Trace was right behind the thin wood.

"You are starting to scare me," Elly admitted.

"You should really talk to your uncle."

"I don't want to talk to my uncle. I want to talk to my best friend," Elly cried, feeling her own eyes starting to burn.

"Well, I don't want to talk to you," she snapped back, pushing past Elly and escaping from the room.

A part of Elly wanted to run after Makiyah, force her to tell her about the letter and what was happening, but as she started to walk she could feel the instability in her legs, the shaking of her hands, and suddenly she had to sit down. Bracing her shaking hands against the bed, Elly could feel her mind and body swirling out of control as she fell onto the bed.

Makiyah pushed the tears from her cheeks as she stormed out of Elly's room, furious with herself for ever agreeing to come down here to help. While it didn't feel as if she had a choice in the matter, Makiyah regretted betraying her friend. Every fiber of her being wished her mother had never told her the truth, ran away the moment Julianna died, but there was no going back now.

She pushed the door open to the kitchen, Trace and Jane in

whispered conversation that immediately stopped as they both turned to stare at Makiyah in the doorway.

"We need to talk," Makiyah affirmed, gathering all her courage to stand up to Jane and Trace. She wouldn't continue to lie and spy on her best friend for them, not anymore.

"Yes, we do," Jane agreed, motioning for Makiyah to take a seat at the small, round kitchen table.

"What happened tonight?"

"I did as you asked. I got us an invite to Niyanna's house, that is where we were when-" Makiyah paused, her leg shaking anxiously. "When Niyanna threatened to kill Elly."

"What?" They both said in unison.

Immediately, Jane was up from the table, nervously pacing the kitchen, her mind racing with all the implications of Makiyah's confession. If Niyanna was here to kill Elly, then she probably wasn't the only one who thought that it was open season on her granddaughter. She thought she could protect her, that no one would dare come to her home, but she was wrong.

"Trace this changes everything," Jane finally said. Trace nodded in agreement, thankful that his mother now saw that Elly going with him was truly the only way to keep her safe.

"What do you mean?" Makiyah asked, fearing she once again betrayed her friend.

"Did you find anything at her house?" Trace deflected.

"Oh, uh, yeah. A letter," Makiyah reached to her back pocket. Only then did she realize that Khalil still had the letter. "Oh no," she whispered.

"What is it?"

"Khalil has the letter."

"How did that happen?" Jane snapped.

"I - I - I don't know," Makiyah stuttered. "He just sort of took it, I guess." Everything had happened so fast, Makiyah was having a hard time recalling it all.

"What are we going to do about him?" Trace asked, his voice seethed with anger.

"He saved Elly's life that night, we both know that," Jane retorted.

"There's something else, " Makiyah whispered, knowing that she had to tell them but that it went against every bone in her body. "I think she is in love with Khalil."

"You know what he is right?" Trace scoffed.

"Yes, I do. The problem here is that Elly doesn't."

"There is a lot Elly doesn't know," Trace retorted, glaring at Jane. He still wasn't sure why his mother kept waiting to tell Elly. They were running out of time and fast.

"I decide when we tell her," Jane affirmed.

"Well, it better be soon because she's asking a lot of questions that I don't know how to answer." Makiyah instantly saw that she had gone too far, Jane's eyes flaring with anger.

"Maybe it's time for you to go."

"No, mother, Makiyah is useful here with us. We will need her when the time comes, trust me. I remember -" Trace paused, glancing at Makiyah, seeing Ava in her eyes and remembering the moment he learned the truth.

"Just stop, I need to think," Jane snapped. "You both go to bed. We will talk about this tomorrow."

Jane glared at Trace and Makiyah as they both retreated from the kitchen. Looking at the window, the night a dark blanket over the world, Jane felt its weight on her heart. Glancing down at her weathered, scared hands, Jane admitted only to herself that her time was coming to a close. Not only would she have to tell Elly the truth, but she'd also be leaving her alone to carry the weight of it all.

A single tear slowly rolled down her cheek as she felt the last ounce of power fade away.

25

Chapter Twenty-Five

Elly felt as if she slept for days, as she pulled her sore body from the sheets. Her room was flooded with light, as the sun was high in the sky. Stretching her sore muscles, pinching her fingers on her tight neck, Elly surveyed the empty room. The last thing she remembered was fighting with Makiyah, then she passed out.

Suddenly, flashes of memories from last night invaded her mind. The threats by Niyanna, the look in Khalil's eyes, and Makiyah's refusal to tell her the truth. An overwhelming feeling pounded down on Elly as she felt as if she couldn't breathe. Grasping her chest, the pain pulsating through her body, Elly tried to calm her breathing.

"Are you okay?" Makiyah was in the doorway, watching Elly as she struggled to catch her breath. Rushing to her side, Makiyah pulled Elly's hands into her own. "Just breath, Elly, just breath, it's going to be okay, just calm down."

Slowly, Elly could feel her body start to calm down and her breathing returning to normal, as Makiyah slowly breathed with her, tightly holding her hands.

"What's happening to me," Elly breathed, her voice barely a whisper as her thoughts escaped through her lips.

"It's okay, Elly. You are going to be okay," Makiyah assured.

"How do you know? How do you know anything, what is happening?"

"It's a really long story."

"Tell me, Makiyah. I need to know what is happening and what was in that letter?"

"Elly, I just - I'm not the right person to tell you."

"What does that mean?"

"It means that all this is really family business and I should just stay out of it."

"Well, sorry, that's not an option as you are literally in it. Now tell me, Makiyah."

Elly could feel her chest starting to tighten, her breathing starting to labor, as she could feel her anger growing, a heat spreading like fire over her body.

"There is a deeper, darker truth to your life. Your mother tried to hide it from you. She never wanted you to be a part of this life, but now that she is dead that protection she gave you died with her."

Elly glared at her friend, shocked by her words.

"What truth?"

"I can't tell you," Makiyah affirmed, fear flooding her face. "They won't forgive that."

"Who? My Uncle? My grandmother?"

"Both of them, they need to be the ones to tell you."

"I want *you* to tell me," Elly demanded, feeling a deep knot of anger building in her chest. She could feel it rising, threatening to explode as she glared at Makiyah. She tried to control it, but it was taking over every nerve of her body.

"I can't," Makiyah whispered. Elly's eyes held the unspoken plea for her best friend to tell her the truth, but Makiyah could never betray Jane or Trace. They would kill her.

"See, that's the problem," Elly scoffed, holding back her burning tears, "You can."

Grabbing her running shoes from under the bed, Elly stormed from the room. She could feel something about to explode within her body. She needed it to stop, so she did the only thing she knew to do. She ran.

Running from the house, fast and hard she took off with no direction in mind. Passing through the fields, Elly ran full force to the edge of the forest. She gasped for breath, her lungs pleading for air. Then she heard Makiyah calling after her from the house. Feeling the cold tears on her burning cheeks, Elly turned and disappeared into the woods.

26

Chapter Twenty-Six

Makiyah nervously paced the driveway outside the back door, wringing her fingers together, as she watched the old, red pickup coming down the drive. She dreaded the thought of having to tell them that Elly ran away into the woods…*again*. Makiyah tried to follow her, but the woods were thick, dark even in the early afternoon. She had tried to follow her trail, but even without knowing, Elly was better than the rest of them ever would be out there.

The moment Jane and Trace pulled up, they knew something was wrong.

"What happened? Where's Elly?" Jane asked, jumping from the truck.

"I'm sorry, so sorry," Makiyah cried.

"Where did she go?" Trace asked, bracing her shoulders and forcing her eyes to his. "Tell me."

"She ran off - into the woods." Instantly, Makiyah could see the fear and anger flash across Trace's face.

"This is ..." Jane gasped, but then stopped herself from saying the words. Attempting to calm her anger towards Makiyah, before she did something she would most likely regret, Jane took a deep breath.

"Did you even go after her?" Trace accused.

"Yes ... well, I tried at least."

"Okay, Trace we still have time. It's a few hours before nightfall, let's all split up and try to find her," Jane dictated. "I'll call Austin and tell him to get back now."

Trace disappeared into the garage and returned with a shotgun. Motioning towards Makiyah, they both took off towards the woods.

"Keep in touch," Jane yelled after them, as she finally reached Austin on the phone. He was thirty minutes out. Jane hung up the phone and disappeared into the garage to get the other weapons ready. It had been years since she went hunting, but it was like riding a bike.

Elly stumbled through the trees, tripping over the large tree roots as if they were speed bumps. She aimlessly made her way around trying to find the treehouse, thinking that if she got lost again, Khalil would come to rescue her as he had last time. A memory of last night flashed across her mind, the look on Khalil's face as he told her to leave, but she refused to accept it.

However, after an hour of walking around she had to accept she had actually gotten lost in the thick darkness of the forest. Now, she was sure she was walking around in circles, as she attempted to find the path out of the forest.

Hours passed, as Elly watched the yellow-faded light starting to transform into pure blackness. A full, milky-colored moon casted a haze over the forest. The night air felt cold against her bare skin, wearing only a pair of ripped jeans and a light-weight white t-shirt that was now dingy with dirt marks. But, Elly could feel the burning sweat soaking her t-shirt, as she pushed her body to the breaking point.

She was starting to feel helpless, lost as she scrambled through the roots in a failed attempt to find any sort of direction. Slipping on a moss-covered root, Elly fell into the groove of a tree. Suddenly, she lost all energy to help herself up, cursing herself for ever thinking that going back into the woods was a good idea. Khalil had made it very obvious that she needed to stay away, his words echoing in her ears - *you should go, you should go...*

Leaning back against the tree, she started to cry again. Not even finding her mother dead on the kitchen floor had she felt this helpless and overwhelmed. This feeling of abandonment by Khalil made Elly want to curl into the tree and never emerge again for fear of what the world would be without him in it, which is actually how she felt when she lost her mother.

But, there was more this time. The betrayal of her friend, the secrets and lies that fogged her mind, and this feeling that something horrible was about to happen and she had no way to stop it or protect herself from it. It all bled together making it impossible for her to even move.

Then, she heard it - the crack of the branch. Quickly, Elly silenced her cries, wiping the tears from her cheeks, as she scanned the forest. The forest at night held many shadows as she strained to see any movement. Then, another crack and a rustle of leaves. Fear started to raise in Elly's chest, as she realized that something was out there.

Then, the yellow lights came into view, as Elly's own eyes grew wide at the figure that stepped into the light. The breath caught in her lungs as the giant wolf stared right at her, only a few feet away. *It's only a dream...*but, Elly knew it was real. She could feel the heat of its breath, smell the iron on its tongue, and every nerve in her body stood on edge.

Elly didn't think, her body instinctively pulled all its strength to get up and start running. Tearing through the woods, the branches slapping against her face and her feet stumbling over the roots, Elly ran as fast as she could without looking back. But, she could hear it running after her.

Just when she thought she couldn't run anymore, her lungs burning and her feet pained, she saw him in the distance. Khalil was running towards her as relief washed over her, quickly followed by fear as she realized that now they would both be attacked by the wolf. She tried to scream at him to run away, but he continued towards her, pulling his arms around her waist and lifting her off her feet. Then, she felt like she was flying as he carried her through the darkness.

Then he stopped, pulling her effortlessly behind him as he stood face to face with the wolf. Elly watched in horror knowing that at any moment the wolf would lunge, attacking Khalil. She pulled at Khalil's arms, her own screams foreign to her in that moment.

A low growl escaped Khalil's throat, causing Elly to instantly release her hold of his arms. Slowly, the wolf started to back away. Elly's mind swirled as she tried to make sense of everything that was happening. It seemed as if Khalil was communicating with the wolf, as it continued to back up. The glow of the wolf's eyes glistened in the night. Elly stepped towards Khalil, pulling on his arm again to urge him to move, as the wolf turned and disappeared into the night.

Khalil turned to Elly and she saw the same yellow glow in his eyes. Stepping back, Elly unsure of what she was seeing, she started to slip on the corner of a root. As she fell, Khalil moved as fast as lightning catching her in his arms. Elly gazed up at him, his eyes returning to their original deep brown. She thought that maybe she imagined it all and even went as far as to think she was dreaming even now.

"Elly, are you okay?" Khalil asked, keeping her safe in his arms. She blinked waiting to wake from the dream, but it wasn't happening.

"What just happened?" Elly's voice was raspy, the dust of the forest clogging her airway. Khalil was so close to her that she could smell the musty sweat on his bare skin and as he breathed she took in the stale smell of iron. It was the same smells she got right before she saw the wolf.

That's impossible.

Khalil saw the realization in her eyes, the fear cascading down over her face as the curtain lifted revealing the truth he so desperately was trying to hide. He knew the moment she knew she would run. Gently, he placed her down on her feet, waiting for her to run, but she didn't. Elly just stared at him. Then slowly, she raised her hands to his face, feeling around the curve of his chin as she stared into his eyes.

"It can't be real," she whispered. "Can it?" Khalil nodded,

confirming Elly's mystical theory that Khalil was a werewolf, just as in the story he gave her when they first met about Bisclavert. Suddenly, she knew the reason he chose that book.

"So, that's how you found me in the treehouse?" He nodded. "And, is this how you got me down from the treehouse?" He nodded again. "Wait, is this why Niyanna said you would kill me?" Sheepishly, he nodded, the pain flooding his face.

"Now that you know my dark secret ... will you run?" Khalil steeled his heart, waiting for the final crushing blow to their relationship, knowing that Elly would fear him as everyone did.

"No," Elly affirmed. "Your dark secret doesn't scare me."

"I am a monster." Elly saw the shame in his eyes.

"Bisclavert was never a monster," she assured Khalil, whose lips slightly curled into a smile. "You have always protected me and been a friend. I trust you."

"I feel more than friendship for you," Khalil confessed.

"I do too," admitted Elly.

They both stood together in the woods, Khalil for the first time feeling as if he could stand as himself before Elly. She had learned his darkest truth and she didn't run away. She accepted every part of him without hesitation. He pulled Elly into a hug.

Suddenly, Elly heard her name being called in the distance. Jane's voice rang through the forest. Khalil stiffened in Elly's arms. For a moment, he had forgotten who she truly was.

"You should go, it's not safe out here," Khalil confessed.

"Who was that out there? It was another werewolf, right?"

"That was my brother, Rex," Khalil revealed. "If he finds you out here again, he will kill you. You are not safe here anymore Elly," Khalil admitted.

Elly could feel that pressure building again.

"What will happen to you now that your brother saw you protecting me?"

"I'm not sure, but you have to promise me to stay away. It's not safe." Khalil and Elly both heard her grandmother calling again. Knowing their time was limited, he added, "Your grandparents can keep you safe," he assured Elly. "Just remember, I'm not like my brother. I'm not a part of that world, nor do I ever want to be. No matter what they tell you, just know that I want to be with you. Never forget that." Elly nodded. "Promise me," Khalil pleaded.

"I promise, but Khalil -" There was another call, closer this time.

"I have to go now." Just before Khalil turned away he reached down and lifted Elly's chin with his fingers. "Never forget."

Elly stood frozen in shock as Khalil disappeared in the darkness at lightning speed. Mentally she went over the facts ... he has yellow eyes... he has super speed ... he has her heart.

"Elly!" Jane cried appearing between the trees, a large shotgun under her arm. She pulled out her cellphone. "I found her," she said into the phone. Jane pushed the phone to her ear listening to the voice, nodding in agreement as Elly just blankly stared into the darkness where Khalil had just been standing.

"We have got to get back to the house," Jane urged, pulling Elly from her fog and dragging her through the woods.

Just as they reached the edge of the forest, Elly saw Trace and Makiyah emerging from the forest further down on the property. Even at this distance, Elly could see the large shotgun cradled in Trace's arms. Up at the house, Austin stood guard by the door.

The moment he saw them he leaned his shotgun against the back door as he ran towards them.

Elly could feel the painful pull on her calves as they walked up the hill towards her grandfather. Meeting in the middle, Austin paused for only a minute, before pulling Elly into his arms. She could feel the tension in his muscles, smell the fresh cedar on his clothes, and hear the humming in his lungs.

It was all the adrenaline she told herself, explaining why her senses seemed to be heightened. Everything felt as if it was in slow motion, as she pulled away from Austin and for the first time noticed the fear in everyone's eyes. Her uncle wore a thick, leather strap across his chest and she could hear the clink of the metal knife as he shifted it on his back. Sweat rolled down Makiyah's temples and she could smell the hints of mint and hear the labor in her breath.

Jane reached for her arm, but Elly narrowly pulled out of reach. Elly saw the glowing green in her eyes, faded and dim, but it was still there as she had seen in her uncle's eyes when they arrived home last night.

"We need to get inside," Jane urged, reaching for Elly again. But, Elly had already started walking towards the house.

Feeling as if time started to speed up again, Elly felt the dryness in her throat, the soreness in her body, and the emptiness in her stomach. Pushing through the back door, on a mission to quince her thirst and hunger, Elly ignored everything else.

"Elly we need to talk," Jane demanded, as she entered the kitchen behind her, strategically placing the loaded shotgun by the back door. The others stood behind Jane, each appearing both defeated and relieved at the same time.

"Look, my life was threatened yesterday," Elly retorted, her chest tight with anger. "I've just been lost in those woods for hours. I'm sticky, hungry, thirsty, I just need a moment," she snapped.

"We understand, Elly, but this is important," Trace affirmed.

As much as Elly had been desperate to know the truth, now she felt as if she had learned it on her own. Khalil was a werewolf. She looked at each of them, knowing that they had to know the truth as well. This is what they wanted to tell her and this is why Niyanna wanted to kill her. It all made sense to her now and she was too tired to talk about it, or more likely defend her feelings.

"Please, I need a shower."

They all glanced at each other, then Jane nodded in agreement. As Elly headed for the door, Trace motioned for Makiyah to follow her and she picked up on the unspoken order to not let Elly out of her sight again.

Chapter Twenty-Seven

The water ran hard against her sore skin, as Elly washed away her fears. A part of her had been screaming at her to run away from Khalil, but a bigger part, the one she listened to, told her she could trust Khalil above anyone else. He had protected her, saved her from Niyanna ... saved her from his brother. At every opportunity, Khalil had shown Elly that he was a good person, who cared about her above all. He even went against his brother in order to save her life. While thinking of Khalil as a raging werewolf was terrifying, deep down Elly knew he would never, could never hurt her in any way. She still left safe with him.

As Elly wiped the fog from the mirror, her pale face coming into view, she realized that she was different. Looking, she found it hard to pinpoint the specific things that looked different to her, but overall she knew she changed. Maybe it was the more prominent flecks of green in her eyes or the broadness of her shoulders that Elly unconsciously noticed at that moment, but she attributed the feeling of change with her feelings towards Khalil. For her, they went hand in hand.

As she came out of the shower, Makiyah was there staring at her from her perch on the window seat. "Oh, you scared me," Elly said, slightly jumping as she didn't realize Makiyah would still be in the room.

"Are you feeling okay?" Makiyah cautiously asked.

"No, I'm not," Elly confessed. Relief rushed over her body as she said it out loud.

"I am so sorry," Makiyah started, but Elly held up a firm hand.

"No, Makiyah, I understand it now." Makiyah's eyes widened in shock.

"But, how - what do you mean?" She stuttered.

"You know?" Elly assured before she revealed Khalil's secret. Makiyah slowly nodded, still disbelieving that Elly had learned the truth out in the woods.

"How do you know?"

"Khalil was in the woods, he told me everything," Elly divulged.

Instantly, Makiyah's face fell into fear.

"It's okay, I'm okay, he would never hurt me," Elly assured her friend.

"No, Elly, I don't think you fully understand," Makiyah warned.

Just then a knock vibrated through Elly's room. They both glanced at the door, their conversation interrupted by Jane, who was now standing in the open doorway.

"Let's talk," she commanded, stepping aside and ushering them both out of the room. Jane glared at Makiyah as she passed.

Allowing Elly to walk ahead some ways, Makiyah whispered, "I need to tell you something."

"Not now," Jane hissed.

In the kitchen, Jane pushed a full plate of food towards Elly across the small, round table tucked away in the bay windows of the kitchen. Immediately, Elly started to eat, as she utilized the time to gauge just how angry her grandparents and uncle were at her at this moment. This was now the second time she had basically run away, followed by staying out way too late.

She assumed she'd be in trouble, which is why she never saw it coming...

"How are you feeling?" Jane asked, her hands tightly folded together in front of her on the table giving her an overly formal appearance.

Trace was in the other seat towards the back of the table, leaned back against the large black windows, as Austin and Makiyah leaned against the bar, clearly more removed from the conversation. Elly glanced at all of them before answering.

"Tired." It was the only truth she could reveal.

"I know a lot has happened to you recently," Jane empathized. "I know you've had a lot of questions."

Elly suddenly realized she was not being chastised, but that Jane was finally going to answer all her questions about her mother's murder. Adrenaline started coursing through her veins as her mind prepared to learn how her mother was killed. For weeks she had tried to figure out what happened, only to be avoided or deflected by her grandmother or uncle. Now, she would learn the truth.

Jane glanced out the window before she continued, "There is more to your mother's death, yes, that is true. But it goes well beyond her murder," Jane began, nervously glancing every few words out the window. Elly glanced at the window but still only saw the black night staring back. She got the feeling her grandmother was looking for someone. Elly feared it might be the person who killed her mother. Suddenly, she had the epiphany that it had to do with Khalil.

"That feeling you are having right now," Jane motioned to Elly's twitching leg. Elly immediately stopped having never realized she was doing it.

"What do you mean?"

"We all feel it," interjected Trace. "The increase in adrenaline tingling through your body and heightened senses ..." Trace gave Elly a tight, sorrowful smile, "the nightmares."

"I don't understand." Elly caught the next words in her throat, unsure if she was ready to reveal that she knew Khalil's secret. While she was assured Makiyah knew, she wasn't sure the rest of them knew the truth. If she mentioned Khalil in relation to her mother's murder, she might open a door she can never close. In an effort to protect Khalil, she swallowed the question.

"You are changing. Regrettably too soon, but ..." Trace's voice trailed off, turning his attentions to the night outside the window.

"Your mother's death has propelled your change forward," Jane admitted. "I am sorry for that. We were hoping that bringing you here would slow it down, but ..." Jane glanced at Austin.

"It's important that you understand that this is not a choice," Austin affirmed, having learned at a young age there was no escaping your destiny. "If you chose to not accept your fate, it makes no difference to them." Elly stared at the hardened look in her grandfather's normally soft eyes. She could feel the magnitude of his words that caused her fear to grow.

"It's in your blood," explained Jane. "It's in all of our blood, including your mother."

"You cannot run from it, as she tried. It will follow you," Austin affirmed.

"I don't understand what you are talking about," Elly asserted. "What does all of this have to do with my mother's death?"

"It has everything to do with it," Jane confessed.

"She was trying to protect you," Trace explained. "She never -"

"Stop it," Jane hissed at her son. "Your mother wanted to protect you, yes," Jane affirmed, glaring at Trace, an unspoken demand to keep his mouth shut about Julianna's failed plan to hide Elly away her entire life. "We differed on how, but now none of that matters. Right now, you need to know what is happening to you. You need to understand that this is your only path, otherwise, they will come for you next."

"Who will come for me?"

"Those that you will hunt."

"What?" Elly detested hunting and refused to ever even hold or look at a gun. The fact that they owned shotguns made her uncomfortable.

"You are special, Elly, more than you realize," Jane explained. "Just like people pass down their skin color, our family passes down a very particular, unique gene. This gene affects your body and your mind, giving you heightened senses, such as the ability to see at night."

Just then a white glow passed over them as the clouds parted revealing the full moon. Elly felt her heart rate jump, the tingling sensation return to her fingers and toes, as her eyes grew wide under the moonlight. As the clouds passed back over the moon, the night fell dark again and the feeling dissipated.

"What is happening to me?"

Slowly, Elly started to understand what they were saying, as she put the pieces together of how she had been feeling. The night terrors that caused her body to soak the sheets through, her ability to run long distances without feeling winded or tired, the fact that she could smell anything within a five-mile radius, and then there was the feeling she just had of intense adrenaline surging throughout her entire body.

"Your body is going through a type of metamorphosis, for lack of a better word. We thought we had some more time, another year, maybe, but sometimes you never know." Jane hesitated, as she saw a single tear rolling down Elly's cheek. "When your mother died, all that power she possessed passed to you."

"Power? What do you mean? I have powers?"

"Not in the literal sense, no," Jane assured. "Your mother's presence kept your gene dormant for a time, but the moment she died." Jane failed to say the words out loud, but she didn't have to because Elly was starting to finally understand.

"I've been feeling it too," Makiyah confessed sheepishly in the corner.

"What?" Elly's eyes widened as she turned towards Makiyah.

"I started having the nightmares a few months ago," she

confessed. "My mother had never told me either, so it took time to understand what was happening, but when your mother died. Well," she shrugged, "she told me everything. She said I needed to know because now we would be in danger."

"Danger? Danger from who?"

"We use these abilities to protect people," Trace stated, glancing at Jane to make sure he wasn't going too far. "These abilities are used to help us do one thing."

"And what is that?"

"Kill werewolves."

28

Chapter Twenty-Eight

The tension in the room was palpable, as Elly could feel the heat rising on her skin, her cheeks bursting with a spike of adrenaline that rushed through her veins at the idea of killing a werewolf. Gasping her hands over her ears, Elly pushed the thought from her mind. *It can't' be true*, she thought. Deep down though, Elly knew it was.

It was the look of fear mixed with sorrow on Makiyah's face that confirmed the real, full truth for Elly. She thought learning that Khalil was a werewolf was the catalyst behind everything that was happening to her, but she was wrong.

"There are animals in this world, dangerous ones. Our bloodline was put on this Earth to balance the scales. It is our calling to protect those who cannot protect themselves."

"Not all animals are monsters," Elly whispered, thinking of Khalil, assured he was not a monster.

"These animals are, I assure you. They killed your mother, thinking that would end our line." Trace affirmed, frustration growing in his voice, as he started to realize that Elly knew the truth about Khalil.

Elly's heart dropped as she realized the reason behind her mother's death. She was murdered because of something Elly barely understood, but at that moment she understood enough to hate it.

"They want to kill us all," Austin divulged. "No longer are we the ones hunting them, but they are now hunting us." His ominous words rang through Elly's mind as she recalled Khalil's words - *I am not like my brother.*

"They didn't know Julianna had a daughter, which is why you had to come here. They must not find out about you or you will be in greater danger," Jane asserted.

Suddenly, Elly's vision of Khalil's brother, Rex, flashed across her mind, as she realized that they already knew. Jane saw the instant fear in her eyes. Even if Khalil was not like the others, and there were others, his brother was.

"What is it?"

"What does that mean?" Elly deflected, knowing that she could never tell Jane that Khalil was a werewolf. She already could see it in her eyes, that she would kill him. Elly was already concerned that her uncle was aware, he definitely had his suspicions, but she held on to the fact that he was still alive meaning that maybe he wasn't sure yet.

"Unfortunately, that means you will have to leave," Jane confessed.

"What? Why? I just got here," Elly protested.

"Your Uncle is here to take you to a place where you will learn all about your abilities and how to use them. You will learn to protect yourself." Jane's pride built within her chest. "You will become a warrior, just like your mother did."

"My mother was a warrior?" Elly gasped, unable to believe that her mother would ever hurt a fly, let alone hunt down and kill someone. Her mother was also the first to forgive, instilling in her the power of words and kindness her entire life. It was hard to believe that the woman who grounded her for weeks for pushing another girl at school could be a fighting hunter.

"Your mother was the greatest warrior anyone *had* ever seen." Jane beamed with pride, which was quickly overshadowed by a thick veil of resentment. "It came with a lot of responsibilities."

"What if I don't want to go?" Elly challenged.

"Elly, let me explain something to you. If you go out there unprotected they will not care. The first opportunity they have, they will kill you. They will not take the risk of you killing them, no matter that you are a child."

"Who are they?"

"There are many different types of creatures, mostly only known to people as mythical folklore ... stories ... fantasies. But, every story comes from truth. Just as we exist, so do werewolves and vampires." Jane paused, noticing the lack of shock on Elly's face. "But you already knew that didn't you?" she glared at Elly, who pursed her lips together as if trying to refuse the words from leaving her mouth. "You need to tell me, your life could be in grave danger," Jane pleaded.

"This girl at school - Niyanna," Makiyah interjected. "Elly, she threatened you because she is a vampire," she explained. "That's what the letter I found was about. It confirmed that she was a vampire and-" she hesitated, glancing nervously from Elly to Jane and back to Elly. "She was ordered to kill you."

"What?" Elly gasped. She thought Niyanna only threatened her because of Khalil, but now she realized that a *vampire*, not just a girl, had threatened to kill her. She also realized that Niyanna thought Khalil would kill her, which meant that he also knew what she was. He knew what she was, yet he still loved her.

"Not to worry," Jane assured. "Your uncle has handled that already."

"What did you do?" Elly demanded.

Letting out a deep sigh, Trace just stared at her with knowing eyes. He didn't have to say the words, Elly knew.

"If you didn't know about Niyanna, then how?" Jane probed, unwilling to let it go.

Jane waited for Elly to reveal the truth, confirming her fears about Khalil, but she refused.

"It's Khalil," Makiyah confessed, knowing that Elly would never say the words. Instantly, she saw the betrayal in Elly's eyes. Desperately, she wanted to cry out that they already knew, but she didn't get the chance.

"No, you don't understand, he's not like them," Elly pleaded.

"They are all the same," Trace affirmed.

Trace had been right from the beginning, which caused a wave of fear inside Jane, as that meant she had missed it the first time ... and she never misses.

"You will leave first thing in the morning," Jane interjected.

Learning now that not only was Khalil a confirmed werewolf but that Elly clearly had feelings for him as well, was another wave crashing against Jane at that moment. If Elly knew about Khalil, then he definitely was aware of her, which put them both in more danger than they knew. Elly would need to leave as soon as possible now.

"I was hoping we'd have more time, but it appears the wolves are already descending, literally. So we must move quickly now."

"I need to say-" Elly stopped the words before it was too late, quickly rethinking before she continued. "I need to say goodbye to Maddie." Jane appeared confused. "She's been my only friend here and I'd like to at least thank her for that before I go."

Jane nodded in agreement. "You can go by first thing in the morning, but you will need to pack tonight." Elly nodded.

The moment Elly made it back to her room, alone, she broke down. Hot tears flooded her cheeks as she held back the gasps and cries. She did not want anyone to hear. In a matter of hours, Elly had learned that a magical, mythical world that only existed in stories did in fact exist in her real life. In addition to the fact that her mother was killed by these creatures and now they were after her as well. But, the most crippling part of all was the fact that in her own story she was the hero and Khalil the villain.

Overwhelmed by her range of emotions, Elly was finding it difficult to ground any of her emotions or thoughts. She was filled with anger over her mother's deception, unable to believe her mother had kept an entire part of her life a secret. It was the final breaking point of lies for Elly, as she realized that to keep this secret she lied about so many other things. Now, that she needed her truth the most, she was gone. She was angry at her mother for never giving her the choice to have her explain it all.

In the darkness of her room, Elly did not sleep, her mind racing. Elly used the time to create her own plan for her life, instead of the one her grandmother and everyone else seemed to be pushing upon her to do. She knew there was going to be a risk, but from the moment she learned the truth she knew deep down she wanted nothing to do with this life. She understood her uncle's unspoken words. She knew her mother never wanted this life for her, that is why they went away and why she never talked to them. She was running from it all to save her daughter.

She knew if she could just get to Khalil, explain what was happening, that she wasn't going to be this person they said she had to be, then they could leave together. He was stuck in this world, just like she was now. Neither one of them wanted to be part of this war. That was the only parting thing her mother had left her that she knew for sure - *get out*.

As the sun started to peek through the trees, Elly pulled her sore, tired body from the bed one last time. Packing up all her things in the single duffle bag, Elly glazed around the room remembering the first moments she arrived. She remembered how much she wanted to be free of this place - runaway. Now, she was getting her chance, but it didn't feel right. She couldn't shake the feeling that she was about to make a horrible mistake.

Chapter Twenty-Nine

Trace drove Elly over to Maddie's house, a decent-sized farmhouse with a wraparound porch and large pocket windows poking out like eyes on the roof. The boards creaked under her weight as Elly made her way to the door, her uncle, upon her endless request, stayed in the car.

"Hey, Elly," Maddie said, opening the door. "What's going on?" She looked confused as she glanced over Elly's shoulder to her uncle sitting in a large, menacing black truck.

"Oh, I just needed to talk to you, can I come inside?"

"Sure," Maddie opened the door wider. Elly gave a slight wave to her uncle as she disappeared into the house.

The foyer smelled of vanilla and fresh soap, as Elly glanced around at all the family photos hanging tightly together on the walls, and small trinkets cluttering each surface. There was a large church bench along the staircase wall that was cluttered with jackets and backpacks. A litter of shoes was tucked away underneath. Elly followed Maddie into the living room just off to the right of the foyer.

Taking a seat on the soft, flowered sofa, Elly desperately looked around.

"What are you looking for?" Maddie asked.

"I need to ask you something." Maddie heard the urgency in Elly's voice.

Suddenly, Elly heard a hard thud above them and the thumping footsteps of Lily as she thundered down the stairs. Swinging on the banister, she practically flew into the living room. As much as Elly didn't want to talk in front of Lily, she was in a rush.

"I'm leaving ... It's a long story, but I have to get a message to Khalil. I was hoping that you could help me."

"I can help," Lily affirmed joyfully, her hair bouncing on her head as she moved up and down on the couch cushion.

"Really? How?"

"Khalil is my friend," she smiled.

"Since when?" Maddie interjected.

"Since ..." she started, dragging out the word, "he helped me pick apples from the trees a few weeks ago." Elly and Maddie both looked at each other in shock.

"Uh, okay, do you think he'll be down there today?" Elly asked.

"I don't know," Lily shrugged.

"I can drive over there, what do you need me to tell him?"

"I need Khalil to know that I am leaving, but that I do not want to go. I need you to get a message to him that I am in trouble. Can you do that?"

Maddie nodded.

"Elly, wait," Maddie reached out touching her arm as she stood to leave. "What is going on? What kind of trouble?" Maddie asked.

"I'm sorry Maddie, but it's complicated."

"Is this about what happened at Niyanna's house?"

"What? How do you -"

"Lauren told me about it, said she saw you with Niyanna and Khalil. She said it looked like Khalil was about to hurt Niyanna, she came back inside in tears."

Elly's blood started to boil. "That is not the truth. Niyanna threatened me, Khalil was only trying to protect me. You were right to tell me to stay away from her and you should too, and Lauren. She is dangerous."

"I mean she's a little extra sometimes, but dangerous?"

"Yes, dangerous, trust me."

"Oh, she is very dangerous, Maddie. I'd stay away from her," Lily added, a large, knowing smile spreading over her face.

"How would you know?"

"Khalil told me. He said to stay very far away from her because she's a vampire," Lily said, raising her hands and showing her teeth as she started to giggle.

It was clear that Lily thought it all to be a joke, but Elly knew otherwise.

"Oh, Lily, stop that," Maddie giggled. "She's just a little different, that's all."

Elly and Lily looked at each other, an unspoken glance that they both knew Niyanna was more than just different.

"Thank you so much. And thank you, Maddie, for being a really good friend."

"Will you ever be back?"

"No."

As Elly and Trace drove back to the house, Elly started to formulate the next part of her plan. She had to find a way to get out of the house so no one would see her and get to the treehouse.

"Elly, I hope you understand we are all doing what is best for you," Trace said, invading her thoughts.

"What?"

"We just want to keep you safe," he assured, looking to Elly for understanding.

"What did my mother never want?"

"She never wanted you to be in danger. She thought she could hide you away, but it didn't work," Trace affirmed.

"Was it a wolf or vampire that killed my mother?"

"A wolf," Trace confirmed Elly's fears. "Wolves are more uncontrollable," Trace explained. "Vampires tend to keep more to themselves and as long as they don't pose a threat we typically keep away from each other ... but wolves ..." Trace's eyes clouded in darkness. "They are a different breed. Wild. Vicious. They have to be put down, it's the only way." Trace noticed Elly wince at his words. "No matter what you feel, or what you know, they all turn at some point."

"What if you are wrong?" Elly thought of Khalil.

Trace let out a deep sigh, knowing Elly's connection with Khalil was not what she thought it was. She felt drawn to him because she was meant to kill him.

30

Chapter Thirty

Walking through the doorway Jane immediately read the look on Trace's face. Elly was young, so Jane was trying to be empathic to what was happening to her life, but it was clear that her feelings towards Khalil were going to cause a problem. It would take time, but soon Elly would understand everything in a new light, then she would see that her connection to Khalil was not friendship. Once Elly knew the truth, she would understand that she had to kill him, no matter what.

Jane nodded towards Makiyah as Elly retreated to her room. Makiyah followed Elly up the stairs, Jane having already told her what she needed to do. Makiyah didn't like following Jane's orders, but she was doing it for Elly, not for her. Elly still needed support and protection, which is exactly what Makiyah had been brought here to do.

"Elly, are you doing okay?" Makiyah asked as she followed

Elly into her bedroom. Makiyah watched as Elly fiddled with the duffle bag on her bed.

"What do you think?" Elly snapped.

"I know this is a lot, I felt the same way."

"No, you didn't," Elly retorted, feeling her anger grow towards her friend. "Your mother wasn't killed, your life completely tossed upside down, have your best friend lie to you..."

"I know and I am so sorry. Please, just don't shut me out," Makiyah pleaded. "I only learned about all this a few weeks ago. But, I think you should know something."

Makiyah knew Elly thought she had betrayed her by telling Jane and Trace that Khalil was a werewolf, but she needed Elly to know that they already knew. Just as Niyanna knew who Elly was, Khalil knew who she was as well. They had all lied.

"Really, I can't - I can't take another thing," Elly protested, holding up her hands to physically block her friend from coming any closer. "Makiyah, please just leave me alone right now."

"I'm your friend, Elly. I have always been your best friend. Please don't forget that."

Makiyah left Elly alone in her room, knowing that Elly was not going to change her mind right now. She needed time, Makiyah understood that more than she realized. Of course, things were very different when her mother told her that she was born to hunt and kill werewolves. In the weeks after Julianna's death, her mother immediately changed from the jovial, loving mother she grew up with to a fearful, anxious woman that refused to leave the house and constantly checked out the window as if she was waiting for something horrible.

When she'd ask her mother about it, Ava would only tell her

that they were no longer safe. That if they could find Julianna, they could find them as well.

"How did it go?" Jane asked Makiyah as she returned to the kitchen, her eyes still red with tears.

"She's still hurt. I told you all of this was a bad idea," Makiyah complained, glaring at Trace.

"Elly needs you right now, even if she is upset, she still needs her friend. Unfortunately ..." Jane paused ... "regrettably, I am not close with my granddaughter and she no longer has her mother to explain all of this to her, so she will need someone she trusts and that is you."

"What about Trace?"

"No, it has to be you. You will be able to go with her, watch her, and
report back to me," Jane affirmed. "Her uncle has other business he must deal with now," Jane added, looking towards Trace in the corner of the kitchen as he cut slices of apple with his large hunting knife.

"I thought - my mother said I didn't have to go," Makiyah protested.

"Sorry, but I've already made arrangements for you to attend with Elly. As I said, she will need you more than ever."

Makiyah's heart sank as she realized her worst fears - *she was not going home*. As she walked away from her mother in the airport terminal just three days ago, she could see it in her eyes but she refused to believe it.

"It's time," Jane announced, looking at Trace. "They will be waiting for you." Trace nodded, as he tossed the rest of the apple in the trash. "I will get Elly."

Trace gave Jane a forced hug before he retreated from the kitchen to the large black truck in the driveway, Makiayh reluctantly followed. Her bags had long since been packed and ready to go, only she thought she'd be going home.

Jane gently pushed open the door to find Elly staring out the window. She knew this would be her last moments with her granddaughter, their time together too short. Jane wasn't sure what bringing Elly to this place would do, but she had hoped that it would provide Elly with protection and more time before she had to go. They knew the moment Julianna died that Elly would be in danger, but Jane thought she could protect her, realizing now that she was wrong. Elly was more than she ever imagined. She worried that Elly wouldn't be able to handle it, which is why even though she wanted to keep her here, she had to let her go.

"Elly, it's time," Jane announced. Elly turned, the tears were still fresh on her cheeks. "Oh, my dear." Jane slid beside her granddaughter, pulling her into her chest as she cried. "I know, I know," she said softly as she gently ran her fingers over her hair.

"I don't want to go," Elly confessed, the tears still flowing freely down her hot cheeks.

"I don't want you to go either, but we have no other choice."

"Why can you not protect me here? Why can't I stay with you?"

"Oh, my dear sweet granddaughter, we all go through this time. Where you are going, they can protect you, train you to protect yourself."

"To become a warrior."

"Yes," Jane beamed with pride. "Makiyah will be going with you, so you will not be alone."

"I don't want her to go," snapped Elly.

"You need to trust your friend," Jane affirmed. "And know we are all here for you, your grandfather and uncle. We have all been through what you are about to go through."

"And what is that exactly? No one has even told me where I am going, just that I have to go. Do you know what that feels like?"

"Yes, in fact, I do, and I implored your mother to not keep this from you. If you had grown up knowing things would be different."

"Don't do that - don't blame my mother for just trying to protect me. She was doing what she thought was best, so how does that make her any different than you?"

"The difference is I *know* what is best, your mother was going against everything. She was trying to change all the rules," Jane snapped, feeling herself starting to lose control. Quickly, she closed her eyes and took a deep breath attempting to calm herself before things got out of control. "Please, Elly, trust me on this."

Elly glanced back out the window, thinking of what she could say to continue to stall her grandmother. Then, she saw the movement she had been waiting for this last hour.

He was here.

"Fine." Elly grabbed her duffle and followed Jane downstairs.

Austin was waiting by the back door, his eyes were red with tears, as he pulled her into a large, comforting hug. If he thought he could win, he would go against Jane and demand that his granddaughter stays under their protection. But, he had learned that his efforts were futile.

Walking out the back door, Elly looked to the forest straining her eyes to see the moving shadow in the distance. Jane followed behind her, carrying the duffle bag as Elly marched to her new destiny. But, she had a plan. Any moment now she knew Khalil would save her from this path. She wasn't sure how, but she could feel that he was close and couldn't explain it, but knew that he would do something.

Just as her hand rested on the truck handle she heard him calling her name. Turning, she saw Khalil running from the forest, through the field towards the house. Jane stepped in front of Elly, but she pushed around her and started to run towards Khalil. Jane called after her, starting to follow, but Trace held her back.

"Let her go, she needs to hear it from him," Trace assured Jane, who relaxed in his arms knowing that he was right. She'd never be able to let go of him until he told her the truth.

"Are you sure he'll tell her?" Jane asked.

"He cares for her, so yes, he will tell her. No matter how much he'll want her to stay, he knows this is the only way to keep her safe."

Trace felt a flicker of pain in his heart, as he once had to make the same decision with Ava. It was one he always regretted making but would make every single time to keep her safe. Just as Julianna had made the same painful decision fifteen years ago. Just as Khalil would do now.

"Khalil, you came."

He stepped towards her bracing her shoulders with his hands.

"Maddie told me you were in trouble, what's going on?" He looked up to the house, seeing Jane, Austin, Trace, and Makiyah standing around the truck all staring at them.

"They are making me leave," she choked out, tears burning her eyes as she tried to push them back. "I'm not sure where I am going, but I don't want to go." Before Elly could explain, Khalil's body went stiff as he turned back towards the forest. Gently, he slid Elly behind him as he glared out into the distance.

Suddenly, a tall, dark man appeared out of the woods. He held a striking resemblance to Khalil, with the same deep brown eyes and dark complexion. However, this man was much larger than Khalil, his frame casting an ominous shadow across the ground.

"Is everything okay?" Elly asked, the words of her grandmother echoing in her ears. "Khalil?" Elly pulled at his arm, fear rising in her chest as she realized that Khalil was protecting her from this person, which meant that he was dangerous.

"Khalil," Rex called. When Khalil didn't move, Rex started the arduous walk up the field towards them both. "What are you doing?"

"Rex, go back home, this doesn't concern you," Khalil called back to him. Suddenly, Elly realized it was his brother. It was a werewolf. Her body started to prick with adrenaline, the hairs bristling on her arms. She could hear the lullaby echoing through the woods.

"Oh, brother, but it does very much so." Rex stopped just a few feet from Khalil and Elly.

For every step that Rex took towards them, Jane and Trace had matched him stopping just behind Khalil and Elly. She could feel them behind her and realized they were surrounded. Each piece of her plan was dissipating in front of her eyes, as her thoughts of escaping this life as her mother had were now slowly fading away.

"You should go," Trace warned, slowly sliding his hand towards his back underneath his long, black jacket.

"Yeah, that's not going to happen," Rex retorted, taking a step closer, as Khalil responded by pushing Elly further behind him and away from his brother.

In a flash, Elly saw the yellow glow in Rex's eyes and felt a low growl vibrating through his body. Rex was significantly larger than Khalil in every way as if Rex had been a blowfish now puffing up to show he was bigger than the other predators. Staring back into Rex's glowing eyes, feeling the pressure and fear, Elly knew she never wanted to feel this way. Jane had been right to say she needed to learn to protect herself.

"Rex, stop this right now," Khalil urged.

"Brother, please, you know this is the only way. This is a kill or be killed world we inhabit."

"No, it's not. I chose to believe that it can be different," Khalil affirmed. "We do not have to be the monsters they think we are and she does not have to be the killer they expect her to be."

Elly's eyes widened, as she learned that Khalil knew she could be different. He too believed that they could hide away forever both concealing their truths, allowing the world to continue with their stereotypes and ideals, as they blissfully ignored it all.

That was the world Elly thought she could live in, until the moment Rex emerged from the trees. He knew and Elly could feel that he was the horrible thing that had been gnawing away at her all this time.

"They are the monsters," Rex screamed, pointing back at Trace who swiftly pulled out the gun from behind his back, Rex in his target. "Why can't you see that, brother? They will turn her into one of them. She will become a killer and one day she will kill you."

"No, I won't," assured Elly.

"Elly, go to the car, now," Jane demanded, but Elly refused to move.

"You can't change the world," Rex affirmed, standing with his hands raised as he glared at Trace, daring him to prove his point to his brother.

Khalil turned to Elly, pulling her close to his face. "Elly, I need you to know I would never hurt you," he affirmed.

"I know that."

"But, I think you should go with your uncle." Khalil glanced at Trace, standing unmoving with his gun pointed directly at Rex, as Jane stood just behind him, reaching her hand out to Elly. "They can protect you."

"I don't want to go. I wanted to stay with you," Elly admitted. She lifted her hand to his warm cheek, feeling the stumble on his face mixed with the smoothness of his skin under her fingers. She gently drifted her fingers over his face as she took in the last moments she would see him. She knew the moment she walked away she would never know if she would see him again, and even then what they would both have become someone else by that time.

"I'll always remember my promise," Elly declared.

"Never let them change you," Khalil added, placing his own hand on Elly's soft, cold cheek. "We will see each other again, I am sure of it."

"I hope you are right."

"Khalil, I think it's time you and your brother leave," Trace announced, slightly adjusting his arm as it was becoming stiff from holding the large gun.

Trace knew if he had to shoot Rex in front of Elly that Khalil would change, possibly hurting Elly. He also knew that if Elly saw what she would become she would resist even more. Right now, Khalil was her friend, someone who protected her, but when she learned the truth, he would become a monster, as they all did.

"It's time," Khalil affirmed. "Never forget."

Khalil turned towards Trace, nodding in agreement, as he stepped back from Elly. She wanted to reach out to him, hold onto the world she thought she knew, and ignore what it really is, but she knew that was wrong. They couldn't pretend that they could be safe together in this world, but Elly knew one day they both could change it all.

"I won't," Elly affirmed.

Khalil stayed there, watching as Elly retreated to her uncle's large, black truck with her grandmother by her side. He knew it was a risk, that they would try to change her mind, mold her into a killer. But, he couldn't protect her anymore, not now that his brother was here. He'd have to trust that the person he knew, his friend, would prevail.

Makiyah slipped into the truck behind Elly. Khalil could still see her face through the front windshield, as the tears started to fade down her flushed cheeks. Jane joined Austin by the back door, his gun raised towards Khalil, unmoving.

"Brother, you have no idea what you started," Rex affirmed, as Khalil stood by his side. Trace dropped his gun and returned to the truck. Austin still had them in his target to ensure they didn't try anything while Trace's back was turned. After all, they were monsters.

Rex placed a firm hand on his brother's shoulder, as Khalil continued to stare at Elly as Trace pulled himself up into the truck. "Forget her. The next time you see her it'll be at the end of the barrel."

Khalil shrugged his brother's hand from his shoulder. "You are wrong," he insisted. "She is different."

"She is different," Rex agreed. "But, not in the way you think. She is destined to be the best of them. To kill us all, including you. Which means, in turn, you will be our only chance of survival. You should've killed her now, it will be harder after she learns."

"Stop it, I will never kill her," Khalil professed. "It doesn't have to be this way."

"You can't change the world."

"Watch me."

Author Bio

Anne Brooks grew up in a small town off the Gulf Coast of Florida, where she cultivated a passion for the water. She grew up immersed in the arts learning to sing and write stories at a young age. She completed her Bachelors in Psychology at the University of Florida. She worked in social work for a few years, before making a career change to early elementary education. She has taught for over thirteen years.

She lives with her husband and two children in her hometown. Nurturing her love for writing by night, she labors to create a balanced life of work, family, and reaching for her dream of being a writer.

www.ingramcontent.com/pod-product-compliance
Lightning Source LLC
LaVergne TN
LVHW012059070526
838200LV00074BA/3666